UNLOCKED DIVE

BROKEN BOYS OF CIRQUE - BOOK 2

A.K. Blythe

Unlocked Dive

© 2024 by A.K. Blythe.

This is a work of fiction. Characters, names, dialogues, and incidents are the product of the author's imagination or are used fictitiously. Any resemblance to actual persons, whether living or dead, businesses, locales, or events other than those specifically cited are unintentional and purely coincidental or are used for the purpose of illustration only.

The publisher and author assume no responsibility for errors, omissions, or contrary interpretation of the subject matter herein. The author and publisher assume no responsibility or liability whatsoever on the behalf of any purchaser or reader of these materials. The publisher and author do not have any control over and do not assume any responsibility for third-party websites or their content.

Cover by Quirky Circe.
Editing by Brazen Hearts Author Services.
Proofreading by Brazen Hearts Author Services.

ISBN: 979-8-9904667-1-5

Author's Note

This story was written in two parts.

The first, immediately after finishing Wristlocked (and before I'd even seriously contemplated the self-publishing monster that is marketing, editors, ARCs, cover artists, and the dozens of other pieces that suck up an indie author's time and resources). This was a phase of dream-driven urgency, the characters clamoring to be heard, to pine and hurt and fall in love. Of sleepless nights where the words came crowding into my brain, my fingers itching for the keyboard or a pen.

Then I decided (thank you, Becky) to put Wristlocked out into the world. Cue six frantic, overwhelming months of immersing myself in indie-authordom. I was not prepared.

The journey was, of course, full of its own rewards—not the least of which was diving back into the world of Gia, Lyot, and Gale and rediscovering all their twisted, tortured charms. But Echo and Byrd languished during this period. An itch at the back of my mind that I could never quite silence but kept pushing down. *Later. Soon. Yes, I miss you too (I promise).*

And of course, when I finally came back to them after Wristlocked ARCs dropped, they punished me like any jilted lovers—with sullen silence and rebellion.

We fought. I had plans. They refused to cooperate. I wanted the easy magic back. They wanted cajoling. This went on for *weeks*. Bastards.

Eventually, we found our way back to each other, and they rewarded my persistence by giving me everything I could've dreamed for them. Their happy ending was worth every page of their struggle, and I wouldn't have them any other way.

I hope you love them as much I do. I hope they make you giggle and cry and blush and squeal.

Are you ready to dive in?

For everyone who's ever needed someone else to put them back together.

In the words of a wise young tattoo artist:
Being more than whole together doesn't make you less than whole on your own.

CONTENTS

Glossary of Circus Terms

- **ACCA** – Fictional circus college located in Las Vegas that is the setting for the book Wristlocked.

- **Aerial rope** – Apparatus for aerial circus art using one vertically hung rope, usually covered in a canvas sheath.

- **Aerial silks** – Apparatus for aerial circus art using a long length of specialized fabric, usually hung from the middle to make two long "tails."

- **Aerial straps** – Apparatus for aerial circus art using a pair of woven straps hung from a swivel, usually with closed loops at the bottom.

- **Base/Flyer** – Designation in duo disciplines to distinguish between the person providing the anchor or structure of a trick and the person performing the dynamic aspect of the trick.

- **Chinese Pole** – A vertical pole on which circus performers climb, slide down and hold poses. The poles are generally between 3 and 9 meters (10 and 30 ft) in height and approximately 2 to 3 inches (5 to 8 cm) in diameter. They are traditionally covered with textured rubber to improve grip.

- **Cirque/cirque** – When capitalized, "Cirque" in this book is short for Cirque du Soleil, a world-wide circus company with both touring shows and "permanent" shows in Las Vegas. When not capitalized, "cirque" is another word for "circus."

- **ENC** – École Nationale de Cirque. A professional circus school located in Montreal, Quebec, Canada.

- **Outdoor Rig** – A freestanding aerial structure (usually with four legs and a truss) to support an aerial apparatus for outdoor practice or performance.

- **Point** – The part of the rigging that attaches to the apparatus. Can also refer to the place in a gym or on a stage where the apparatus will hang once attached.

- **Pole** – The section of an aerial rope above the athlete's body (taut with their weight).

- **Rigging** – The system of ropes, pulleys, carabiners, anchors, and swivels used to suspend an aerial apparatus, adjust the height, and lift or support a performer.

- **Rosin** – Crystallized tree sap in rock/powder form that is used to make things sticky. Used by aerialists to improve grip.

- **Tail** – The section of an aerial rope below the athlete's body that hangs loose.

*Circus moves are hard to describe with words. If you are really curious about what these art forms look like there are a ton of super talented aerialists on Instagram and YouTube and I encourage you to check them out!

1

Echo

R *eckless. Fearless. Flawless.*

I was a god on the rope, a hero at home, and the envy of every aerialist at the gym. They called me "Echo" because I only needed to see a trick once to repeat it.

I was invincible.

Until I wasn't.

Nineteen feet from the rigging point to the floor.

Five broken bones in my arm, wrist, and hand.

Seven screws and a plate to put me back together.

Two surgeries. Four days in the hospital. Eight weeks in the cast. Three months of OT.

Countless immaculate falls. One that mattered.

Ten fucking inches to the left.

In Dilaudid-drenched dreams, my grip is sure and familiar, strong on the rough canvas of the rope. Gravity is an enemy so long vanquished, we've become friends.

Consciousness is hitting the ground all over again, reality detonating the air from my lungs and pain returning with un-gentle hands.

I hide in the dreams as often as I can. The hospital room feels like weakness. Like worry in my mother's damp, shining eyes and anger at the sharp edges of my father's frown. Like a body I don't recognize weighed down by tubes and wires and blurry pain. Gabe flickers on the periphery, and once, a small, calloused hand that must be Asha's squeezes mine. But guilt and pity are ugly bedmates, and I only fuck beautiful guys.

On the third—*three hundredth?*—day, I resurface alone. My family is gone, the drama of my disaster already subsumed in the quicksand of their everyday lives. I'm not dying; I'm already dead. And dead is boring when only the corpse is grieving.

"That's morbidly dramatic."

Aaron. Shit. How much of that did I say out loud?

Fucking drugs.

It must be late in the day—Aaron's shift starts at four. He's the best and the worst of my three nurses.

Lorena works the graveyard shift and is swift, competent, and sparing with her heavily accented English. Moira, the day shifter, is perpetually exhausted, with two kids at home and an airline pilot husband she talks about the way people describe vacations they know they'll never take. Aaron is young and cocky, with dark skin and full lips that quirk adorably with every stupid, perfectly professional smile. I hate those lips. I want to see them wrapped around my cock. *Before* Echo would have had him on his knees the first day.

Broken Echo has a tube in his cock and thanks fucking Christ that Aaron wasn't the one who put it there.

"It must be the clothes," I say, scrambling to diffuse the fallout from my ramblings. "I mean, I know I have a great ass, but surprisingly, hospital-gown chic isn't really the best way to show it off." I watch for the familiar quirk of his lips, but Aaron only shakes his head. He never bites at my attempts at flirtation, and I don't like the way those cold teeth turn inward, gnawing pieces from my once-untouchable ego. I should stop trying, but my mouth refuses to accept the inevitable. Once upon a time—*four days ago*—I said whatever the fuck I wanted, and people lined up to gobble that shit down.

At least Aaron never feels sorry for me. Under my grieving corpse is a spoiled twenty-year-old kid who's barely had enough hardship in his life to call himself a man. I *know* Aaron's seen worse tragedies than mine, probably on a weekly basis, and the last thing I want is his pity.

"Actually, your mom left you some clothes this afternoon." He gestures toward a familiar gym bag resting on the cheap steel-frame chair beside the bed. "They're sending you home first thing in the morning."

"Bored of my morbidly dramatic ass already? You haven't even seen it in jeans." *What the fuck is wrong with me*? I let my head fall back on the pillows, closing my eyes as if my mouth might take the hint and follow their example.

"I'm pretty sure it's sweats and a T-shirt." Maybe it *is* pity. The kind that lets him smooth over my bullshit without making it awkward, before he goes home to whoever is waiting to take all the things I want from him.

"You must be ready to get out of here," he continues. "We don't usually keep orthos over forty-eight hours."

"Sounds like my dad's been pissing in corners." This elicits a deep chuckle, and I crack my eyes before I miss what it does to his mouth.

"Yeah, man. That dude can be pretty persuasive when he's scared."

"I think you mean scary when he's pissed."

Aaron shrugs. "That too. He obviously cares about you."

I let my eyes drift around the empty room, the flowers just starting to curl at the edges in the slanting light. My dad has always been proud of me, excited to have me as a son, but I'm not sure it's the kind of love Aaron's thinking of. But no need to dump my daddy issues all over him on top of my obvious insanity.

"He gets the job done." Let him take that how he will. It's mostly true in the ways that matter.

"Anyway, you want those clothes? The T-shirt will be kind of a bitch with the IV, but we can make it work. And I can pull the catheter now that they've switched you to oral meds." He taps the chart in his hand and gives me an encouraging smile.

I can only spare a brief second to mourn the loss of the Dilaudid drip because my mind is stuck on his second offer.

"Are you sure you're not just looking for an excuse to touch my dick?"

Oh my god. Shut the fuck up, Echo.

But his quirk of a smile is slightly less professional this time. Or maybe that's my dreams fucking with me. Probably a good thing they're taking me off the drip.

Every sexy nurse porno I've ever seen had it dead wrong.

My dope-soaked dick doesn't even twitch when Aaron wraps his responsibly gloved fingers around it and pulls the fucking piss tube free. The whole thing takes five seconds, and then he's helping me into the boxer briefs and sweatpants my mom picked out like I really am a helpless toddler.

He doesn't offer to kiss it better, and I don't ask, my mouth apparently—*finally*—grasping the nature of our new reality.

2

Byrd

"Please tell me you at least got laid before you left the city."

"Reggie."

She ignores the warning growl in my voice. Probably because I sound more tired than threatening.

"It's been over five months, Byrd."

Ouch. Actually, *double ouch*. Reggie is the only person in my life besides my family who still insists on calling me Coen. If she's breaking out the nickname, it means she's trying to make a point.

"We only signed the divorce papers yesterday," I remind her.

"After being separated for *five months*. And now what? Your plan is to wallow for another five, alone in the middle of nowhere?"

"It's a three-quarter-million-dollar cabin in the redwoods, Reggie." I smile at the thought. "It's perfect for wallowing."

"Unacceptable." Even through the Bluetooth in my 4-Runner, I can tell she's not amused. "I have a job offer for you."

"I'm not coming home." I'm already past Santa Rosa, the last real bastion of civilization in Sonoma County. Only winter-blue hills and bare vineyards line the last stretch of highway between me and towering solitude.

"It's not in Tilburg. In fact, you can do it from your mansion in the woods." Her voice softens. "But you should come home sometime, Coen. We miss you."

It's nine hours later in the Netherlands, which means she's probably curled up in her loft bedroom with a glass of wine and her laptop. I think about changing the subject, asking her if she's started the new season of *White Lotus* yet, or if she's rewatching one of her nineties teen soap operas for the hundredth time.

"What kind of job, Reggie? I have wallowing to do."

She snorts, letting me pretend it's a joke because she's known me since way before Lara and she's a good friend.

"There's this kid..."

"I'm not handling private auditions anymore," I cut in. "And I'm on sabbatical from Cirque."

"It's not an audition. Well, more of an evaluation. He's already been accepted to Cici."

"Then why does he need an evaluation?" The Netherlands Circus Conservatory, which Reggie runs and affectionately calls "Cici," has a pretty stringent audition process.

"It's a special case. He was supposed to start last fall, but he was injured right before the start of term. Busted his distal radius, scaphoid, and two metacarpals."

"Shit. Training? Or fucking around?" Talented circus kids are rarely risk-averse and are prone to dangerous hobbies.

"Training. Home gym." There's a sharp lilt to the last words, and I shift in my seat, glad Reggie can't see the guilty reaction. Commercial gyms go under after a claim like that and work hard to prevent accidents. Home rigs are completely unregulated, rarely insured, and always a little dangerous. Not that that stops those of us who can afford them. I'll be training at the cabin with no one around and spotty cell service by tomorrow afternoon, and Reggie knows it.

When I don't say anything, she continues, "He's been rehab training since the beginning of the year, and his parents are adamant that he'll be ready to join the next class in the fall."

"You held his spot?" I'm not totally surprised. The school only takes about twenty kids a year out of hundreds of submissions. If they gave him one, he must have earned it.

"We want him. The kid's a fucking magician on the rope." The banked excitement in her voice stirs an unexpected flutter of interest in my own beaten heart. "He could have gone anywhere, but he chose our little corner of the circus world."

"Why?" I'm genuinely curious, not trying to sound like an asshole, but Reggie bristles.

"Because we might be small, but we're a good school, asshole."

Yeah...my enthusiasm might be out of practice.

"You should know," she adds. Reggie and I met at NCC, and I grew up a circus kid in Tilburg. I do know.

"So you want me to check him out? Make sure he's actually ready?" I'm almost to Cloverdale, where I'll ditch the 101 and start to lose cell service. "What if he's not?"

"You've got four months. Make him ready."

"I'm not a coach, Reggie. And I'm sure as hell not in any position to be a therapist if it goes south."

"You're a good guy, Coen. You make people feel comfortable in stressful situations, and you recognize when to push and when to go gently. You've also got one of the best eyes for talent in the business, and you know the rope. Shit, you haven't performed in years, and you still train like a pro every week."

"That's a lot of very flattering bullshit that still doesn't explain why you don't have one of your own coaches do the evaluation."

"Because he's in California. Mendocino is a lot closer to LA than Tilburg."

"There are a lot of great coaches in LA."

"Jesus, Coen. Take the fucking job. You need something to do in that house besides *wallow* and think about the bitch who left you."

"She's not a bitch." The response is automatic, although I'm not sure I still believe it.

"Fine. The soul-sucking vampire in Lululemon that you were always way too good for." Believe it or not, Reggie never liked Lara.

"Stop." I sigh. "I'll take the job. But don't pretend I'm not doing you a favor."

"You're my hero, and I adore you. I'll send the paperwork right now."

"I'm driving, Reg."

"So? Sign it when you stop for gas."

"I'm not doing that. I'll look it over when I get to the cabin and send it back tomorrow."

"Good enough. Now say thank you, because you know I saved you from becoming a reclusive sasquatch, and tell me you love me."

"I'll get back to you on that after I've spent a week with a teenager in my sasquatch sanctuary."

"He's not a teenager. He's twenty." She laughs like she can see my eye roll through the phone. "Oh, and there's one more thing..."

"Seriously?"

"Just remember you already said yes."

"Reggie." I'm so close. I can smell the fog-drowned forest. "His name is Jericho Wash. He's Gabriel's little brother."

3

Coen

12 Years Earlier

"Gabriel Wash."

"What?" I turn my head to look at Reggie without unfolding from my half-assed seated pike. Unlike me, my friend is actually stretching in preparation for our morning class.

"The freshman you've been staring at for the last half hour? His name's Gabriel Wash. From California."

"Like a movie star." It slips out, and I duck my head, knowing she'll never let it pass.

"Oh my god, Coen. You're adorable since you discovered guys."

"Fuck off. I did not 'discover' guys." I give her a sideways grin. "Turns out they were always there."

"Yeah, but you never blushed like this when you were only ogling girls." She pokes me in the ribs, and I twitch away, swatting at her hand.

"Maybe because they weren't from *California*." I match her teasing tone, but my eyes drift back to the new boy. He doesn't really look like my imagination's blond, blue-eyed vision of a Hollywood star. He's small and slender, with dark eyes and darker ringlets brushing his delicate cheekbones. But in a plain white T-shirt and black joggers that hug the curve of his ass, he still manages to look exotic with one arm wrapped in the scarlet silks across the gym.

"You do know that not everyone from California is a movie star?" Reggie laughs. "It's a big state with a lot of other cities besides Los Angeles."

"So which one's he from, then?" I don't bother to hide my curiosity. Reggie and I have been inseparable since she bounced up to me on the first day of school and made me her official guide to all things Tilburg.

"Los Angeles." She manages to keep a straight face when I give her a reproachful look, but her brown eyes sparkle with amusement.

After two years, I still don't know how Reggie manages to know everyone and everything that's happening at NCC the minute it develops, but she always does. She claims it's because she's observant and a good internet stalker, but I give more credit to the brilliant brain hiding under her wild mop of sun-brown curls. I'm half-convinced she'll be running the school someday, even if she is an American. I didn't even know there was a state called Iowa before I met Reggie, but apparently, it turns out frenetic geniuses with perfect handstands and unruly mouths.

He *is* from LA, of course, and he laughs, quick and sharp, when Reggie tells him I compared him to a movie star. It delights him, and the sound makes my skin warm and skittish.

His eyes are a deep, cryptic blue, giving nothing away, but he angles the lithe line of his shoulders toward me when he talks, and my fingers itch to explore the pale shadows where his throat disappears into the collar of his T-shirt. Even though I tower over him, the minute I see him up close, I stop thinking of him as a *boy*; he radiates all the languid confidence of a man in every studied movement.

Reggie carries the conversation, amusement plain in her arched brows and the twitching corners of her busy mouth. But Gabriel's eyes stay glued to me, flashing every time I look away and dropping to my mouth whenever I'm brave enough to open it.

For all my sideways longing and bold talk in the safety of Reggie's room, I've never actually flirted with another guy, and although I'm fairly certain this one is a dangerous place to start, I'm already falling into his orbit.

I am, of course, not the only one drawn to the darkling diva that is Gabriel Wash. He dominates the first-year class, holding court like a Delphic raven among songbirds. My gaze follows jealously when he's charming, and every wicked arc of his quick temper heats my captive blood until I'm brazen with need.

Reggie begins to lose patience with my obsession, less impressed with the quicksilver shift of Gabriel's moods.

"He's fascinating," I tell her, watching him bite his lower lip in concentration during an acro demonstration by a guest instructor.

"He's demanding," she replies, shaking her head.

"He's so confident," I sigh, staring at the way he tips his head back to laugh while lounging against the wall of the pub.

"He's arrogant," she says, turning back to the bar to call for another pint.

"He's beautiful," I groan, burying my face in one of her pillows while she scrolls Netflix on her laptop for something new to watch.

"He's selfish and fragile, Coen."

He's fragile.

This, we can agree on, and it's the contrast between the daring and the delicate that captivates me. He's so *different* from Reggie's uninhibited cheer and my own careful patience, and even as his attention baffles me, his layers beg me to unwrap them.

Despite her disapproval, Reggie is stoically supportive and loyally unsurprised when Gabriel actually returns my interest.

"*Of course* he likes you, Coen," she assures me. "You're incredible." She beams a smile at me, and she means it, so I let it slide when she can't help but add "and you worship him" under her breath. It's not like I could argue with her, anyway.

It's Gabriel who first calls me "Byrd," and though he tosses it out in his usual way, teasing me about my accent and my Dutch surname, I feel the thrill of being marked, claimed by him. Within weeks, the nickname spreads throughout the school, transforming me from steady, unremarkable Coen Baardwijk into something more—someone worthy of watching. Someone *wanted*.

And when he finally lets me inside him, a mess of tangled curls and satin limbs and greedy heat, something unfurls inside me that tastes like taking flight, and the whole world breaks open at my feet.

"He looks like a spider."

"It's a *character*, Reggie. It's sexy."

"A constipated spider."

"Oh my god, shut up." I squint at the stage where Gabriel has convinced the administration to let him practice his piece for the Circolo auditions next month. "He does not look constipated."

Reggie snorts, unimpressed by my loyal declaration. "When are you going to start working on your own act? I know Fleming's been bugging you about it." When I don't answer, she elbows me, hard enough to nudge a sliver of discomfort loose from its carefully constructed cage. "It's our senior year, Coen. You know if I was an aerialist and met the brief, I'd be gunning for the chance. A show like this could launch your career."

"I know." I keep my eyes on the twisting limbs and rippling silks above the stage. My tempestuous boyfriend will want to squeeze every nuance from my reaction later so I can soothe his manic self-doubts with praise. It would be so much easier if he could see himself the way I see him.

"Please tell me you're not passing it up because of *him*."

Even if she didn't know me as well as she does, my guilty shift would've given me away. "I can't audition against him, Reg."

"That's stupid. He's here for two more years. He'll have plenty of other chances."

"You don't get it."

For almost a year and a half, I've been basking in the reflected glory of being Gabriel Wash's boyfriend, and it's everything my starving heart craved. Reggie can roll her eyes and try to mask her impatience behind well-meaning advice, but if he's jealous and possessive of my attention while being careless with his own, it only keeps me chasing his high.

"*You* don't get it. If he loved you as much as you love him, he'd want you to go for it. And if he had any balls, he wouldn't be threatened by you going up against him anyway."

"He has plenty of balls," I mutter. "I've seen them, remember?"

"Ha-ha. I know you've heard the rumors."

"The ones Dolph has been spreading? He's just jealous."

"You don't think it's at all weird that the only other silks guy in Gabriel's class sprained his ankle right before RPP selection?"

"Students get hurt all the time. It doesn't mean anything."

"It means your boyfriend got to be the only sophomore with a solo act in their showcase."

"So he obviously pushed a kid down the stairs? This isn't one of your Netflix teen dramas. That shit doesn't happen in real life."

"What doesn't happen in real life?"

I jump to my feet with a wide-eyed warning for Reggie and take Gabriel in my arms, pressing a kiss to his neck and licking the salt from my lips. "That was the best one yet, babe."

He ducks his head, pushing me away.

"You weren't even watching."

Reggie studies her nails, pointedly ignoring his narrowed gaze.

"I was just asking Coen about his own audition piece. Coach Fleming has been hounding him. He's being annoyingly secretive, but I'm sure you've been helping him come up with ideas?" Her blithely feigned innocence fools exactly no one.

"You want to audition?" Gabriel rounds on me. "I thought you decided against it."

"I did." My fingers skate over his jaw before he bats my hand away, and I swallow the dull sting of rejection. Rebellion flickers in its wake. "But I am getting a lot of pressure to change my mind. Not just from Reggie."

I shift awkwardly in the silent standoff that follows, the futile hope that the two of them might someday stop tugging me apart beating against the mounting pressure in my ears. With his uncanny knack for knowing when I'm approaching critical, Gabriel breaks the tension with one of his electric smiles.

"I guess you should do it, then." His arms snake around my waist. "But let's talk about it later. Right now I need a shower. Wanna come help me get all nice and *clean*?" His tone promises scandal and sin, and my ears heat as blood rushes to all the inconvenient places.

"I'll let Fleming know to add you to the list," Reggie calls as he drags me away, but I barely notice through the eager thrill hijacking my limbs. My brain is already drowning in images of wet, naked Gabriel.

I win the spot.

Gabriel is understandably furious, raging against my selfishness and accusing me of putting my fledgling career before our relationship. Only the withering disappointment in Reggie's eyes when I dare to broach the subject keeps me from turning the Circolo showrunners down.

The weeks leading up to the performance are a torment of casual cruelty and sullen withdrawal, chipping away at my precarious pride. My act becomes a liturgy of heartbreak, every move wrought to the cadence of lonely desperation that fuels my hours.

My rehearsals leave Reggie in tears, but the coaches and the audience eat it up, and my parents are beamingly proud on opening night. Even my teenage sister manages to attend without adding any heedless drama.

But the one person I needed to show up is conspicuously absent, and none of the accolades can protect me from the fallout.

I spend my last six months at school nursing a shattered heart and graduate with only the merciless final lesson etched beneath the pieces:

Holding on to love means giving up the spotlight for a brighter flame.

4

Echo

"I'm not going."

"Jericho." My father is losing patience.

"Echo." My mom's voice is softer, pleading. "You already agreed to it. You've known since December that this was coming."

"I was still on drugs in December."

That's a lie. I flushed the painkillers three days after getting home from the hospital, on the day I should have been flying to Amsterdam. It was that or down the whole bottle.

Instead, I got way too drunk with my friend Asha until it seemed like a good idea to go through the NCC student social accounts and pick out all the guys I would've fucked if I'd actually been there.

I should have taken the fucking Percocet.

When Regina Blake herself called my dad before Christmas to lay out the conditions of her offer, of course I said yes, even though I despised the idea. It felt like auditioning all over again, only this time, I wasn't confident about passing. My father was so smug that the school was willing to pay for four months of personal training to make sure I passed the evaluation. It proved they were invested in me and had faith in my full recovery. All I had to do was show up and do what I always did—be perfect. Be Echo.

I'm starting to hate my fucking name.

The cast was two months gone at that point—two months of occupational therapy to get me back to the point where I could close my fingers tight enough to feel the fiber core of the rope through the canvas sheath—and Regina gave me until the end of March to get ready. To build back the corded strength in my forearm and remember all the ways I could fly.

I haven't been back to the Center. I'm still too much of a liability for their insurance. It's also full of people who've never seen me falter, and I can't fucking face it. Can't bear to see myself rendered small and ordinary where I've always been larger than life. My dad bought a new mat, four inches thicker and twice as wide as the one I cursed with my calamity, and tossed me back in my studio, careless with all the confidence I no longer possess.

Start small.

Start safe.

Start over.

It's been fucking torture.

Basic movements I haven't had to think about for years make me sweat and tremble. My hand, my *right hand*—the thought-less foundation of my whole identity—cramps and slips and *terrifies* me. Everything feels intangible, a new barrier claiming space between my body and my brain, making me clumsy and aberrant in my own skin.

After the first month, I fled to Audrey's to cover my scars.

"It's way too soon," she tells me, fingering the tender grooves where the skin is beginning to fade from ugly red to underbelly pink.

"It's been almost six months."

"I should make you wait at least nine, probably a year."

"Fuck that, Audrey. Since when have we followed the rules?"

"It's gonna hurt like a bitch."

"It always hurts. You're the one who says that's part of the fun."

"I'm a masochist. You're a hedonist. Trust me when I say this is not your kink."

"Maybe my kinks have changed."

Audrey gives me a steady look, and Asha snorts from her perch at the piercing counter. I throw a grin at my friend like it hasn't been weeks since I've seen her. Like I haven't been shutting her down every time she wants to come to the studio, unwilling to face the humiliation of watching her move effortlessly through the tricks we used to do together. Knowing I have nothing to throw at her now to trigger the competitive envy she thrives on.

Yeah, I'm a coward, but ours is a complicated friendship, forged over years of chasing each other up and down the rope even before puberty and grace solidified my advantage. At the

Center, Asha is the queen bee to my king cock, and I'm not letting myself wonder how she likes ruling alone.

She's also Audrey's little sister and the reason I've been able to ink myself since three years before it was legal. Audrey started tattooing me in their basement when she was barely an apprentice with borrowed gear, and she's the only one I've ever let mark my body. She's every bit the badass bitch she needs to be as the only female artist in a shop that caters mostly to bikers and bangers, but she loves me. Possibly more than Asha does. Audrey calls me her passion project, even though ninety percent of what I've let her do is simple words and numbers. She likes the story they tell and how her ink and needles make her a part of it. She charges me half what her time is worth, even though she knows I can afford to pay, and in return, I tag her in all my shirtless Insta posts.

"You've been dying to get your hands on my right arm for years," I remind her. "This might be your last chance."

"Aren't you training? Asha says you're still heading off to school in the fall."

"Mostly conditioning," I admit with a shrug, glancing over at Asha. I wish she'd fuck off and stay out of my shit today. "No one-arm stuff with a wrap. No release moves." I keep the words casual. Audrey may or may not understand the implications, but Asha definitely will. "I've got another month before I'm allowed to get serious enough to fuck up the tat." *Lies. Cowardly, stupid lies.*

Audrey is caving, moving around the space and gathering her tools. I sink gratefully into her chair and hook the armrest stand toward me with my foot.

"And you're one hundred percent sure about the design?" she asks, hesitating next to her stool. "I appreciate the tragic symmetry, Echo, but do you really want me to immortalize your broken wings?"

I almost laugh. My wrist is held together with surgical screws and a steel plate. Long after my tattooed skin and the bones it covers have decayed to dust, that metal will be the last *immortal* part of me, buried treasure at the bottom of my coffin.

"It's part of the story, Audrey." *Truth*. "Can't call it art if you chicken out at the hard parts."

Maybe it's the words or the smile I give her—rueful, with just the right touch of conspiracy—but she stops trying to talk me out of it and gets to work.

She starts at the edges, letting me sink into the familiar buzz and drag before laying into the scar. It doesn't help.

The first bite of the needle through the virgin flesh is way, way worse than I'm prepared for, and I'm sweating and cursing within seconds. Audrey only grips my hand tighter and doesn't stop, but I can read anger in her tightly furrowed, pierced brows and the bitter line of her plum-painted lips.

I want to say I'm sorry, but I'm not sure if she's mad at my ruined wrist or at me for making her add a new layer to my misery.

By the time she's done, the anger is gone, poured into my skin, and when she wipes the last of the blood away, there's a dreadful wonder in her expression.

What the hell are tattoos, anyway, but a torrid affair between art and pain?

And we've just consummated a masterpiece.

I keep it covered at home. I'm supposed to wear the arm warmer anyway, and I don't need my morbid new tattoo to make my mother start crying again. I don't know what my dad would think. He's always liked my ink and what it represents, in that way that arrogant fathers are secretly proud of their sons' little rebellions. The alpha wolf grooming his favorite pup to take over the pack someday—as long as the pup picks his battles wisely.

But I'm pretending I'm unbroken, so my wrist stays covered, and I hide in the studio and run laps around the walls while my rope hangs limp and idle. I do squats and sit-ups and C-shaping drills until my muscles ache and I can emerge breathless and exhausted. I tell my parents that yes, it's going great, and yes, I can't wait to get back in a real gym, and yes, *yes*, of course I still want my place in Tilburg.

So they're understandably confused by my current change of heart.

"I was still on drugs in December."

"Enough." My father, less than amused by my flippant comment, slaps his hand down on the kitchen counter hard enough to rattle the decorative bowl of oranges against the marble. "You spoke to Regina yourself last week. You're committed."

"Echo," my mother tries again, resting a manicured hand on his sleeve. "You told us you were ready. What's happened in the last six days to change your mind?"

I drop my head onto my folded arms with a groan. I'm not ready. I was just willing to fake it and hope that somehow, magically, my confidence might reemerge if I got the fuck away from the scene of the crime. But something *has* changed.

Byrd fucking Baardwijk.

Regina "Call me Reggie" Blake, lord and master of my precarious future, was so excited to tell me who she'd recruited to handle my evaluation.

"He's been one of the top talent scouts for Cirque du Soleil for the past six years, and he's an old friend of mine and a Cici alumnus. He has a private studio in Mendocino where you can focus on your training without any distractions."

Except, when I look him up online, I discover that my new "coach" is definitely going to be a serious fucking distraction.

His headshot on the Cirque website isn't so bad—wavy chestnut hair pulled back from a face a little too fine to be called rugged, even with the short beard clinging to the strong line of his jaw. Full lips, curved up at one corner like the photographer caught him halfway to forgetting the professional setting, with the faintest crinkles tickling the corners of his clear hazel eyes. Almost devastating. Not quite dangerous. Sexy but approachable.

Thirty-two years old. Probably straight. Totally not my type.

But his bio says he performed on the rope for three years with Zircus Weber out of Germany, and since it's the twenty-first century, I go internet stalking. There isn't much from his touring days, but I find an old promo reel in the bowels of YouTube.

Byrd Baardwijk, shirtless on the rope in black and white, with wavy hair falling in his eyes and muscles coiling across his shoulders and along his back, dancing through the ether above a dark stage.

I jack off to it twice, and then another half-dozen times over the next few days, and nowhere in my filthy fantasies is the shattered, useless version of myself I now inhabit.

So I tell my parents no, but I lose that skirmish too, of course.

One week later, I'm standing in a cold drizzle next to a Charlie Brown statue outside the smallest airport I've ever seen, waiting to go to battle with the last of my pride.

5

Byrd

I forgot about the idiots on the 128, gawking at the lush scenery and crawling past the turnouts at thirty-five miles an hour on their way back to the city. So I'm irritated, irrationally nervous, and twenty minutes late picking up Jericho Wash.

"He's nothing like his brother," Reggie had assured me. *"I wouldn't send him to you if I thought he was going to dig up old graves."*

From anyone else, I'd take it with a grain of salt and think they were placating me, but Reggie was the one who picked up the pieces when Gabriel and I went down in flames at the end of our senior year. I trust her judgment, the way I should have back then, but I'm still on edge. She sent me the kid's file along with the contract documents, including a link to his first-round audition video, but despite her reassurances, I'm too chickenshit to watch it.

I tell myself it's for all the same reasons I always go into auditions blind—I like my eyes fresh and my critical brain uncluttered by expectation. But my objectivity is unraveling with every winding mile, tidal memories undercutting the promise of novelty.

When I pull around the curb outside the airport, my eyes slide right past the young man in faded jeans, smoking a cigarette with his white Stone Island hoodie pulled up against the insistent drizzle. I'm looking for a slight build, for dark curls and drama. I'm expecting *recognition*. But the Santa Rosa airport is ridiculously small—one gate, one building, with a pickup lane only four spaces long—and I'm late. After a quick glance at the shadowed overhang guarding the single entrance, I realize this guy is it.

I bring the 4-Runner to a stop in front of him and roll the passenger window down, then lean across the console to call his name.

"Jericho Wash?"

He lifts his head and meets my eyes, and something hot that should feel like relief but is too electric carves itself across my chest. He has the porcelain skin, but that's the last resemblance. The eyes are still blue, but where Gabriel's were dark and fathomless, these are bright and brilliant, the color as unreal as the shock of hair escaping beneath his hood to cling wetly to his face. He looks like a character from one of the video games James and I would play on Sundays while Lara was out with her girlfriends. Something out of *Final Fantasy* or *Assassin's Creed*; beauty like the edge of a knife.

Then he pulls the cigarette from his lips with a half smile, and the wide mouth breaks the illusion, rendering him human, if no less dangerous.

"Toss the cigarette and grab your shit." It comes out colder than I intend, or maybe it only sounds that way through the pounding pulse in my ears.

He ignores me, leaning his elbows on the open window, filling my space with the rich, bitter scent of tobacco and, underneath, something liquid and clean.

"It's organic," he says, meaning nothing. Meaning the cigarette, meaning the way his shoulders fill the window frame and the cerulean tips of his hair drip water on the warm leather passenger seat.

"Just get in," I reply after a long moment of forgetting how to breathe, straightening with a jerk of my head that frees me from his gaze. "Leave the window cracked."

He pinches the filter between his teeth with another smile and turns to the huge black tote bag gathering moisture on the curb. I keep my eyes on the rain while he bends to gather the short straps and tosses it carelessly into the back seat.

You're going to have to watch him do a lot more than that, idiot. What are you gonna do when the sweatshirt comes off?

He climbs in beside me, and I hold out my hand, feeling awkwardly ancient when he stares at it for a long second before giving me his own.

"Byrd." *Obviously.*

His fingers are long and elegant, warm from the pocket of his hoodie, and I can feel the worn calluses on his palm and the faint ridge of new scars under my fingertips.

"Echo," he replies, pulling his hand back and drawing on the cigarette without taking his eyes from my face.

"We call him 'Echo' because he's always following me around, thinking he's gonna be the next hot-shit circus god." I remember Gabriel laughing, and how I laughed with him, marveling at his cleverness. Now all I can think of is how Echo and I both carry the weight of Gabriel's ambiguous attention in our names. I wonder how much he knows, and if he'll hold it against me—and what it means that I care.

"Have you ever been to the coast up here?" I ask, pulling into the exit lane with way more attention than warranted by the nonexistent traffic.

"Mermaid country?" Another crooked smile tips those wide lips. "Yeah, spent a couple of weeks in Mendocino over the summer when I was a kid."

Mermaid country. It makes him sound young, and it throws me back to the first time I drove up the 1 and discovered the sinuous coves with their blooming cliffs. I remember the lure. Lara never got it. She liked the cabin because it let her claim my undivided attention, but she always missed the lights of Sausalito and the carnival of culture across the Golden Gate.

"I used to call it Neverland," I confess, "when I first started coming here."

"Got a thing for lost boys?" The tone is light, teasing, but when I glance over, his eyes are on the cigarette in his hand, or maybe on the hand itself.

Once upon a time, I thought I was in love with Peter Pan.

"I prefer adults these days," I say instead. He stubs the cigarette out on the window's wet edge and tucks the butt away in the pack before shifting to face me.

"Find many of those at the Cirque auditions?" he asks, folding a leg up onto the seat so his knee presses close to the gear shift and his jeans stretch tight across his thigh. He catches me looking, and the grin turns wicked. "Or was it all twinks and divas trying to suck your cock to get ahead?"

"Is that what you are? Just another twink trying to suck my cock?"

Reggie was right—I should have gotten myself laid in the city. *Shit.*

He drags his hood down and leans his head against the window, and I see that his hair is straight and thick, and only the spiky edges are that startling blue. The rest is almost black, scrambled from the hoodie and begging to be tamed.

"No one's called me a twink since I was fourteen," he says. "That was the year I gained three inches on my brother, and he never bothered after that."

"He meant it as an insult?" It's not really a question. I can *hear* Gabriel's voice in my head, taunting the little brother who dared to outgrow him.

"Didn't *you*?" He quirks a black-wing brow.

The left one.

I look away, fighting the faint nausea that tries to crawl up my throat.

I remember lying in bed, both of us laughing while Gabriel tried to teach me the gesture. I never figured out the trick of it.

"You don't seem particularly insulted," I observe before the silence can grow awkward. He doesn't. He seems relaxed, curious, but I notice the way he keeps pulling his sweatshirt cuff down over his right hand.

"I'm more interested in what it says about your sexual orientation that you called me a twink."

I take the bait and blame it on the ghost between us.

"So you *are* trying to suck my cock?" I absolutely do not shift in my seat, keeping my eyes glued to the road.

"Would it get me out of this evaluation?"

"No." Before I can ask if he *wants* to get out of it, he continues.

"And it's not my mouth that's broken." Self-loathing flickers across his face, so quick I'd have missed it if I wasn't obsessing over every molecule of him.

"Obviously not." I can't help a wry smile—or fight the way it widens when his gaze drops immediately to my mouth.

"Maybe we can work a few hand jobs into my training rou-tine?" His laugh is ragged at the edges, and he wiggles the fingers of his scarred hand at me while I shake my head and try not to come apart.

I am so fucked.

"Got another cigarette?"

6

Echo

By the time we climb the steep, winding driveway, faded light creeping through the dripping redwood canopy, I'm fucking high on Byrd Baardwijk.

I can't stop checking him out, and I can't stop flirting with him—not when he keeps *responding* in his adorably reluctant way. Like he can't help himself either. Like I'm still irresistible in spite of everything.

I keep catching his eyes on my mouth or flickering down to my crotch, and remembering the way he said "cock" like it didn't scare him, the bare traces of his Dutch accent making my toes curl. He smokes two of my cigarettes, the filter pinched between his thumb and fingertips, and I fantasize about sucking the nicotine off his tongue.

He parks in front of a two-car garage and grabs my duffel from the back seat, slinging the strap over his shoulder while I'm still taking in the three stories of glass and timber carved into the rugged hillside. He leads me past the deck wrapped around the lower level, up a long flight of wooden stairs, and I stare at his ass and think about ripping his hair free of its messy man-bun and seeing what it feels like between my fingers—or draped over my dick.

"...old two-seater in the garage if you want to run to town. It's about thirty-five minutes to Mendocino if you're not trying to kill yourself, but there's a general store a few miles back down the..." He trails off when he turns at the top landing to find me only inches behind him.

"I can carry this myself," I tell him, sliding two fingers under the strap across his chest and giving it a light tug. "I'm an *adult*."

His sharp inhale traps my knuckles against his chest, and I'm close enough to watch his pupils blow in the dying light.

Please. Please...

"Good to know." His half smile is amused, ironic.

I want to press into him. I want to feel his cock harden against my thigh. *I want—*

He opens the door and turns away.

I want to be someone else.

He gives me a quick tour while I gather the shreds of my vanity. The house is three split levels of high ceilings and half walls, rich and somehow cozy with its dark, exposed beams and tall windows. Byrd's obvious pride in his home is an eager, charming thing, and it's hard to feel resentful of his rejection watching him. Instead of diluting his immediacy, the space only enhances it until I'm drowning in everything Byrd.

"I've got a twenty-four-foot outdoor rig," he tells me. "We should be able to set it up in a couple of weeks when the ground dries out. In the meantime..." He gestures to the rope hanging in the center of the living room over a four-by-six gym mat. "This is what I usually use when I'm here."

I walk up to the rope and wrap my hand around it, my pulse rocketing in my ears.

"How's the recovery going?" he asks, his tone careful and agonizingly gentle.

"Brilliantly. My doc says I'm ahead of the curve and waxes poetic about the joys of youth." I fight to keep my voice light, to keep the bitter mockery from seeping through. Byrd remains silent, and I tighten my fingers until my knuckles whiten and my bones ache. "Apparently, athletes make the best patients, always so diligent about their PT." I let my hand drop and throw him a smirk.

It's all true, and he didn't ask about my soul.

"Good," he says, with a genuine smile that instantly makes me feel like an asshole. "We'll start easy tomorrow anyway. Ready for some food?"

"You cook?" I ask, following him back up the steps to the kitchen. His chuckle curls around the base of my spine, low and luscious.

"They don't have DoorDash out here. Plus, my mom was Italian; cooking is practically a prerequisite."

"I love Italian. Wine and carbs."

"Am I allowed to let you drink wine?" he teases, turning to face me with a wink and walking backward up the last few stairs.

"At your own risk." I push past him, taking the excuse to bump him with my hip as I move toward the butcher block island at the center of the kitchen.

"Not going to tell me you're an 'old soul'?"

I lean against a barstool and roll my eyes. "Fuck no. Who have you been hanging out with? Twinks like me cherish our youth. Besides, it keeps all the pervy old men panting and eager to please."

"Good thing I'm not a pervy old man."

Fuck, he looks good in a smirk.

"My loss." I shrug, and we stare at each other as the air between us blisters. He breaks first, shoving up the sleeves of his Henley and turning to the fridge.

"You like anchovies?"

"What?" Forearms are absolutely clutch for an aerialist, and his have caused all the blood to abandon my brain.

"Anchovies? Puttanesca?" He glances back over his shoulder. "Carbs?"

"Yes. Sure." *Anything you want.* "Can I help?"

"Grab the big pot from the lazy Susan." He jerks his head toward the cupboard in the corner of the counter and goes back to rummaging in the fridge. "Fill it up from the tap and throw in some salt."

"So you're saying you trust me to boil water?"

"Too much for you?" His eyes sparkle with challenge.

While I know he's watching, I strip my hoodie off over my head, flashing my abs and flexing a little. I have ripped forearms too, after all.

"I think I can handle it."

I should probably be insulted that it's all he lets me do, but my culinary skills begin and end with scrambled eggs and boxed mac and cheese, so I wander around the loftlike kitchen as he starts pulling stuff out of the fridge.

"Exactly how old *are* you?" I taunt, spotting a current wall calendar hanging beside the pantry door. *Like I don't already know.*

He glances at me, and then at the calendar, clearly amused.

"A local youth theater group sells them," he explains, grabbing a sauté pan from a hanging rack. Yes, I know what a sauté pan is. They're the ones you use to scramble eggs. "They're a nonprofit, and it's one of their yearly fundraisers."

Well, that's fucking adorable.

I trace a finger over today's date.

"Jericho Wash—Alaskan Airlines 3:49 p.m." written in neat red script. My name in his handwriting makes my dick hard.

I flip through the next few pages while he chops garlic and the smell of frying onions fills the house. *Alice in Wonderland. Toy Story. Charlotte's Web. Peter Pan.* The last one makes me smile. I raise the next page—*Willy Wonka?*—and more red writing stops me cold.

August 1: "Jericho Wash—Evaluation due"

And two days later: "Alaskan Airlines 8:25 a.m."

It's not like I didn't know I had a deadline. It shouldn't make my hand shake and my head ring with panic—four months is plenty of time. Except I've already had twice that and I'm still waiting on my miracle.

Unless I've finally found it.

My eyes rake over the man currently rooting around in one of the cabinets, the hem of his shirt riding up to expose a strip of tantalizingly tan skin above his low-hanging jeans. Maybe he won't be a cure for my busted brain, but my body is one hundred percent willing to let him try. To prove I'm still something more than an expiration date on a glossy page.

The red Sharpie hanging from a thumbtack on a string catches my eye, and I snatch it up. Pulling the cap off with my teeth, I gather the tenuous remnants of my will to scrawl "Echo Was Here" across pubescent Willy Wonka.

I'm *here*. I'm trying. Maybe I can remember how to be Echo again too.

August is a long way off, I tell myself, settling back onto my stool. *Focus on the dreamboat making you dinner.*

It works. Before long, I'm having way too much fun watching him cook to give a shit about the eval. The quick, sure movements of his hands on the knife, the way he swipes a rogue lock of hair out of his eyes with the back of his arm or sucks on a fingertip to taste the sauce—it all has me half-hard, helpless, and *hungry*.

"How'd you find circus?" he asks. Not the way everyone else does, curious and over-awed by its novelty, but like we're sharing a secret, and he's glad of the company.

"My brother. He—" A pan clatters against the stove, and Byrd yanks his hand back with a hiss. "Are you okay?"

"Yes. Fine. Handle was hot." He rolls his shoulders without turning around. "Go on."

"Gabe's actually my half brother. He's a lot older and generally an asshole, but he did silks for years. When I was about six, my dad took me to see one of his performances, and I fucking loved it. Not just Gabe, even though I was still young enough to think he was the shit back then, but all of it. The stage, the spectacle. Kids not that much older than me doing things I'd never imagined. It felt like—" *Destiny.* But I can't say that out loud without feeling like an idiot.

"Recognition?" Byrd has turned around to look at me, leaning against the stove, his hands curled around the oven handle at his hips. His Henley is stretched tight across his chest and his eyes are sober, and if I don't look away, my whole body will fall into his gravity.

Recognition.

"Yes." I look away. "My mom was pissed. She always hated it when my dad gave Gabe attention. His mom was the college sweetheart, right? The first love. Mine was the midlife crisis trophy wife, and I was her favorite weapon." I pause, suddenly guilty. "I mean, she loves me. She's not a bad mom. She just..." My hands flex on the cool concrete island top, and I watch the skin stretch over my scars. "When Gabe flamed out, and then I

got accepted to NCC...I guess I feel sorry for Detta sometimes. Gabe's mom."

"But not for Gabe?"

"No." I meet his gaze but don't elaborate. That story leads
to clouded places I'm not ready to go. Byrd doesn't press me.

"I was married until recently," he says instead, as if he
needs to share some sordid piece of his own history after my
confessions.

"Aren't you a little young for a midlife crisis?" I ask, wanting to make him smile.

"The split was her idea." The smile is bitter.

"Oh." *He had a wife. A wife who left him.* "She sounds like
an idiot." This earns me a real smile.

"No. Just unhappy. She wanted things I couldn't give her."

"Like what?"

"More pieces of myself." Now it's his turn to look away.
"She's the reason I stopped touring and took the job at
Cirque. Did you know I used to perform?"

I nod and shove away the images of his promo reel. The
Byrd in front of me is *real*, absurdly, unfairly forsaken, and
the urge to touch him rages wretched in my chest.

"She wanted me close to home, not out on the road,
surrounded by other performers. 'The beautiful freaks,' she
called them. I knew she was jealous and threatened, but I
understood—what kind of wife would want their husband
gone for months at a time?"

There are a lot of ways I could answer that, but instead, I
shake my head and say, "Wives aren't really my specialty."

He huffs a short laugh. "Or mine, apparently."

"So she got what she wanted, but it wasn't enough?" I
know plenty of people like that. LA is full of them, infinite
vacuums of insecure need. Gabe is one of them.

"No." Byrd shoves away from the stove and busies himself draining the pasta. "It was never enough."

7

Echo

I drink two glasses of wine with dinner and pretend the glinting amusement in his eyes is interest.

Later, I jack off in the crisp white sheets of his downstairs guest room, imagining it's his hand wrapped around my cock. The tan muscles of his forearm shifting with each stroke, his fingers in my mouth, salty and calloused. And when I slip one spit-slick digit behind my balls and press it into my own heat, I come hard enough to forget how terrified I am of tomorrow.

It doesn't last.

I'm awake a few hours later, my heart pounding to the faint throb in my head, the sheets gone clammy with the half-remembered panic of another nightmare.

The house is dark and spectrally silent. Even in our gated community at home, the night is always full of small sounds. The frantic bark of some neighbor's 50K guard dog warning off a coon, the far-off wail of LA's ever-present sirens, the hushed growl of the security trucks making their midnight rounds. Apparently, NorCal doesn't even have crickets at 4 a.m. in April.

The sky here, on the other hand, is a vast orchestra of stars. The silver light filters through the floor-to-ceiling windows that make up the south wall of the living room as I stumble out in search of a glass of water. More than enough illumination to see the rope's black silhouette hanging like a harbinger in the center of the room.

Today.

I'm out of time.

I should have let my parents into the studio to see the wreck I've become. That's what normal rich kids do, right? Let their parents bury their flaws under a shield of money and scotch-scented phone calls. *Give him a little more time. We're handling things on our end. How many zeros on the check?*

Just because I've never needed their protection before doesn't mean they wouldn't have given it. How many times did my dad bail Gabe out of some near-humiliation?

I am not like Gabe.

"Are you scared, little brother?"

My hand flinches back from the rope, and I stumble over the lip of the mat.

Am I still dreaming?

I suck in a breath and shove my hand into my pocket, where I curl each finger into my palm to a slow count of ten. I press my nails into the skin, digging for a pain I can point to, an excuse I can name. Too bad my calluses run even deeper than my scars.

I tiptoe up the stairs to the kitchen, lingering on the landing that leads to Byrd's bedroom. Three steps up, and I could open his door, cross the carpet, and crawl into his bed. Maybe he'd fuck me.

Idiot.

Most likely he'd toss me out, pissed—or worse, horrified. Either way, he'd be done, and I'd be back home. Safe. Alone.

Don't forget damaged and horny.

I remember him surreptitiously checking me out in the car, and the hitch of his breath when I cornered him outside the kitchen door. I can see his forearms flex in the glow of the refrigerator light and the shape of his lips closing over his finger. I still want to know if his hair feels as sinful as it looks.

I still want to be whole again.

Fuck it.

I climb the rest of the stairs and steal my glass of water from the tap. By the faint light of the abalone nightlight he left glowing above the counter, I stare at my name in his calendar and think about August. I notice a tiny circle around the date, and I realize the whole month going back is the same. He must mark off the days every night before he goes to bed. It's such a strange, old-fashioned quirk, like something out of a Hallmark movie. Or an after-school special about the football star who fucks up his knee and makes a miraculous recovery just in time for the big game. Like it should be a lesson instead of a time bomb.

I take the Sharpie and turn the small circle into a cartoon cock and balls.

Then I slink back to bed, going over everything I brought in my duffel to plan the most devastatingly sexy morning-workout outfit I can muster.

After a brief fantasy involving turquoise booty shorts and body glitter, I settle on a white wife-beater and pale-blue joggers that hug my ass. Simple and classic, and I've reaped the benefits of the look at the gym more times than I can count. Maybe I can distract him into ignoring the way my hands tremble when I reach for the rope.

In the watery daylight, the black canvas sheath that covers the braided core is faded with use and rosin to a well-loved gray, only the very top and the tail curling on the mat still dark with the original dye.

Byrd watches from the couch, sleeves shoved up above his elbows where they rest on his knees, and I'm forced to admit I'm way more distracted by his thighs in sweatpants than he seems to be by mine.

"Just run me through your usual warm-up," he says, offering an encouraging smile.

Right.

I want to show off. I want to surprise him. I want my acrobatic prowess to make his dick hard.

I do three basic climbs.

Tuck-ups. Straddle-ups. Single-coil wheel ups all the way to the top. At least those last ones are impressive. I cut the beat sequence short when the hardware starts to wobble at the point and my breath tightens in my chest. For a second, I hang there, letting the momentum ooze out of my body. When the rope settles, I force myself to invert, hooking my left knee so I can peel my clinging fingers free.

There are a dozen tricks I could do from here. Basic ones I can handle even on my off side, but my mind is full of static, and muscle memory eludes me, short-circuited by trauma's sharp current.

"Unlocked star?" Byrd's voice breaks through the buzzing in my brain, calm and casual.

It anchors on my bad hand when I do it on this side, but it's not really a release move since neither hand leaves the rope during the drop. I throw the tail across my waist and regrip, bracing for the rotation, and then pop my leg free. I ride out the short spin, my right arm locked straight to slow and control the drop. It's not as flashy as it could be, but it lets me absorb most of the landing with my left arm and shoulder, trapping the pole in my armpit so it doesn't pop free. I relax into the flag like an afterthought, hanging from my good hand with the other held out to the side, the rope taut between them.

So much for hiding my mess.

I let go and drop the few feet to the mat, flexing my fingers like it hurt and biting my lip.

"I'm okay," I lie, feeling like an asshole when his brow creases with concern.

"Reggie said you were cleared for more intensive training," he says, rising from the couch and reaching for my hand. "Does it still hurt?"

I hesitate, ready to lie again, but his long fingers close around my wrist, and the heat of his touch derails me.

"Nope." I flutter my lashes and tease my knuckles along his pulse, imagining it racing to catch up with mine. "But I won't complain if you want to kiss it better."

He drops my hand and narrows his eyes, but I swear the hint of a blush steals up his throat, and suddenly I *do* feel better. "In fact..." I offer up a slow smile. *That's not all you can kiss.*

"Nice try." He cuts me off before I can push it and ignores my best pout, returning to his perch on the couch. "Do the drop again. Let's see it on both sides."

It goes better the second time, but my brief surge of confidence doesn't last. No amount of flirting can cover up the fact that the old Echo is lost, especially when Byrd refuses to rise to the bait again, and all my insecurities return with a vengeance. I limp through the rest of the workout until he finally calls it quits and sends me off to shower while he runs out to grab lunch from the local store.

Beneath the purgative spray of Byrd's rainfall showerhead, I rewrite the morning. The memory of his hand wrapped around my wrist spills into a fantasy where I'm tugged against his broad chest, his mouth whispering accolades over my skin. Naked, cocooned in steam-drenched glass, I fly flawlessly through every trick and cast the faint surprise behind his eyes as lust instead of cautious disappointment.

Tomorrow I get to try again.

Yay.

But first I get to spend the rest of the day with him—hearing his voice and watching him cook and whatever else he does for fun out here in the boonies. Maybe he'll let me suggest a few things to pass the time. I find the tiniest bath towel he owns to wrap around my hips while I saunter back through the house to my room.

Maybe if I can make him want me, I'll stop feeling so helpless in my skin, and the rest of me will come back too.

Even fallen angels are allowed to dream.

8

Byrd

Losing someone you thought you loved is hell, but I wonder sometimes if it isn't somehow a kinder tragedy. There's something perversely liberating about being the victim in your own disaster—just shift the blame onto the person who did the leaving.

At least, that was always Reggie's preferred tactic.

"I refuse to watch you waste any more time crying over someone who never deserved you. Get up off your ass, Coen, and take the fucking showcase. Screw Gabriel and his guilt trips and his passive-aggressive jealousy. Coach Fleming chose you."

"Your family fucked you up, Coen, just like the rest of us. Your parents gave so much of their attention to Elke, you taught yourself to survive on scraps. I love your sister, but she is a drama vortex, and you know it. You need to learn to be selfish every once in a while."

And a decade later:

"If you keep paying for love with pieces of yourself, Coen, you'll eventually go broke, and there'll be nothing left to spend on yourself. Get the fuck out while she's giving you the chance, and go find someone less expensive."

It was Gabriel's fault, and Lara's, and a half-dozen others in between. I was a perfect boyfriend, a perfect husband—making the sacrifices, putting their needs above my own, doing everything right. Being *good*. And Reggie never let me look too closely at why I chose lovers who excelled at taking, or what it fed me to be the one to give.

So I came to the wild NorCal coast, ready to power through my latest hell and gather back the pieces I'd lost along the way.

Even though what I probably need is a good therapist who isn't my best friend.

But living with Echo Wash is a new kind of purgatory. Selfish doesn't even begin to cover the way he makes me feel.

For the first time in my life, I want to be *bad*. To forsake every cautious warning, every moral binding, and immolate myself on everything he offers up.

From the beginning, the nights are the worst. Finally, blessedly, *horribly* alone, I lie awake and imagine I can feel him breathing through the walls and empty house between us. Behind my eyelids, he's fresh out of the shower—*my shower*—wearing nothing but a towel and his wicked smirk, daring me to watch, to covet. His runaway mouth plays on repeat in my ears, teasing as I make our dinner, and a brazen, savage creature stirs and coils low in my gut. I taste the cigarettes we share on the deck in the evenings, where he marvels at the Milky Way as I watch the smoke curl over his lips and tongue with hopeless envy.

I haven't touched myself this much since I was a teenager, and it does nothing to quell the relentless tension.

In the mornings, he pads barefoot through my kitchen, shirtless and tousled from sleep. He eats cereal standing at the counter, heavy eyed and elfin, while I drink in his tattoos with my coffee and wonder if he's real.

j-flip 8/09/14
unlocked dive 4/18/15
single-coil wheel up 12/06/17
pirouette 2/20/18
double pirouette 6/25/23

Star drops and bombs and saltos and so many more.

A litany of tricks and their dates of mastery scrawled along his ribs and over his biceps to the crook of his elbow. A private record, triumphs carved in pain, and I can measure in heartbeats exactly how close I need to be to read the words.

Only his forearms are different, wrapped in angel wings of black and blue. On the left, whole and perfect; on the right, crumpled and broken, with one word in flawless calligraphy carved starkly into the pink flesh of a new scar.

"Fallen."

If Echo *off* the rope is one kind of torture, Echo *on* the rope is another.

He walks into my living room the first morning like temptation wrapped in thin, pale jersey, all fine skin and black ink—his lean muscles born of talent, rather than hours pumping iron in front of a mirror at the gym. Once I've recovered from the sight of him, I run him through the basics, letting him get a feel for the rope and the space.

He's good, of course—more than competent—but the genius Reggie gushed about is as absent as the cocksure attitude that flees every time his fingers touch the rope. I could look past some loss of strength or lack of stamina. There's plenty of time to build those back. What I don't know how to kindle is the missing spark.

Eventually, I download his audition video to see what Reggie saw and try to make sense of what I'm missing. And then I scroll through every single one of his Instagram videos, and I start to get pissed. Something happened to this gorgeous dynamo with the reckless mouth to crush more than his wrist.

For weeks, I watch and nudge and, with gentle patience, suffer a loss he has to mourn. Here is heartbreak in the bones, and every day, I ache with him, caught between what was and what should be in a helpless now.

"Try it again from the hipkey."

We're working on his unlocked dive. It's a half-release move that shouldn't put more pressure on his hand than he's ready for, although, since it's basically a falling front flip, it does require a certain leap of faith.

Instead of the static hipkey this time, he goes for a dynamic entrance—a quick back beat for momentum and then a smooth threading of the outside leg through his staggered grip on the rope. A little slack to slide into position, and he's poised for the dive, one hand gripping the tail at his abdomen and the other hooked above his head.

"Nice," I say with a smile. Split-grip beats put a lot more pressure on the top hand, and his confident execution is a good sign. He grunts without looking my way and releases the pole. Like every time before, he makes the grab and pikes perfectly through the drop, but the second he catches his full weight, he lets go, landing on his feet and breathing in tight gasps.

"Does it hurt?" I've asked him this a hundred times, and the answer is always a reluctant "no." I don't think he's lying, but his continued refusal to tell me what's going on is seriously starting to grate.

Maybe he can hear the frustration in my voice because, this time, he finally snaps.

"It doesn't fucking hurt, Byrd. It just doesn't *work*."

Bullshit.

"It works fine for beats," I throw back at him, fighting my own temper. "It works fine for windmills and lassos and candy-cane toe climbs." All things that put pressure on the dominant hand.

But none of those require letting go.

"It works fine for jacking off too. Wanna see?"

"Cut it out. I'm not letting you distract me this time." His favorite way to end a session is to flirt until I flee.

"Mmm. You like me distracting." The words are playful, but his tone is acerbic, and his eyes spit fire. "Better than watching me fake it on the rope."

"So stop faking it." I jab my finger into one of the tattoos at his hip, and for once, I don't tremble at the contact. "'Unlocked dive.' You've been doing this trick since you were twelve. You could probably slow it down and land it with your left alone. What the hell is stopping you right now? Because I don't believe it's only your hand." There. I finally said it. *Please let me in.*

"Maybe I'm just done?" He shrugs like it's that easy. Like I won't know better.

"*Fuck that.*" I want to shake him. "It doesn't just go away, this thing you have. It nearly killed me to walk away, and I never had a fraction of your talent." I've never admitted that to anyone before. When he doesn't react, I yank my phone from my pocket and stab angrily until I'm back on his IG feed. I've studied it so many times, it only takes a second to find the right video.

"See this?" I ask, shoving the phone in his face. "This is a flawless unlocked dive." I swipe once. "This? An unlocked double-back salto. That shit is terrifying, and you're *laughing*." Another swipe. "What about this? Four pirouette switches. Practically impossible." I shake the phone at him, all the fury and frustration of the last three weeks vibrating in my skin. "Where the fuck is *this* Echo? *He's* the Echo I want to see."

He's gone ashen, his eyes wide and panicked, and I reel back from the slap of his pain.

"That Echo?" He laughs, edging toward hysteria. "The Echo in that video? *He ruined my fucking life.*"

Before I can force my staggering lungs to draw breath, he's gone, storming through the glass doors and taking the deck stairs two at a time. Guilt and anger war at my insides, hot in my chest and cold in my gut. I realize, too late, that I can still feel the burn of his skin on my finger, and that I might have inadvertently shattered the last lifeline of a beautiful, broken boy.

Or maybe I'm giving myself too much credit.

Typical Byrd, thinking you're enough to heal the missing pieces for everyone in your life.

I want to chase after him, but I pace the room, uncertain. Is it the selfish Byrd's desire? Or the Byrd who needs to fix everyone around him, regardless of the cost in flesh? *What the fuck do I want from him?* Why do I care if he throws himself away? He's not mine. I can't have him in the ways I refuse to admit I want, so what the hell am I doing here?

I've been dodging Reggie's calls for weeks, scared and unwilling to answer the questions I know she'll ask, but maybe it's time to suck it up. Confess my sins and let her handle the fallout. That would be the responsible move.

Instead, I go after Echo.

I catch him at the bottom of the driveway. No longer running, he leans against the crossbeam gate with his chin on his chest and his hands in his hair. My heart cracks wide at the sight, and I'm out of the truck almost before I can throw it in park.

"Echo." I reach for his wrists to tug his hands down and make him look at me, but I catch myself and let my hands fall after a bare brush against his skin. For a brief, brutal second, his fingers clutch tighter in his hair, and then he drops his arms in defeat. The face he lifts to meet mine is ghostly, lost behind the bruised blue of his eyes.

"I'm sorry," I say, uselessly, reaching again—inevitably—to touch his tragic beauty. This time, he's the one who jerks back.

"Don't bother." He spits the words like bitter poison. "I'm not the Echo you want."

My heart is a void, collapsing under his weight.

All the warring pieces of myself dissolve and scatter, and there's no thought, no decision made, just my hands in his hair and his mouth under mine like there was never meant to be space between us.

He gasps against me, his hands coming up to rest against my ribs. Maybe he means to push me away, but now his lips are parted, and I let myself inside. He's nothing but silk and craving—his hair between my fingers, the curve of his neck when I drop a hand to tug him closer, the lethal heat of his fierce, eager mouth. He sucks at my tongue, his own bold and teasing, every cocky promise made real in wet flesh.

His fingers curl at my waist, hooking my jeans to pull me into him. My cock is painfully hard, and if I don't stop now, I'll be taking him against the gate post, five feet from the damn road.

I lurch back with a groan, dragging myself free until my fingers on his throat are all that's left of the kiss. He lets me go, trailing his hand down over the bulge in my jeans before palming his own erection, unashamed. With his other hand, he rubs a thumb across his swollen lips, and his eyes are a cobalt sea of raw desire.

"Echo," I try again. Those eyes flash.

"*Don't* say you're sorry. Don't try to explain."

I can only shake my head. "Will you get in the car?"

"That depends." He tilts his head, and I'm struck again by that aura of unreality, like he's drawn from pixels and dark fantasy. "Are you taking me to bed or back to the rope?"

"Neither," I say. "We're going for a ride."

9

Echo

Driving with Byrd has become one of my new favorite things. Even if it still takes forty minutes to get anywhere, it's not like driving in LA. There are no eight-lane highways up here. No strip malls or stop lights or bumper-to-bumper traffic. Only trees and fog trying to reclaim the blacktop, and on the coast, the vast expanse of the Pacific falling away from the edge of the world.

I like the nearness of him, where I can study the play of muscles in his shoulder and the flex of his long fingers on the wheel unobserved. And the way the charged energy between us bounces around the trapped space until he has to look over at me, the deep green shadows of his hazel eyes reflecting the sylvan scenery.

"Will you tell me what happened when you fell?" he asks, taking the right onto Flynn Creek that will eventually bring us to Mendo. All the roads here are named after the landscape: Flynn Creek, Albion Ridge, Little River.

"I broke five bones in my hand and wrist." *You kissed me.*

"You know what I mean."

"Are you asking how my brain got fucked up too? Maybe I landed on my head." *I kissed you back.*

"You didn't." He gives me a sideways look. "Reggie would have told me."

"So, one kiss, and you think I'll spill all my secrets?" *I will.* That was the hottest fucking kiss of my entire life. I'll give him my whole life story for another taste.

"I want to know what really happened. *How* you fell."

"And I want to know how your mouth feels swallowing my cock." I take a second to admire his reaction: the way his head falls back against the headrest and the sound he makes low in his throat. "I'm pretty sure it's a bad idea to drive these roads with your eyes closed," I tease. He opens them and aims a glare through the windshield.

"You're doing it again."

"What?"

"Trying to distract me."

"Am I distracting? I thought we were discussing the price of my secrets. That was just my opening offer." First rule of negotiating—start high. I'd definitely settle for a hand job.

"No blow jobs. And no more kisses." He flashes me a stern look. "You know this thing can't go any further, Echo. I'm evaluating you for Reggie."

"But you admit there's a thing." Giddy triumph creeps over my limbs, culminating in a rush of saliva at the lingering taste of his tongue exploring mine.

"There's no—That's not the point."

"Whatever you say." *I know you want me now. I know you were as hard as I was.* He glances at me again, clearly suspicious, but lets it lie. We drive in silence while he pretends to concentrate on the road and I stare at his perfect profile.

"It was the video," I say eventually.

"What video?"

"The four pirouette switches on IG. '*That Echo.*'" There's no accusation in my voice, the bitter taste of his earlier words burned away by his molten tongue, but he flinches slightly anyway.

"You tried it on the home point?" he asks, skeptical.

"I'm not a complete idiot," I scoff. "I've only got eighteen feet at home. No way I'd pull four without dragging my feet on the last two beats." Before he can voice his confusion, I continue. "Gabe was at the house that weekend. My parents had thrown a big send-off party to celebrate me heading to Tilburg." I look out the window and remember the last time I felt like my old self, drunk on champagne, with Caleb Fortner bent over the counter in my parents' master bath. And the next afternoon, sweating out my hangover with Gabe in the studio.

"*Gabe* was there when you got hurt?" There's something menacing in Byrd's voice that I don't recognize, and my barely recovered cock twitches. I spend half my time around him trying to keep it in line and failing. Or not trying at all.

Is he feeling protective? *And why the hell is that so hot?*

"He'd seen the video and was bugging me to demo the switches. He's got this thing where he makes it sound like he's complimenting you when he's really being an ass, and..." I hesitate, not sure how to explain. Or maybe I just don't want Byrd seeing any more of my scars.

I worshipped Gabe for half my childhood, always wishing he was around more, and I felt like an idiot when I realized he didn't feel the same. By the time I was old enough to understand him, I was already my own brand of asshole and very, very good at pretending not to care.

"Most of the time with Gabe, I let it slide," I say. "He's a dick, but it can't have been easy, watching his dad replace his mom with a younger, hotter version, and then do the same thing to him."

"Is that what you think you are? A younger, hotter version of your brother?" He throws me a glance I can't decipher, some shadow flickering beneath his carefully cultivated calm.

"Well, younger and hotter, obviously. And then I was better at circus too." I shrug and toss him a cheeky grin. "Sucks to be Gabe."

"So he tried to talk you into the switches, and you said no," Byrd says, fighting an answering smile and refusing to be distracted. "Then what happened?"

"I didn't say no. I did the two I had room for, but that wasn't impressive enough. He started talking up my double pirouette. It was my newest trick, and I worked on that fucker for *months*. I always liked showing it off. I had it tight at that point, too—I was barely losing any height."

If I close my eyes, I can still feel it in my body—the float of the release and the compact blur of the rotations, the rope back under my hands like magic, and my shoulders stretching to absorb the catch.

Muscle memory can be a cruel, ironic bitch. I suck in a breath and push the next words out past the hurt.

"Gabe was filming me on his phone, acting all excited and, I don't know, sort of proud? Like an actual big brother." I laugh, hating the way it sounds, young and needy. *Jesus, Echo. Get it together.* My head falls back, and I stare out the window again, suddenly ready to be done with the story. "So when he suggested I try it into the switch, I agreed. One double on the right, one single on the left. Should have been plenty of height."

"But it wasn't?"

"I was pushing for maximum clearance, and I started the beats too close to the rigging point."

"It threw off the swing."

"Yep. Stupid rookie shit, right? Maybe it was the hangover. But I threw the double anyway, and of course, because of the extra swing, the rope wasn't where it was supposed to be when I came around." Even then, I wasn't scared, my brain refusing to believe the betrayal until I actually hit the ground. "I almost got my left hand on the tail. It wouldn't have saved the pirouette, but it might have slowed me down enough to get my feet under me. And I still should've been okay—it was barely fifteen feet to the mat, and I know how to fall. I've taken a hundred of them."

"Aerials 101," Byrd says, almost nostalgic. I can feel the weight of his attention, even as he navigates the twisting two-lane road, like his ability to make me *important* is as natural to him as breathing.

Who cares if he thinks I'm important? I'm just trying to get my dick sucked, right? But something warm blooms in my chest, and I breathe a little easier.

"Yeah. But those techniques don't work as well on wood floors."

"You missed the mat? How the hell did that happen?"

"About ten inches of me did. And I don't know how. It was a big crash-style mat. Four by eight and six inches thick. My parents wouldn't let me train at home without it. I shouldn't have been that far off-center, even with the bad swing." I shake my head as if I can still deny it after all this time.

"I heard the crack before I felt it, and then everything's kind of a blur. Gabe freaking out and calling my dad, the ambulance, and the ER. I remember the sirens and how they magnified the pain, turning it into these long, wailing waves of agony. I remember thinking I was gonna miss my flight to Amsterdam and I hadn't even started packing, and how my dad would be pissed."

"You were in shock."

"That's what they told me. My head CTs were clear." I laugh again, but even I can tell it sounds forced. *Nothing to see. Nothing to save. Nothing to blame but myself.* "I woke up in the hospital room after the second surgery and realized I'd finally done it."

"Done what?" He's frowning at me again, and his mouth is still beautiful.

"Suicide by ego. Like every other fallen god."

"I guess that explains the tattoo." He glances at my wrist, and I run my fingers over the word carved into the scar.

"It works on so many levels."

"Thank you for telling me." The words are oddly formal, but another layer peels away between us, exposing something vulnerable I'm not ready to examine.

"Did it help?" I want him back to flustered and charmed. I want him craving, not concerned, but the questions fall out anyway. "You gonna fix me now?"

Fix me. Fuck me. Find my soul.

"I want to." His voice is rough and sorry, and I wait for the rest: *But there's nothing left to fix.*

It doesn't come.

We crest the final hill, and the sea devours the horizon.

The last thing I expect to see when we finally pull up another one of those long-ass Mendocino driveways is a real live circus tent. It rises like a personal mirage from the sandy soil of what they call the pygmy forest—meaning stunted pine trees and manzanitas, rather than redwoods. We're only a mile or two inland, and it's flatter here, too. The space around the tent is cleared and scattered with trailers, from a tiny hand-painted ticket wagon to a sleek airstream. Two big box trucks parked at the end of the driveway declare "Big River Big Top" on the sides in a looping script.

"Mendocino has its own circus?" I ask as Byrd parks the 4-Runner next to one of the trucks.

"It's actually a European-style traveling company." A chuckle rumbles from his chest at my amazement. "My friends Shilo and Cheyenne run it with Shilo's ex, Halston. They hire acts from all over the world and tour the Pacific Northwest from June to October every year."

"Is that how you met them? Back when you were performing?" Although the lot has a lived-in feel, with camping chairs and milk-crate tables tucked beneath awnings on a few of the trailers, no one seems to be around.

"No," Byrd replies, starting toward the airstream. "I met them after a show on one of my first trips up here with Lara. But they let me play in the tent sometimes, and it's always fun to connect with the performers they bring out for rehearsals in the spring."

"The 'beautiful freaks'?" Remembering the first night in his kitchen, I flash a grin at him, and his answering smile makes my heart leap.

"We're the best kind," he says, and I don't miss how he includes himself, and me, in the statement.

"Byrd! I thought I heard voices." A tall, totally ripped woman with short graying hair exits the airstream and throws her arms around Byrd.

"Hi, Shilo." He returns the hug with genuine affection before releasing her and gesturing to me. "This is Echo Wash. He's here for the summer, and I thought he'd enjoy checking out your scene."

"Welcome to Big River Big Top," Shilo says, shaking my hand. She has the calloused palms of an aerialist and asks the universal question. "What's your poison?"

"Rope. Some silks. Tumbling too, but I always preferred to be in the air." My standard answer, so practiced I don't have to wonder if it's still true.

"One of us, then." She winks at Byrd. "Maybe you can talk this guy into getting back where he belongs so I can hire him one of these days."

"I'm too old to start over with performing, Shilo," he protests, shaking his head.

"Bullshit." She smacks him, not particularly gently. "I'm forty-five, and you don't see me rolling over." Turning back to me, she asks, "What do you think? Seen him on the rope yet?"

Fuck yes. But I pretend I'm not swooning like a total fanboy. "Only conditioning at the cabin. I think I intimidate him."

Byrd coughs and Shilo laughs, and when I catch his eye, the heated warning there sends sparks along my spine.

"Where's everyone else today?" he asks, changing the subject.

"Cheyenne drove to SFO to pick up our first contract—duo hoop act from Hungary. They won't be back until late. Hals is on a grocery run. You probably passed him on your way up Little Lake. Josha and Milla are around somewhere. They're supposed to be running a light check this afternoon." She backs up a step before shouting "Milla" in a voice used to being obeyed.

A teenage girl in sparkly leggings and a long blond ponytail skips out of the tent, followed by a guy around my age with close-cropped auburn hair in jeans and work boots. He's pulling on a button-down shirt with the sleeves already rolled up, and even with Byrd's aura drenching my skin, I check him out by reflex.

"Almost done hanging the lights," he tells Shilo as they approach. "Hi, Byrd."

Byrd is currently wrapped in the exuberant teenage girl but manages to extract a hand to shake.

"You brought a friend," the girl, Milla, says, giving me a once-over from her spot under Byrd's arm. "He's kinda cute. Very anime. I like your tattoos."

"*Milla.*" Shilo shakes her head. "Sorry about my daughter. We're still working on her manners." But she sounds more exasperated than embarrassed.

"Echo." I offer my hand first to Milla—"*Ooh, cool name!*"—and then to the guy, Josha. "Welcome to Big Top," he says, echoing Shilo's earlier greeting, and he blushes when his hand touches mine. It's kind of adorable, but I can't help glancing over at Byrd to see if he noticed or cares.

Is he trying to set me up? Does he really think throwing me at some small-town virgin will change the insistent chemistry that fizzes between us? He doesn't protest when Milla and Josha decide to drag me back to the tent to help with their light check.

"Go have some fun."

No way I'm letting him get away with that when he had his tongue down my throat less than an hour ago.

"Sending me off to sit at the kid's table?" I tease, low so no one else can hear. His lips twitch, and for one brief, lunatic second, I consider stealing another kiss just to see his reaction. As if sensing my wild intent, he shoves me gently away, but his eyes fall to my mouth like he's tempted.

"Try to stay out of trouble."

"No promises."

10

Byrd

"We missed you last year." Shilo hands me a beer from the fridge in the airstream before cracking her own and leaning against the built-in table.

"I know. I'm sorry." I spent most of the past eighteen months scrambling to salvage my marriage, and trips to the cabin weren't part of the agenda.

"You and Lara are done?" There's sympathy there but no sorrow. Like everyone else in my life, Shilo was never a fan of my ex. "It's too small in here to watch you pace," she adds, eyeing me. "Let's take a walk."

"I think we'd been done for a while," I sigh, following her down the steps and back toward the tent. "I was just the last one to know."

"Well, 'cheers' to finally knowing." She knocks her can against mine and falls in step beside me. "Tell me about the kid."

I try not to flinch at the word. She has a son only a year younger than Echo, and hell, I think of him that way half the time myself.

Except when my tongue is in his mouth.

"He's one of Reggie's. He was supposed to start last year, but he took a bad fall and had to defer."

"So, you're his rehab coach? How's that going?"

One of the things I like about Shilo is her ability to cut through the bullshit, a little like an older, harder version of Reggie. Unlike Reggie, however, she doesn't pull her punches just because she loves me.

"I think I'm in over my head," I admit. *In more ways than one.* "He's been self-isolating, and the cabin isn't helping. I'm hoping that bringing him around you and the crew might help him remember what he loves about circus."

"The barely controlled chaos?" She chuckles.

"You sound like Cheyenne."

Shilo is a total control freak. For her, chaos has always been something to conquer, not celebrate, and she's damn good at making magic out of her victories.

"I guess she's finally rubbing off on me." She smiles fondly. "And I'm also guessing that you want me to talk to Echo? Share my inspirational tale of wreckage and recovery?"

"One of these days, yes. I think it'd be good for him to hear." Shilo busted her hip in a fall that could have ended her career a few years ago. "But not today. I don't want him to think I ambushed him or spilled his secrets."

"You gonna fix me now?"

"In fact," I add, "probably don't spread that around at all until he's ready."

She gives me a look. "You're protective of him."

"Yes." No point in denying it. We've reached the tent, and she gestures to the canopied entrance.

"Want to go inside?"

Do I want to see what Echo is up to, she means. I can't deny that either, so I follow her into the high shadows with a nod. She parks herself on one of the wrought-iron audience benches. On a show day, the tent would be packed with them, but currently, only a handful are scattered around the space.

The stage is set up opposite the door, in front of the heavy blackout curtains that section off the "backstage" area. Stage lights hang from the king poles and the rigging truss, a few more waiting their turn at the edge of the stage. There are crash mats stacked against the sidewalls, a sawhorse to one side next to a folding table piled with tools, and her son Gem's Chinese pole anchored in the alcove where the concessions wagon usually sits. Controlled chaos.

Milla and Echo are taking turns at star drops on the shimmering gold silks hanging center stage. Josha stands at another folding table set up off stage left, messing with the light board and occasionally calling out for one of them to climb or drop or hold a certain position as he bathes the stage in sunset hues.

"Milla's looking good," I venture after a few minutes.

"So is your boy."

He's not mine.

But she's right. The star drops are flashy but not dangerous, and Echo's movements are sure and almost languid, taunting Milla to match his easy grace with her coltish limbs. After the final drop—a backward shooting quad that Echo wisely declines and has Milla's blond ponytail brushing the mat and Shilo shaking her head beside me—Josha pulls up the girl's music so she can run her routine. Echo gives her a fist bump before vaulting off the stage and moving over to lean against the table.

Shilo watches the act in silence, her critical gaze softened by affection. I know I should pay attention, that she'll want my professional feedback on her daughter's burgeoning skills, but my eyes keep straying to Echo and Josha in the shadows—measuring the inches between them and caught by the way Josha ducks his head and laughs when Echo leans over to whisper in his ear. Something ugly curls in my gut, and I shove at the ungracious impulse.

Luckily, Shilo is too engrossed in her daughter's performance to notice my distraction. Until I blow it by opening my mouth.

"How come Josha's still around? I'm surprised you didn't lose him to the big city once he graduated."

"Thank god we didn't," she replies, glancing over. "Hals would throw a fit if we had to replace him. Josha's the only thing holding half this shit together." She gestures vaguely to the surrounding scene. "And the only one I trust to drive the flatbed."

I grunt, trying to smooth my features. I know a gig like Big Top takes a lot more than artistry and out-of-town star power to stay afloat, and Josha is the carpenter, mechanic, and engineer in one dedicated package. More than that, after growing up as close to next door as exists around here, he's part of Shilo's family.

He doesn't deserve my scowls, and I know better than most the electric lure of Echo's charm.

"How's Milla's big crush these days?" I ask, softening slightly and tearing my eyes away from the blue glow of Echo's hair. Shilo laughs.

"Dead and buried. Or at least buried," she amends. "Josha came out to his family last year, and she had to stop pretending he was going to change his mind someday."

"How'd that go? The coming out part?" Like Shilo, I've known Josha was gay for years. I should be proud of him, not wondering if this makes him more of a threat.

"About as expected." She shrugs. "His parents hardly noticed. His brother gave him shit for a couple of days—Jeremy is fourteen and still learning how to be a decent human being—but his sisters rallied around him and put the little punk in his place." She follows my gaze back to where both guys are now fussing over Milla while she preens. "Think Echo might teach him a thing or two before we head out for the season?" There's no threat to the curious question, but I almost choke on the growl that rumbles in my chest.

"Maybe." *Too stiff.* I can feel her eyes on me, and I take a swig of my forgotten beer.

"Or maybe not," she muses.

I shift my shoulders, awkward and edging toward miserable. Echo is leading Josha through the heavy backstage curtains, leaving Milla cross-legged on the mat, playing with her phone.

"You know Cheyenne was only twenty-five when I met her," Shilo says, freeing me from her gaze to spear me with words instead. I guess I'm not fooling anyone today.

"But no one was paying you to evaluate her."

"No. Hals and I were paying her to perform. And still married to each other with two kids."

"So, what?" I ask, sharper than she deserves and trying not to picture someone else's mouth on Echo's skin. "You win the inappropriate relationship trophy?"

I'm immediately ashamed. "I'm sorry. That was a shit thing to say."

"It was, but I'll forgive you. And I won't tell Cheyenne you said it."

I absorb the gentle rebuke, but before I can apologize again, she continues. "My point is, no one here will judge you, Byrd."

"Except myself."

And maybe Josha. Fuck.

"Always your own worst critic." She squeezes my arm. "And that's saying something, considering your marriage."

"Now who's being a dick?"

"Hey, like I said—no judgment. But you deserve to be happy, Byrd, no matter what that looks like." She gives me a nudge with her elbow and collects my half-empty beer, and for the second time today, I go in search of what I'm not allowed to want.

I find him with Josha, of course, leaning against the box truck by the 4-Runner. Echo is smoking one of his damn cigarettes, and their heads are tilted together, shoulders brushing. *Too fucking close.*

"Time to go," I say, climbing into the driver's seat and fishing the keys out of the cupholder. Josha blinks at me, no doubt surprised by my uncharacteristic rudeness, and pushes off the truck.

"Nice to meet you, Echo," he says, all country manners and shy smile, impossible to hate. "See you later, Byrd."

Echo waves him off with a wink and takes another drag before dropping the butt and stubbing it out with his shoe.

"Pick that up and get in the car." Jesus, I sound like an angry father. *Or a jealous boyfriend.* He walks over and rests his elbows on my window, a hint of a smirk tugging at the corners of his regrettable, delectable mouth.

"What happened to you?" he asks.

"Nothing. Get in the fucking car." I can't look at him when he's this close without remembering his taste on my tongue.

"Not until you tell me why you're so pissy all of a sudden."

"I'm not *pissy*." It's such an obvious lie I could laugh at myself. If I wasn't so pissed.

"You're gripping that steering wheel so tight, my cock is getting jealous, and I can hear your jaw grinding from here."

"Jesus. Can you stop talking about your dick for five minutes? Save it for someone your own age." I put all the derision I can into the words and let myself meet his eyes. Instead of backing off, he tilts his head, studying me.

"Someone like Josha?" he asks after a beat.

"You two seemed to be getting along." It's meant to sound casual, but it comes out through gritted teeth. I can't keep sitting here, exposed, while his eyes dig through my defenses like our ages are reversed. "Please just get in the car?"

He laughs then and opens my door, reaching between my legs for the lever that slides the seat back.

"What are you doing?"

"Getting in the car." And then he climbs up to straddle me while I'm still reeling from his hand on my thigh and the sight of his midnight neon hair in my lap.

My hands fly to his hips, locking him in place before he can shift forward and feel my rapidly growing erection. Undaunted, his fingers slip beneath the hem of my T-shirt to skim over my abs and trace the line of hair running down from my navel.

"This is not what I meant," I choke out, anger evaporating like oxygen as my brain scrambles to adjust to the turn of events.

"You think I want a blushing virgin?" he asks, his lips against my ear. "That's never been my style." He leans back with that arched left brow, daring me to ask the obvious question. For once, Gabriel's specter is no more than a far-off flicker.

"Then what is?" Apparently, on top of losing the ability to formulate a coherent thought, I am also now a slave to his wicked mouth.

"I like to take guys who think they're in charge and show them that they're not." There's a hint of confession beneath the smolder, perfectly tailored to slink past my rapidly crumbling barriers. "Breaking them is almost as much fun as fucking them."

I can almost see it—the banter and the battle of wills and the inevitable triumph—*That Echo*. Cocky and reckless and chasing the same.

"Sounds more Narcissus than Echo," I observe, "and it doesn't sound like I'm your type either. No one's ever accused me of thinking I'm in charge." Not *accommodating, considerate, careful* Byrd.

"I think my tastes are changing." He slides his hands up my chest and laces them at the base of my skull before running his thumbs through the scruff of beard along my jaw. "The only part of you I want to break is your self-control."

On the last word, he rolls his hips, bringing the hard ridge of his cock against mine, and the groan that escapes me sounds like surrender.

"Echo." It's a warning. A desperate plea. My hands are clenched around the firm slope of his ass, and my hips rock helplessly under him. His lips are on my throat, blazing along my rocketing pulse.

"Break for me," he breathes, and I feel the last of my sanity siphoning into his storm.

"So you can fuck me?" The words are thrown out like fingernails scrabbling for purchase, heedless of the cost.

It works. He rears back, eyes wide with shocked heat, and his body goes still.

"Would you let me?" he asks.

No. Yes. Not in the car. Nothing comes out but a shuddering breath. Understanding ripples across his features.

"How many guys have you been with?"

"Three." *Don't ask me about them. Especially not him.*

"Have you ever bottomed?" This time, he punctuates the question with another rock of his hips, as if testing my resolve.

"No." *I have to tell him.* I can't touch him like this with Gabriel's shade between us.

If you tell him, he'll never let you touch him again.

That's the whole point.

Is it? I shake my head a fraction, and something flashes in his eyes.

He answers my denial with a kiss, twining his arms around my neck and pressing all the lethal lines of his body against mine. I forfeit the internal battle on a groan—my hands are under his shirt, sliding over his sleekly muscled back to grip his shoulders, and his mouth is melting, I'm melting, the world is melting.

"It doesn't matter," he whispers, close enough to drown in. "You can have me any way you want."

11

Echo

Byrd kisses like he can't believe I'm real, savor on his tongue like syrup and smoke.

I'm greedy by comparison, sucking at his lips and teeth, hungry to harness all the things he holds hidden. Everything coalesces, urgent at the edges of my skin—the shift-surge of his thighs under mine, the euphoric torture of his zipper through my sweats, the half-moon bite of his fingernails on my shoulders crushing me into his hard heat.

Does he want to crawl inside me the way I want to do to him?

I drag my hands from the gorgeous wreck of his hair, fumbling at his jeans in the not-space between us. He sucks in a breath, breaking free of my mouth, and stops me with a hand on my wrist.

"Wait." His voice is ravaged. "Stop."

"No." After weeks of torment, I'm ready to climb him right here in the car—fuck lube, fuck condoms, all I can think about is getting his cock in my hands, in my mouth, *everywhere*.

"Echo." He drops his forehead to mine, breathing hard, and my name from his lips spells divinity and damnation.

All my life, I've been able to reach out and *take*. Skill. Admiration. Desire. Everything I ever wanted, effortlessly mine. The tremor of his fingers digs into my scars, and I won't survive if he rejects me now.

"Byrd...*please*." *I want to be myself again, not this messy, hollow thing.* "Isn't it killing you not to touch me?"

It's killing me.

"I am touching you." He knocks his head gently against mine and strokes his thumb along my thigh.

"Not enough."

A choked laugh escapes him, and he pulls back, searching my face. I'm too far gone to show him anything but the raw bones of my need, rattling at the edge of connection. How much he sees, I have no idea, but he releases my wrist, and his next words send anticipation lurching giddily up my spine.

"Put your arms behind you and grab the steering wheel."

I give his button one last tug and do as he demands.

"If you let go, I'll stop," he warns. "And whatever you do, don't lean on the horn."

He grips my neck then, his thumb heavy against the pulse point under my jaw, and skims his other hand down my chest, skating over the bare skin at my hip. When his fingers slip behind the elastic of my sweats, I make a sound embarrassingly close to a whimper, and his mouth quirks.

"Is this better?" he asks.

"*Not enough.*"

He drags his knuckles over the head of my cock, and my hips buck, straining for contact.

"How about this?"

"Jesus fucking Christ, Baardwijk." I'm clutching the steering wheel at my back hard enough to feel every stitch in the leather. "Just put me out of my misery."

And then he wraps his fingers around me, and *ohfuckyesohjesusfuckinggod,* I'd fall into him if he wasn't holding me in place. I might anyway. I'm wound so fucking tight, the whole thing's gonna be over in, like, thirty fucking seconds, and I don't even care.

His hand is warm and calloused-rough, and he's done teasing. He jacks me firm and steady, squeezing the base of my cock and twisting his palm over my crown on the upstroke to gather the precum leaking from the tip and smear it down the sensitive underside.

His eyes are locked on my face, full of wonder and hunger finally unleashed, drawing me up and over into rapture. I'm completely unmoored, babbling a nonsensical string of curses and ragged pleas, and my balls are tight and aching. As he increases the pace, I fly past all my salacious fantasies. The head of my cock swells, and I'm thrusting into his hand and...and...

When I come, *he* makes a sound so primal, I feel it on the back of my skin. Like it's not just me coating his fingers and coming apart.

Holy fucking shit.

I collapse against him, peeling my hands from the steering wheel to clutch at his hips.

"I think you might be better at taking charge than you give yourself credit for," I say, burying my face in his neck. His breath is rough and unsteady in my ear.

"Maybe my tastes are changing," he murmurs. His fingertips stroke the fine hair at my nape, and the late-afternoon sunlight slants warm and drowsy on my back. "Is it enough?"

Instead of answering, I grip his wrist and suck my cum from his fingers, and I imagine that his galloping pulse beneath my cheek means everything I want it to.

I watch him quietly panic on the ride home, his lips still bruised from my kisses, while a local radio station plays shitty jam-band music from the nineties. My post-orgasm haze has long faded by the time he finally breaks the silence.

"Put your shirt back on. Please." His voice is huskier than usual, with a note of desperation to it that makes me grin.

"It's sticky." Actually, it's more crusty than sticky now, but the point still lands. I swear he fucking blushes, but he changes the subject before I can press my luck.

"You looked good on the silks back there, with Milla."

Fine. Let him pretend he didn't have my dick in his hand if he wants to.

"Gabe taught me to do star drops as soon as I could invert at the top of the silks. I've been doing them since I was seven." *And there's no unlocked release.*

"*Gabe* taught you?"

"Yeah." The memory makes me grin. "My dad almost killed him. I'd only been in classes for about two weeks, and we weren't supposed to be in the studio without an adult watching us."

"Gabe didn't count as an adult? He must have been, what? Seventeen?"

"Not to my dad. He was still in his overprotective phase back then. But I'd seen Gabe perform the trick at his show, and it looked so cool. I wouldn't have been able to learn it at the gym until I hit level three, and Gabe was getting ready to go off to NCC. I was impatient."

"Imagine that." He catches my smirk with a sidelong glance and turns quickly back to the road. "Did you and Gabe do a lot of training together?"

"Not really. By the time he got back to the States, I'd switched to the rope, and he was an actual adult with no room in his life for a little brother."

This time, he does look at me, the sympathy on his face making me squirm.

"I told you, I grew out of that hero-worship shit a long time ago," I remind him. *Stop looking at me like a stupid child. Go back to jealous, horny Byrd.*

"Why did you apply to Cici?"

"You mean because it was Gabe's school?" I shrug. "Maybe I like proving that anything he does, I can do better."

Something hungry flickers behind his woodland gaze, but he only turns up the music and ignores me for the rest of the drive. By the time we're climbing the front porch to the cabin, it's cold enough that I've pulled my cum-stained shirt back on, and I'm itching for him to say something. Anything.

"I'm sorry."

Anything but that.

"That you gave me a hand job, or that you feel guilty about it?" I ask, masking my frustration with my fallback snark. He doesn't answer, leaning against the glass doors in the living room with his hands shoved in his pockets and that familiar wary look in his eyes.

I'm fucking sick of it.

I step into his space, gratified by his sharp exhale and the heat that inevitably flares between us when I reach up to cage his head with my hands on the glass. "Don't be sorry. I'm not. Just tell me you have lube in this house."

"I don't even have condoms." He shakes his head. "But you know it doesn't matter because I'm not fucking you."

I open my mouth, and he almost smiles.

"And you're not fucking me."

"So that wasn't foreplay? Back there in the car?"

"It was a mistake."

"You're so full of shit." I press into him, wedging my thigh between his. "Stop pretending you don't want this as badly as I do."

"Echo, I've crossed so many lines already. If I'm *pretending,* I'm doing a terrible fucking job of it." He brings his hand to my jaw and brushes his thumb over my lips. "But Reggie is expecting me—*paying me*—to give her an unbiased evaluation. How the hell am I supposed to do *that* job if we start having sex?"

"Who cares? The evaluation is fucked anyway. You already know I'm not good enough for her school anymore."

"I don't know that. There's still plenty of time."

God, he actually believes it. That somehow, he can still salvage my future. And all of a sudden, it clicks into place. *He's not trying to reject me.*

The salvation he's holding out for isn't his, it's mine.

I drop my arms and step back. Time to try a different tactic.

"You know when I don't feel fucked up?" I ask. "When you touch me. When you look at me like something worthy of wanting."

"You *are* worthy of wanting. When I'm around you, all I *do* is want."

"Then give me something. Prove it, and I'll show you."

For a long moment, he searches my face, and I try to hide my creeping fear. Finally, he leans in until his lips brush my ear, his words low and feral.

"The whole time I was jerking you off, all I could think about was taking you to bed and spreading you open with my tongue and fingers until I had you begging for my cock."

Well, fuck.

"And you say I have the filthy mouth," I gasp, heat thrilling over my skin and buzzing like static at the base of my spine.

"I love your filthy mouth," he admits. "And it's your turn."

I haven't been on the rope with a hard-on in years, and for a second, I'm fourteen again, with Jason Kase's voice in my ear telling me, *"The opposite-side climb-over gives better friction."* But hey, it's the easiest way into the unlocked dive anyway.

I do three of the inverted climbs because fuck it—it feels good, the rough weave dragging over my keyed-up cock with every hook and pull. When I slip into the prep position, I throw a smirk over my shoulder and catch him staring at my ass with the rope wedged tight between my cheeks.

Don't think. Just do it.

Be Echo.

I dive, my right hand releasing above my head and finding the tail between my legs like a thousand times before, my abs contracting to control the drop.

"If you let go, I'll stop."

I don't let go. My eyes find Byrd's, and my relief looks like pride in the reflection there.

I wrap a leg and do a fireman's slide to the mat. He's there when I land, wrapping his arms around me and dropping a kiss into my hair.

"Is it enough?" I ask, pressing my face onto the slope of his shoulder.

"Yes," he says. "Tonight, it's enough."

"Does it change anything?"

"It shouldn't." He sighs and pulls away. But underneath the reluctance is his faltering resolve.

"Why not?" I don't want it to end. I want to soak up this small moment of triumph and turn it into sweat and spit and slick, tangled limbs. Not to break him, but to give him back a piece of something as sacred as the feel of the rope sure in my hands.

"Have you ever just taken what you wanted?" I ask, as if I can't already guess the answer. "Just for yourself, and fuck the consequences?"

"Are you asking me to be selfish?"

I drop to my knees on the mat at his feet, offering up all my damaged, desperate fervor. "I'm not asking for anything," I say. "I'm telling you to *take*."

12

Byrd

I think I'm going crazy.

Echo on his knees, mouth begging to be fucked.

Ican'tIcan'tIcan't.

I can.

"I can't." I'm crouched in front of him, running my hands over his hair, his face, his neck, and he's closing his eyes, head falling back. And then he stands, pushing away, away, away, and walks to his room without a word.

I make him dinner and bring it to his room. He's sitting on the bed, watching something on his phone, wearing headphones that he doesn't take off when I enter.

"Thanks," he says. "I'll do the dishes." And then ignores me while I hover in the doorway, torn.

When he emerges, I flee up the stairs to my own room and spend an agonized half hour listening to the water running and pots banging and the clink of plates being fitted into the dishwasher.

Now the house is quiet, and I'm lying in the dark, slowly losing my mind.

Fifteen years and a half-dozen lovers, and it's always been me on my knees.

Gabriel was the first, needy and perpetually unattainable, even when I thought he was mine. Lara was the last, fragile and weighed down by her fears, always looking for reassurance.

And now Echo—vital, immediate, *real*—offering something I never knew I wanted. Am I brave enough to take it? Am I foolish enough to keep pretending I can resist?

"Have you ever just taken what you wanted?"

"You need to learn to be selfish every once in a while."

Will Reggie forgive me if I betray her trust to take her advice? Will Echo forgive me if—*when*—he finds out I loved his brother first? Do I even care anymore, when my body is an anguished roil of need, sweating in my sheets and shivering in my cool, dark room?

It's after midnight when I swing open his door and step through into a dream.

Echo is sprawled on his stomach, angelic by moonlight with his face pressed into the curve of a bicep and the sheets low on his hips. With a deep breath, I lower myself next to his pillow, my fingers hovering between the sharp angles of his shoulder blades like I could touch his vanished wings.

He stirs when the mattress shifts beneath my weight, turning his face toward me and opening his eyes. There's no surprise. No recoil or rush of breath. He looks at me like he's been waiting to wake and find me in his bed. All his vibrant color is bled away, leaving him a creature of liquid and shadow, sleep-soaked and warm, and I drop my hand to his back and brush along his spine until my fingers tangle in his hair.

Without a word, he throws an arm across my waist before tugging me closer and shifting to bury his face in my lap. A low, drowsy hum rumbles in his throat, vibrating over my groin and frying my last remaining brain cells. Heat pools everywhere his bare skin touches mine—the inside of his elbow curled around my hip, the smooth contour of his chest against my thigh, his ear brushing along my abdomen above the elastic of my briefs. His breath is hot through the thin cotton as he nuzzles my cock, and my fist tightens in his hair.

He rolls his own hips lazily into the bed, the sheet slipping to reveal half his naked ass, and the sight of the pale skin and round flexing muscle sends me back onto the pillows with a groan.

Echo lifts his gaze at the sound, rubbing his jaw lazily over the swollen head of my cock as he takes in my expression.

"You done saying no?" he asks, voice husky with sleep.

"Yes." I brush my thumb over his lips, and he catches it between his teeth, swirling his tongue around the pad. It's enough to have me thrusting beneath him, grinding my cock against his throat and into the hollow under his jaw.

He grins, a white flash in the dim, before dropping his head to lick along the groove at my hip. I run my hands over his silky shoulders, kneading the firm muscles as he works his way across my abs with wet, sucking kisses and trailing teeth.

When he hooks his fingers in the waistband of my shorts and exposes my hard length, I go still, irrationally shy under his dark, heated gaze. His breath breaks free in a rough sigh, feathering over the sensitive skin.

"Wow," he whispers, gifting me another grin. "This is going to be fun."

It starts slow, with his tongue teasing circles over the delicate ridge beneath my crown and trailing down the thick vein to suck gently on the softer skin at the root. His free hand skims over my hip and up my ribs, pausing to tug gently at my nipple before continuing its exploration.

The heat of his mouth is tantalizing, his hair tickling my inner thighs, and I'm strung taut with barely contained urgency, one fist in the pillow at my head and the other frantic in his hair. It's unexpected and maddening, this languid torture when always before, he's been riot and need.

"Echo." It's a warning growl that rises from the dark corners of desire. He swirls his tongue once more around the head of my cock and raises his eyes to mine, mischief and moonlight dancing in the blue.

"Need something?" He wraps his fingers around my base and squeezes, far too gently.

"You know what I need." My voice is almost unrecognizable, low and dangerous. A shudder runs through him, and he flicks his tongue against my slit.

"So take it."

It's challenge and sass and *retribution*, and he watches me, lips parted, while I fit the pieces together in my lust-addled brain.

Be selfish.

The fist in his hair tightens, and my other hand drops to cover his, feeding him my cock with one invading thrust, until the blunt head hits the back of his tongue and he starts to suck in earnest.

And holy fucking hell if my soul doesn't leave my body for a second before crashing back to relish every gluttonous, carnal second of Echo's slick, wet throat constricting around my flesh.

It's been years since I've had anything but Lara's perfunctory mouth on my dick, and this is altogether different—rough and messy and entirely erotic, my fingers threaded in his hair, my body clenching from ass to abs as I try to keep from driving into his mouth and ending it too soon.

"*Fuck, y*ou feel good." I'm mesmerized by the bob of his ebon head and the way he swirls up my cock with his whole body, rutting into the sheets every time he dives back down like he's the one being driven wild. Saliva coats his fingers, and he releases the base of my shaft with a final squeeze, tugging lightly on my balls before trailing a finger into the crease of my ass. When he presses against my tight rim, I lose what's left of my control, fucking into his mouth as my rhythm dissolves and I clutch at his skull, locking him against me.

"I'm gonna come," I warn through gritted teeth, with no intention of letting him go. And then he fucking *purrs,* a low rumble that starts in his chest and vibrates through every inch of my buried cock until it hits the tight coil of my balls, and I'm done, pulsing and arching and roaring my release while he swallows me down.

"Jesus Christ," I gasp, once my brain can form words again. "Don't you have a gag reflex?"

"Mmm." He climbs up my spent and quaking form to plant a kiss in the hollow of my throat and grind his erection against my thigh. "We train that shit out as baby twinks these days." Another kiss, nipping at my jaw. "Didn't you ever practice on dildos as a kid?"

"No, Christ. You really are a deviant."

"Lucky for you." He licks along my lower lip until I open to his questing tongue, and he feeds me the taste of my own undoing.

13

Echo

I wake up alone and wonder if he was a dream.

But no, his scent lingers on the pillows, almonds and apricots, and the sheet is crusted where I spilled my own release over his fingers before drifting back to sleep last night. My dick remembers, and my morning wood is more than ready for another round.

I tug on a pair of clean sweats—it might be the middle of nowhere, but I'm still not sure how he'd react to me walking around naked with a hard-on—and pad up the stairs. He's not in the kitchen. Did he crawl back to his own bed after I fell asleep? I have no idea what time it is—I didn't bother to check my phone—but the entire time I've been here, I've never woken up before him. I haven't been in his bedroom, either, and I'm taking the first hesitant step up the last flight of stairs when I realize the shower is running.

Fuck yes.

Byrd's bathroom is ridiculously large, with a claw-foot tub, a walk-in shower, and one huge window looking out over the forested hillside. It's built for pampering and dirty fantasies. I've certainly indulged in my share of the latter, but I'm still not prepared for the way the sight of him, wet and naked with his back to the door, steals the breath from my lungs. I immediately regret my decision to bother with pants.

Caught on the threshold, I drink him in—the dark dusting of hair on his thighs and the swell of his ass; the grooves of muscle along his spine; the way his biceps flex and his broad shoulders shift as he runs his hands through his hair. His skin is tan and perfect, unmarked, and the urge to score him with my fingernails and lick the wounds floods the back of my tongue.

I must make some sound, a groan or a whimper, or maybe he feels my scorching gaze, because he half turns, looking over his shoulder, and his eyes darken. Without giving him a chance to protest, I shed my sweats and cross the room to open the shower door and slip inside. He turns fully to face me, still rinsing the last of the shampoo from his hair, and I give him a slow, deliberate once-over. His dick twitches where it hangs heavy against his thigh, and I'm shot through with the memory of him, swollen on my tongue, and the sweet-bitter taste of his cum.

It's enough to make me close the distance between us before dragging my nails through the wet curls on his chest and licking up the column of his throat. The sensation of his rough stubble under my lips makes me shiver, and even though he's only got maybe thirty pounds and a couple of inches on me, when he drops his hands to my shoulders and runs them down my back, I feel, for a bright, fleeting second, strangely young and almost small.

It's like he's somehow more *finished* than the guys I usually fuck—his lines of muscle and bone drawn sharper, bolder, and all his textures rougher and more fascinating.

I want to claim them. I want to pin him against the tiles and pillage him with my cock until I've stolen his secrets and made them mine.

I am definitely making it to the store today.

"How did you sleep?" he asks, amusement in his voice like he can hear my thoughts. I drag myself back from the abyss to meet his gaze.

"Like the dead," I say. "But I was kind of hoping to wake up with my dick wedged between your cheeks." I punctuate the admission by squeezing the ass in question and grinding my erection into the crease at his hip. His own cock thickens in response.

"I thought you liked being the little spoon," he teases, nuzzling at my jaw. The memory of my back pressed into the warm curve of his body while he jacked me off with a hand curled around my throat flashes through me, and I hum in his grip.

"I like it all. *Any way you want me*, remember?"

He doesn't protest when I back him up against the wall, instead taking my face in his hands and bringing his mouth to mine. I'm still not sure he'll ever let me top him, but fuck if I'm going to stop trying. And in the meantime...

God, I could get drunk on his kisses.

For everything he holds back elsewhere, he kisses with abandon. This one starts as an indulgence, deliberate, tasting every corner of my mouth until the answer to the question is an overwhelming *yes*. I fall against him, boneless, my hands on the warm tile at his back, my throbbing cock nestled against his, and his hands on my jaw the only things holding me up.

He moans into my mouth, and my pulse quickens, sparking along my limbs and flooding me with need.

More.

And *mine.*

Gasping for control, I pull away and reach for the body wash on the small corner shelf.

"My turn," I tell him, flashing a breathless grin. "Hands on the wall."

When he hesitates, I kiss him again, harder this time, and then bite down on his lower lip. He drops his hands with a hiss, his pupils dilating to swallow the gold-green fire in his eyes. The steam swells with the scent of almonds as I squirt some of the soap into my palm and stroke it up his shaft, and his head falls back against the tile.

"Let go, and I'll stop," I warn, half teasing, half not, and then step into him, wrapping my hand around us both.

He shudders as I glide my fingers up and squeeze our heads together, before rubbing my thumb in a rough circle over his slit. My other hand holds him still against the wall while I pump both our lengths, rocking my hips and reveling in the sinful glide of skin on skin.

"*Fuck.*" It's half curse, half growl, and now his eyes are locked on my hand. "So fucking hot." His fingers flex and clench at his sides, and his voice is strained. "You have such a beautiful fucking cock."

"*Holy shit.*" My grip stutters, steadies, slows. "I'm gonna come if you keep talking like that."

"Jesus. Don't *stop.*" His hand comes up and closes around mine, and I don't care that he's breaking the rules, because now he's thrusting all along my cock, and our fingers are interlaced and firm, and I'm surging into the exquisite friction, matching his rhythm.

I need him to come first. I'm frantic for it, so I wrap the wet fall of his hair in my fist and yank his head back.

"Come, come, come," I chant breathlessly against the hollow of his pulse, and then I sink my teeth into the swell of muscle at the crook of his neck.

"*Echo.*" My name is a hoarse howl to a pagan god, torn from his throat. His head slams back into the tiles and his dick pulses under my fingers, and *thankyoufuckinggodIfuckingmadeit.*

Because it's too late to stop. I'm spiraling, soaring, shooting, shattering. But at least he falls to pieces with me.

"You broke the rules," I say eventually. We're both sitting on the floor under the spray, sprawled and senseless, and thank god for on-demand hot water heaters, or we'd be freezing too. "Does that mean I get to spank you now?"

"I'm breaking a lot of rules." *For you.*

He doesn't say it, but I hear it anyway. I'm too cum-drunk to feel guilty.

"So what next?" I ask instead. "Shopping for lube?"

"Next, breakfast," he replies, laughing and shoving at my thigh with his foot. "And then we train."

If I was expecting Byrd's magic dick to automatically fix me, it doesn't happen. The traitorous battle between instinct and insecurity still rears its head, short-circuiting my brain any time my hand is called on to release and regrip. But *something* is different. When the panic hits and I search for Byrd, he's full of confidence now, instead of concern, and it's hard to hold on to my fear when he refuses to show me his. So I breathe and push and steal wet, sloppy kisses in between tries.

We spend a long, hot afternoon in mid-May setting up his outdoor rig, shirtless and laughing and taking every excuse to put our hands on each other. It's there, under the dappled redwood shadows, that I really see him fly for the first time, and something shifts inside me.

Freedom.

I miss it.

We spend at least one day a week out at Big Top as this year's performers trickle in and the new show starts to come together. I do silks with Milla, talk shop with Shilo and her wife Cheyenne, and listen to the stories of the new arrivals.

Byrd keeps his distance when we're in public, but his eyes follow me in the tent and around the lot, and more than once, I catch Shilo watching us with a knowing look in her eyes.

Josha is actually becoming a friend, although I still flirt enough to stoke the rougher edge of Byrd's desire, and I relish every time I push him to the brink of his control.

He's deliriously generous with his mouth and hands but maddeningly stingy with his dick. He'll let me get him off, and one night in the kitchen, after a few beers, he puts me on my knees and uses my mouth until I'm choking and tears are running down my face. But even though I come in my hand before he's even done with me, wild with the glorious unleashed brutality of it, he refuses to touch me for two days afterward and ignores all my reassurances.

And for all his talk that first night of spreading me open until I begged for his cock—something I am totally down for—he still won't actually fuck me. Like it's some hetero holdover line he's drawn in the sand of his honor and refuses to cross, no matter how I taunt and plead.

So I train and tease and fuck myself on my fingers when I wake up alone, and I wonder if I'm using him or falling in love.

14

Byrd

"We're having company?" Echo asks as I hit the end-call button on my phone and toss it onto the couch next to me with a sigh. He's been lying on the mat since my sister's call interrupted our training session, toying with the tail of the rope like a lazy kitten.

"Looks that way. James is going to pick Elke up in Oakland and drive her up. He'll spend the night at an Airbnb in Navarro, and she'll be here for who knows how long. Hopefully, not more than a week."

"You and your sister don't get along?" There's no judgment in his voice, only curiosity.

"We get along fine, most of the time. But she's...a lot. You'll see." Elke has reliably questionable intentions, no filter, and creates chaos by simply occupying a room. I have no idea what she'll make of Echo.

"And James is her boyfriend?" He bats the tail in my direction with a smirk. "Is he hot?"

"James is my brother-in-law. Ex now, I guess. And a good friend."

"The video game guy?"

"Yes."

"So..." He catches the rope on its next swing and pins me with his sapphire gaze. "Is he hot?"

"He's straight. And too old for you."

That cracks him up, of course, and he peels himself from the mat and stalks toward me on all fours. My dick starts to pay attention, and I palm myself through my joggers. "He's also Lara's brother, in case you missed that part. You're going to have to behave while he's here."

"I always behave." He climbs into my lap and straddles my thighs, arching that damn brow at me until I reach up to smooth it away with my thumb.

"Don't," I say, unthinking.

"Why not?" the cheeky little brat asks, waggling it at me. While I fumble for an answer, he pulls the elastic from my hair and starts to card his fingers through it.

Because it reminds me of your brother.

"I'm serious," I warn. "About James." *That too.*

His grip in my hair tightens, and he tugs my head back, eyeing my mouth, as my hands find their way down the back of his shorts to squeeze his ass. Which might not be helping me get my point across. "Elke will be enough drama. I don't think I can handle the fallout if James figures out..." I trail off, and Echo goes still, his lips an inch from my own.

Shit.

"That you're with a guy now? Or that it's me?" His tone is dangerous, and his eyes have gone flat and hurt.

"Echo." I could almost laugh if he wasn't looking at me like that. "*No one* could be ashamed of you. You're a walking wet dream, and you know it." I dig my fingers into his ass again and tug him against my erection in demonstration. "But James is very protective of his sister. Despite how long we've been friends, I'm pretty sure the *only* reason he still talks to me now is because the divorce was Lara's idea."

"And what? You think if he sees you've moved on, he'll be pissed?"

"Or hurt. And I don't need to rub it in his face. I also think it won't kill you to keep it in your pants for one night."

"It might." He drops his hands from my hair to his thighs. "I've never really done the whole 'in the closet' thing."

He's pissed, and the guilt makes my own temper flare. "Jesus Christ, Echo. I'm not asking you to pretend to be straight. You can't tone down the flirting for a few hours while he's here?"

The disappointment in his eyes as he pushes off my lap burns acrid in my gut.

"You play nice in public all the time," I plead, frustrated. "Why is this so different?"

"I guess it's not." He reaches the rope and starts to climb. "But if you think anyone at Big Top is fooled, you're deluding yourself."

I want to stay angry, secure in my righteous belief that it's not asking too much to respect James's sensitivity for one night. I want to grovel, to beg forgiveness for asking Echo to sacrifice pieces of his identity the way I've spent my life doing for others.

Instead, I tread lightly, expecting him to withdraw, and tell myself it's easier with distance between us.

His response is to wage war with his body.

Taking advantage of the warming weather, he abandons his shirts entirely. My days are spent watching him walk around in ass-hugging joggers and faded jeans slung low on his hips to reveal the irresistible V of his obliques below the lean expanse of his torso.

He attacks the rope during every practice, pushing himself to the edge of his fear as if determined to prove it was never there to begin with, and every movement is calculated for seduction. Wheel ups and scorpions and arabesques—anything that lays him out, arched and exposed.

One afternoon, he rediscovers his ninja roll, landing the internal rotation of the half pirouette in a perfect back balance, his body displayed in a vaulted line from toes to fingertips. The look in his eyes has me crossing the mat, tugging his head back and down with a fist in his hair, and capturing his delighted mouth while he's still in the air. For one moment, we're back on the same side, and I'm lost in the verdant taste of his joy, sweet and splendid on my tongue.

Each hour I resist him is punished when we inevitably come together, a toll paid in lust and flesh. His grip painful in my hair as he razes the sensitive skin of my throat. His teeth fierce on my nipples and bruising my lips. His fingers sunk in my ass, stroking my prostate as he works me with his tongue and compels ecstasy from every agony.

By the day of James and Elke's arrival, I have to wear my hair loose and a collared button-down to hide the marks of his retribution, while Echo oozes sin in a deceptively simple white V-neck tee, thin enough to reveal the shadows of ink across his ribs.

"At least I'm wearing a shirt," he snarks, sliding a pile of diced onions into a bowl and passing it over. We're making lasagna, and he's been alarmingly docile all day. I can't tell if he actually plans to behave himself or if he's setting me up, and I'm no longer certain I care.

"You need a haircut," I observe, although I like the way he tosses his head to clear the blue-tipped strands from his eyes. It's an excuse to touch him, to rub the dark silk between my fingers and brush my thumb along his winged brow. His eyelids flutter, and he leans back against the counter, gripping the edge when I slide my knee between his thighs.

"Do they have any decent salons around here?" He tilts his head as I run my jaw up his neck, tickling him with my stubble. That damn purr starts in his chest, the vibration hitting the base of my spine, and I pull back before I get carried away and start burning the onions.

"There are a few that cater to the weed wives and big-city transplants. I'm pretty sure at least one of them survived the Covid lockdowns." *Blood back in the big brain, Byrd.* I move back to the stove.

"Maybe I'll do it for my birthday."

"Your birthday?" I look over, hand halfway to a can of tomatoes. He's still leaning on the counter, watching me through half-lidded eyes, the hard outline of his cock pressing against his jeans.

"Twenty-one in two weeks. You'll finally be able to take me to bars."

"We've already been to both pubs in town." Patterson's is a regular dinner stop for us on our way home from Big Top, and one Sunday afternoon, he dragged me to Dick's to shoot pool after a grocery run. He's never been carded.

"Well, soon we can do it legally. Maybe we can go down to the city and hit up one of the famous San Francisco gay clubs."

"Would you like that?" I was married to Lara the whole time I lived in the bay. I know the places he's talking about, but I've never been inside one. "A birthday trip?"

He pushes off the counter and closes the distance between us to rub his hand over the front of my jeans.

"What I'd really like is to ride your eight-inch cock until I come all over your chest and then return the favor, but I'm not holding my breath." He presses his lips to mine, stealing my groan, and then shoves me gently before returning to his station at the cutting board. "In the meantime, I guess I'll settle for a haircut."

"I'll make an appointment," I choke out, clearing my throat and dragging my eyes back to the stove. We definitely need new onions.

"I can't wait."

"Do you only shoot buildings?" Echo and Elke are sitting at the kitchen island, scrolling through pictures of my sister's latest project on her tablet and finishing off the third bottle of wine while James and I tag team the dishes.

"Well, all the money's in weddings, so I do a lot of those, but my passion is architecture," Elke tells him. "Especially urban architecture in Europe. I love the juxtaposition of the ancient and the modern."

"She wanted to go to design school as a kid but didn't have the patience to stay in one place for that long. Or to learn all the math." I swat away the wine cork she throws at me with the dish towel in my hand. "Show him the Amsterdam series you did last year so he can check out his new playground."

Echo shoots me a look, but I'm not rescuing him. He's handled her enthusiasm and her incessant questions surprisingly well all night, turning his easy flirtatious charm her way. He's been confident and polite with James as well, his trust-fund manners on full display.

Even now that he's a little drunk, I'm the one struggling to maintain the facade. The whole time I'm drying and putting away the dishes and catching up with James at the sink, I can't keep my eyes off him. His flushed cheeks and wine-stained lips heighten his already-dramatic coloring to paralyzing levels, and I'm jealous of every brush of his arm against Elke's, every bump of their knees under the island.

When he catches me staring for the hundredth time, he bites his lip to hold in a smile, arching his brow. It's getting easier to banish Gabriel every time Echo claims the gesture, overwriting old memories with new. My lips quirk in response, and I shake my head as he bends back to Elke's iPad.

"So," he says, shoulders trembling with suppressed laughter. "Amsterdam?"

"So," Elke responds, deadpan. "Are you fucking my big brother?"

I freeze, fingers tightening reflexively on the wineglass in my hand, as James's head comes up beside me and Echo's eyes flash to mine.

"Not yet." He holds my gaze a second longer before turning to her with a shrug. "He's playing hard to get."

"Really? That doesn't sound like Coen."

"Elke."

They both ignore me.

"Oh yeah," Echo continues. "He's been a paragon of self-control. Apparently, he's immune to my wiles."

"Tell me more."

"Elke, give it a rest."

James is watching us now, the dishes forgotten in the sink.

"This is you playing nice?" I add to Echo when he finally looks at me again.

"You said keep it in my pants." He turns on his stool, knees opening, and spreads his arms. "Fully covered."

"You're quite the brat, aren't you?" Elke giggles like a god-damn teenager, and I can feel James tensing at my side. "I bet you could teach Coen a thing or two."

"You have no idea." Echo tilts his head at me. "Gonna send me to my room now?"

"That might be a little awkward since it's currently my room." My sister tosses me a devious smile. "But I'm happy to switch and take the couch."

"Jesus, Elke." *Damage control.* "Can you keep your mouth shut for five fucking seconds?"

"I'm only trying to help."

"No you're not. You're trying to stir up shit, as usual."

"Wait." *James.* "Before you two get into one of your sibling battles, can I ask a question?" He doesn't wait for my reply. "I thought Echo was supposed to be your student?"

"He is." *Here we go.*

Is it too late to turn back the clock and stop myself from star-ing at Echo for five seconds too long? To prevent the inevitable collision of curiosity and pride? I should have taken James out to dinner and left Echo and Elke to babysit each other.

You wanted to show him off.

"So this is all bullshit? Or is 'student' some kind of new euphemism for fuck toy in the gay community?" Sarcasm drips from James's voice.

Echo bursts out laughing. "Don't you live in San Francisco?"

"What's that supposed to mean?" James glowers at him.

"He means," I say, placing a hand on my friend's arm before he can stomp across the kitchen and start something we'll all regret. "It's 2024, and you design video games in the Bay Area. Half the guys you work with are gay."

"I know that." He shakes himself free of my grip. "I'm not a homophobe. I just didn't know my sister's husband was one of them."

Echo's eyes shoot daggers above a contemptuous smirk, while Elke frowns like she's not the one who lit the match.

"Technically, I'm bisexual," I say dryly, letting the "husband" comment slide. "And I would have told you years ago, but Lara wouldn't let me."

"Lara knew?"

"Of course she knew. I would never keep something like that from any partner, let alone my wife."

"Is that why she really kicked you out, then? Because she stopped being enough? You wanted to fuck men?" His tone grows louder and nastier with each question, but before I have a chance to try and calm him down, Echo jumps back into the mix.

"If he's not trying to suck *your* dick, why do you care who he fucks?"

"I'm curious about that too," Elke pipes up from the peanut gallery.

For fuck's sake.

"I care if he was trying to stick his dick in some kid's ass while he was married to my sister."

"I wish," Echo murmurs, not quite under his breath.

"Fuck off, James," Elke explodes, jumping up from her stool. "You know as well as I do that Lara was the problem, not Coen's dick."

"*Enough.*" My voice cuts across the kitchen, shocking them all into stillness. "James, I was *never* unfaithful to Lara, and you know better than anyone why we fell apart. You were there."

Coloring, he looks away.

"Elke, please never talk about my dick again." I shake my head at her cross-my-heart gesture. "Echo..." *I tried to warn you.*

"Yeah, yeah. I know." He's still flushed, brilliant and untouchable in his rebellious truth. "Go to my room."

Byrd

"I remember when you and Lara bought this place." James leans his elbows on the deck railing and stares out into the dark trees. It's an overture, if not quite an apology, and I try not to think of Echo in the same spot, smoking with his head tipped back and his eyes full of stars.

"We had some fun trips those first couple of years." Taking the spot next to him, I mimic his pose. "Remember that girl you brought up for Fourth of July that time? Jennifer?"

"Juniper." He chuckles. "God, what a disaster. I thought Lara would skin her alive when she threw up all over the new shower."

"Yeah, well, she was, what? Twenty-two?"

"Barely." He glances over at my face. "I guess I shouldn't be throwing stones."

"I guess not."

"Look, man." He sighs. "I'm sorry if I lost my shit in there. You kind of blindsided me, you know?"

"I know. I was trying to keep it under the radar. I forgot Elke doesn't really have that setting. Or Echo, I'm learning."

"So is there really something going on with you and this kid?" He holds up his hands when I level a look at him. "I'm asking as a friend."

"I know you think you are, James, but I also know anything I tell you will make it back to Lara eventually, and I'd rather not throw any more hurt on that pile."

"Fair enough."

We stand in silence for a while, listening to the creak and rustle of the forest. A night owl calls, and something answers with a shriek. A bobcat, I think.

"You could have told me, you know. Whatever Lara wanted. I still would have kicked your ass at Elder Scrolls on Sundays."

"You know Lara," I say, mourning the missed opportunity to be truly myself with my last real male friend. "It wasn't what you'd think of *me* that scared her, but what you'd think of *her* for being with me." *Maybe it's not too late.* "Anyway, now you know."

"Now I know."

"If you think you can keep from hulking out again, you can come back inside for ice cream. I was going to make a pie, but..." Echo kept feeding me blueberries until we both needed a shower and a change of clothes. By the time we got back to the kitchen, no pies were being made. "We ran out of time."

"I think I'll pass tonight, Byrd. I still need to check into the Airbnb and wash off the drive."

"Thanks for playing chauffeur." I chuckle. "Four hours in the car with Elke is its own adventure."

"That sister of yours never shuts up, does she?"

"Not so much, no."

"Well, I'll have the radio to myself the whole way home tomorrow, and I'll be able to listen to my podcasts in peace."

"You still hooked on *Higherside Chats*?"

"Best shit out there." He punches my shoulder, a slightly awkward bro move, but I take it for the peace offering it is. "Still on for brunch in Mendo tomorrow?"

"You could come out here instead, if you want. The PlayStation was the first thing I set up when I got here. I have all of our games. Let Elke make us brunch."

"What about the kid?"

"*Echo*," I say, a little sharply, "is not to be trusted in the kitchen without expert guidance. But he could run the juicer for mimosas without getting into too much trouble."

Way to convince James to drop the "kid" comments.

Still, scrambled eggs do not count as brunch.

"Maybe check in with your houseguests before we make any plans," he says, "I'm a little scared of those two."

"You and me both, brother." And we're laughing as he hugs me goodbye and heads down the long steps to the driveway.

Elke is alone on the couch in the lower living room, flipping through one of her photography magazines, when I come in from the top porch. She looks up and gives me a wry smile as I start down the stairs to join her.

"Guess I still know how to clear a room."

"Did he come back?"

Echo chose not to hide out in his-now-temporarily-Elke's room when he stalked out of the kitchen earlier, instead disappearing through the sliding glass doors and over the edge of the lower deck. I didn't hear either of the cars start up, thank god, since he'd definitely be over the line after keeping up with Elke all night.

"Echo? No."

I start for the doors myself, hoping he stayed on the property and I won't have to wander the neighborhood in the dark.

"Hold on a second," she says, patting the couch next to her. "I need to talk to you."

"I need to find him." I do. It's a physical pull, tugging at someplace below my solar plexus, sending me out before Echo evaporates into the night like an angry wraith.

"And this is exactly why you need to stay and listen to me, Coen." It's the concern beneath the exasperation that catches my attention. "Echo's a big boy. He'll survive an hour of disappointment on his own, without you chasing after him like a lovesick puppy."

"That's not what I'm doing. He's my responsibility, and I need to make sure he's safe." And not trying to do something monumentally stupid like walk all the way to Mendo or start climbing the rig after three-plus glasses of wine.

"Was it also your responsibility to start fucking him? Part of Reggie's assignment?"

"No, of course not." I groan, dropping onto the couch beside her. I'm obviously not escaping without a little-sister lecture, so I may as well get it over with. "And contrary to what everyone assumes, I have not actually fucked him." *My increasingly meaningless line in the sand.*

"But something's going on, Coen. Even James could see it."

"Once you threw it in his face."

"And Echo helped with that too, didn't he?"

"What's your point, Elke?"

"My first *question*, Coen, is why did you try to hide the relationship from James in the first place? That was obviously your idea. And before you go all denial on me, it's also obvious there *is* a relationship, whether you're calling it 'fucking' or not."

I could go around all day on that latter point, but I'm not sure which of us I'd be lying to, so I answer the question instead.

"Because I knew how the night would go if James found out. And I was right. Thanks for that, by the way."

"It went that way because he didn't find out from you. You seriously think if you'd taken him aside right away, or hell, prepared him with a phone call, it still would have imploded so badly?"

"Maybe not." I scrub my hand over my face. "But the long-term repercussions will be the same. James will tell Lara, Lara will get hurt and then be pissed, and then she'll start telling everyone we know, including my contacts at Cirque. And no one will care that he's of legal age. All they'll see is another older guy in a position of power, coercing sex from an impressionable young talent."

"They'll say that until they meet Echo," she scoffs. "It's pretty obvious who's calling the shots around here."

"Please don't let him hear you say that. He's barely house-broken as it is."

"Well, you're the one choosing to mess around with a child."

"He's not a child." *Not in the ways that matter.*

"He was acting a bit like one tonight," she observes.

"You're one to talk. And you've got six years on him."

"Don't get all defensive." She curls her legs up onto the couch and turns to face me, setting the magazine aside. "I don't want to fight with you about what Echo is or isn't. I just want to make sure you're being careful."

"Are you seriously giving me the safe-sex talk right now?"

"No, dork. I'm sure even you can remember how to use a condom."

"I thought we agreed you'd stop talking about my dick."

"I'm talking about your *heart*, you big dumb lug. The one you like to hand away like candy for anyone to break a piece off? I want you to protect yourself *emotionally* for a change. You're terrible at that, and you know it."

"You think Echo is going to break my heart?" I put disbelief in my voice like I can conjure the sheer ridiculousness of the suggestion.

"Well, is he?" she asks, not fooled.

Into a million pieces.

"No. It's not like that." *It's treading dangerously close to those waters.* "Christ, Elke, we haven't even had sex."

"Not yet." She deliberately echoes Echo's statement from before, and the irony is not lost on me.

"That was just Echo being—"

"A brat?"

"—*Echo.*"

"Uh-huh. Well, that's reassuring." She pats my cheek the way our gram used to when we were children and were trying to get out of cleaning up some mess we'd made. Irritated, I swat her hand away. "So, what, then?" she presses. "What is it like if it's not '*like that*'?" And then, because she's goddamn Elke and always thinks she knows better than anyone, she answers her own questions with a statement. "You have to know he's using you."

A pit opens in my stomach, shadowed with self-loathing and thorny with doubt.

"Yes, Elke." I keep my face impassive, my trembling fists shoved between my thighs. "I know."

Of course I know. He hasn't tried to hide it. *"The only time I don't feel fucked up is when you touch me."* He's using my desire to fuel his recovery, and it's *fine*, because his recovery is what I want too. We've never pretended this would last past his evaluation—an evaluation I'm increasingly certain I'll be handing over to Reggie once the last of my credibility is shattered and she yanks me from the case.

But another, deeper part of me is laughing at my foolishness, because Elke is right. Reggie is right. I don't know how to hold back my heart in these situations, and pretending that keeping my dick out of Echo's tight ass is the same thing is both laughable and doomed to fail.

I'm used to ignoring the advice of the women in my life, though, so I lie to us both one more time.

"I can handle my own sex life, Elke." I return her pat on the cheek, equally patronizing. "No one is falling in love."

I make my way across the lawn, following the creak and clatter of the rigging that tells me Echo is, in fact, on the rope. There's no moon tonight, and in the faint starlight that filters through the trees, all I can see is the shadow of his movements and his white T-shirt flashing in the dark.

"Hey," I call softly. He ignores me. "Echo." Firmer this time. "You shouldn't be up there drunk in the dark. It's not safe."

His movements slow, then stop. After a second, he drops to the mat.

"I'm not a fucking child, Byrd. I am capable of making my own decisions."

I know. I still want to protect you.

But what I say out loud is:

"Is that what you did tonight? Made your own decisions?"

"You told me to lay low, to 'keep it in my pants.' You never told me to lie." He moves toward me, coalescing out of the darkness like a mirage of pale skin and turbulent flashing eyes, and stops barely beyond arm's reach.

"You're right. I never asked you to lie." I shove my hands in my pockets to keep them from seeking him out. "It wasn't your fault, anyway. Elke was only picking up on what I wasn't strong enough to hide."

His lips twitch. "Who knew I was so irresistible?"

I did.

You did when you wore that shirt.

"Does it really matter?" he asks. "Your friend is a dick. From everything you've told me, so is your ex. Who cares what they know?"

"It doesn't really matter." Elke's warning lingers, bitter in my throat. "Not to you. You'll be gone in two months, back to fucking in your own league." *And I'll be here, dealing with the fallout of my own weakness.*

"My own league? You mean other *kids*?" He steps closer, his fists balled at his sides. "So, what? I'm your current charity case? Don't do me any fucking favors, Byrd."

My head snaps up, reeling, shocked anew by the insecurities hiding beneath his merciless bravado.

How does he do that? How does he hide his fears so well and then unleash them like a weapon when I'm least prepared? The armor of my own fears is woefully inadequate to withstand him.

"Are you joking? *You're* the one who's out of *my* league, Echo. What the hell are you going to want with a washed-up divorcé carrying around a string of failed relationships once you're off conquering the cirque world?"

"Stop." His hands reach up to cup my face. "I don't give a shit about your past relationships."

"You should." I close my fingers around his wrists but don't pull away. Maybe I've avoided telling him about Gabriel because Elke is right, and I know this thing between us is temporary. Maybe the best thing now is to come clean and blow it all up before it goes any further.

Ask me why, Echo. I won't lie to you, but I'm not strong enough to offer it up unasked.

"I've never even had a relationship to fuck up until now," he says instead, running his thumb gently over my mouth like those last two words aren't crushing me. "And you're fucking thirty-two, so cut it with the 'washed up' crap. I've seen you on the rope. If you wanted to get back into it, the only thing stopping you is yourself. Hell, Shilo would hire you in a heartbeat."

"Even if you're right, you're still leaving in August."

His lips are so *close.*

"Maybe."

"Not maybe. You're getting stronger every day. In another two months, those fears you're fighting will be a distant memory." I squeeze his wrists once, then pull them down, shaking my head. "It would be stupid for either of us to get attached to what's happening here."

"What if I'm already attached?"

I stare at him, ethereal in the darkness, knowing all too well how real he feels under my hands.

I should shut this down right now. Ignore the way my heart is pounding and send him back up to his bed on the couch—hell, back to LA if I was smart. Because no matter what he thinks he's feeling, he will leave eventually, and I'll be the one left behind.

But he's made me selfish. And I want him more than I want to protect my foolish heart.

"Don't," I whisper, but it sounds like *please*.

16

Echo

"Don't," he whispers, but it sounds like *please*, and I launch myself into his arms.

His hands come up under my ass as I wrap my legs around him, claiming his mouth and dismantling his protests with my tongue. I want to kiss away the scars of everyone who's come before me and suck their venom from his wounded soul.

What comes later is a problem for another day.

He carries me back to the mat without breaking the kiss, stumbling slightly when his foot hits the edge in the dark. I'd happily go down with him, but he catches himself and sets me back on my feet. I tear my mouth away long enough to strip out of my shirt and go back to devouring him as I start on his buttons.

He doesn't stop me, for once matching my urgency with his own, tugging open my jeans and shoving them down my thighs before palming my eager cock. The night is warm and dark, the nearest neighbor is half a mile away, and Elke...Elke can have my bed. I'm having Byrd here on the mat, and fuck all if I'm sleeping on the couch tonight.

I tear through the last few buttons and push the crisp cotton shirt from his shoulders before dropping my head to suck along his collarbone as I step out of my jeans. He's peeling his own off now, one handed and clumsy, while he continues to stroke my cock. Our knees knock against each other, and my hands fly everywhere, too greedy to be graceful. His hair brushes against my abs and over his shuttling hand as he bends to tug his last foot free, and the silky texture caressing my crown steals the strength from my legs. I fall back onto my ass, pulling him on top of me with a sound halfway between a moan and a laugh.

"Shit," he rasps, raising up on an elbow to take in my face. "Are you okay?" His shirt is tangled between us, still caught on his wrist, and he shifts his weight so I can tug it free.

"Yes. Do that again."

"Fall on you?"

"Your hair." I push at his shoulder. "Use it on my cock."

"Mmm. Like this?"

"Yes. *Oh.*" I writhe beneath him as he hooks my knee and presses it open, letting his burnished waves fall down over the crease of my thigh and trail along my aching shaft. The whole mess of it pools in my groin, and I lift my head, wishing the moon was up so I could take in the full glory of the visual. Then he rubs the soft stubble of his beard lightly over my balls, and my head falls back with a whimper.

"*Fuck*, that's insanely hot." I reach for him, and he finds my seeking fingers, lacing them together, palms pressed against my open thigh.

"I can make it even better," he says, and nuzzles deeper, running the flat of his tongue up the seam behind my balls. I jolt against his mouth, and he slides his other arm under my free leg, splaying his hand across my hip to hold me still.

"I like you like this." He peers up at me through the fall of his hair.

"Desperate?" I groan, wrapping my hand around myself and pinching the tip. Precum slicks my fingers, and I bring them to his lips.

"Trapped." He catches one in his teeth and sucks it clean. "*Mine.*"

Yours.

And even though I've never been the guy who gets off on surrender, my whole body shudders at the thought.

And then he dips his head and proceeds to take me apart.

His tongue is worship and torture—a delicious invasion, sucking and spearing at my entrance until I'm a dripping, defiled mess.

I'm flayed open, inside out. The stars are all around me, behind my eyes and under my skin, and my cock is weeping, but I don't touch it. I want every nerve ending concentrated *there*, under his mouth, opening to his warm, wet tongue.

"Byrd," I groan. "Are you going to fuck me?"

"Not tonight." He bites into the flesh of my ass, right at the crease below my balls, and a whine escapes me. "No condoms, remember? No lube."

Fuck. I've been stashing the damn things all over his fucking house for weeks. Apparently, I need to start carrying them in my pockets, too.

"Then turn around."

"Why?"

"So I can taste you too."

"Sixty-nine?"

I can sense his amusement, but his voice has dropped that last octave, telling me he likes the idea.

"Not just for straight people," I tease. "Now turn around and feed me your cock."

He ignores my demand, instead crawling up my body to capture my mouth in another dizzying kiss. "Such a greedy boy," he murmurs, rocking his hips against mine.

"Yes," I agree.

I want him everywhere.

I hook my leg around his calf and push at his shoulder. He shifts his weight, letting me roll him over and straddle his waist. His thick erection nestles in the cleft of my ass, where I'm slick with his saliva, and I can't resist sliding back and forth. His tip catches on my rim, and I grind into it, letting it stretch me a little so he sucks in a breath and digs his fingers into my hips.

"Echo," he growls in warning.

I roll my hips one more time, teasing us both, and then relent and flip around to face his beautiful cock.

Leaning down, I wrap my hand around his base and flick my tongue over his slit. I want to take my time, to tease and savor him, but as soon as he feels my lips opening around his blunt head, he thrusts into my mouth, shocking a moan from me. At the same time, he runs his tongue down my length and spreads my ass with his hands.

"How much can you take?" he asks, circling my entrance with a finger. "Can you take my cock and my fingers at the same time?" He presses through the tight ring of muscle, and I rock back into the burn, panting around his shaft as it glides over my tongue. "Do you think I can make you come like this?" Stretching me gently, he works his cock deeper with short, deliberate thrusts. "Filling both your needy holes without ever touching your cock?" Another finger joins the first, and he jacks his hips up, driving himself to the back of my throat.

Holyfuckingshit. At this point, his words alone are almost enough to drive me over the edge, the low gravel of his voice hitting me on a subsonic level. When he adds a third finger and twists, pegging my prostate, my molecules fly apart with the last of my thoughts.

He might have spent his life being emotionally submissive, but I'm starting to suspect there's a sexual dominant lurking behind the filthy talk he gifts me with when he lets his guard down.

I'll take everything he's willing to give.

He brings his knees up, planting his feet, and now I'm clinging to his thighs, choking with every ruthless buck of his hips and writhing into the relentless pump of his fingers. I'm someplace beyond arousal, half gone already, my cock leaking on his chest. The sounds we make together weave an obscene symphony—wet slap and suction, Byrd's harsh grunts, and my own aborted, keening gasps.

Every wave of pleasure rides the edge of pain, and my body thrills to it—to being *used* by him. To feel him straining at the end of his leash and know that I drove him there.

"Fuck, baby, I'm gonna come," he warns.

Baby. Heat spools through my trembling limbs as his rhythm quickens, and I clench around his fingers to the stutter of my heart.

He sinks his teeth into my inner thigh, pulsing on my tongue, and coats my ravaged throat with his release. I swallow every drop, and when his sweat-slick chest arches up against my deprived, delirious cock and his fingers curl cruelly inside me one last time, lightning bursts along my spine.

My head snaps back, releasing him with a scrape of teeth before I bite down and everything goes electric, a white storm exploding from my center to crash against the confines of my skin.

When I regain my boneless body, I'm lying on my back, and the moon is rising over the trees. Byrd is stretched out beside me, head propped on one curled bicep, fingers tracing lightly over my hip.

"Are you okay?" I ask, stupidly, and then burst out laughing. He winces at the hoarse sound.

"I think that's my line," he says ruefully.

"I'm good." *Understatement.* I'm completely, fabulously wrecked. I'm planning to sleep naked on the mat for a week. I drag my hand up to touch a tangled lock falling over his eyes. "I really like your hair."

He laughs softly, leaning in.

"You're fucking perfect," he whispers, sweet against my lips.

"I—" My breath catches. My heart is on the tip of my tongue, his for the taking, and he swallows it whole.

17

Echo

Byrd's sister is seriously cock-blocking me.

I thought I'd won the battle when Byrd let me ditch the couch and crawl into his bed, but unfortunately, all we've done in it so far is snuggle.

"I'll be quiet," I promise, throwing a leg across his thigh and trailing my fingers down his happy trail to the waistband of his sleep shorts. We're finally alone after a second full day of following Elke around Mendo while she takes pictures of restored churches and explores every single kitschy tourist shop in town.

"You're incapable of being quiet." His hand finds its way down the back of my briefs and squeezes my ass. When a finger teases my crease, I arch into his touch with a groan. "See? And this house is basically one open room split across three levels." Capturing my wandering hand, he sucks my middle and ring fingers into his mouth and swirls his tongue between them, then bites down when I can't stifle another moan. "I heard everything you ever did in your bed downstairs."

"Everything?" I swear this man has the self-control of a saint, and he gets off on torturing me.

"Everything. It was torture."

Ha.

"So this is payback, then?" I rock my hips against him, but he only pulls his hand free of my briefs. *Stupid saint.* "Why couldn't you be a pervy priest with a thing for altar boys instead?" I mutter.

"*What*?" He tugs my head back to frown at my face.

"Just cursing your restraint." When I try to lunge for his mouth, the fist in my hair holds me still. "Ow."

For another long second, he considers me, then leans in and traces my lips with his tongue, featherlight and devastating.

"Go to sleep, altar boy." He rolls me over and curls his warm, half-naked body around my back. As if I can sleep with an ignored hard-on and my ass nestled against his dick. "She'll be gone in a few days."

A "few days" turn into a week.

A week of Elke sitting in the grass watching Byrd and I train on the rig. A week of trips to the coast for shopping and taking pictures of buildings and cold windy walks on the beach. One afternoon, we drive to a vineyard in Anderson Valley. She and I get wasted on eighty-dollar-a-bottle wine while Byrd laughs at us, and I pass out in the back of the 4-Runner on the way home. After that, I start letting them go on their adventures without me.

Elke, on the other hand, seems to have no interest in leaving Byrd and me alone. She tracks our interactions with calculating eyes until I find myself pushing the boundaries of appropriate PDA to fuck with her. To my surprised delight, Byrd plays along, returning my kisses with all his usual potency, tugging me into his lap while we watch TV, and reaching up to grip the back of my neck when I slip in behind him and wrap my arms around his waist.

And letting me sleep in his bed every night, for all the good it does me.

"You know I'm in my sexual prime, right?" I throw back the sheet to show him the morning wood tenting my boxers. "It's not healthy for me to go this long without orgasming."

"Go jack off in the shower." But he's not looking at my face.

"Alone?" I give myself a slow, deliberate stroke, and his eyes go molten.

"And quietly." But he rolls toward me, adjusting himself.

Mirroring his position, I move my hand from my cock to his. "What if I send Elke on a beer run?"

"It's eight o'clock in the morning." But he's hard in my grip, and his voice is rough beneath the shape of his smile.

"A coffee run."

"Are we out of coffee?" He thrusts into my hand, and I know I've won.

"We could be if you give me a minute."

"Fine. If Elke goes to the store, *I* will jack you off in the shower. But you're buying the new coffee."

"Twelve bucks for a hand job? Totally worth it." I lean over to steal a kiss before heading to the kitchen. "You could definitely charge more."

In the evenings, when the three of us eat dinner at Byrd's family-sized farmhouse table, Elke peppers me with questions.

"How many boyfriends have you had?"

"Boyfriends? None."

"Girlfriends?" She snorts at my horrified expression. "Fine. Relationships. More than one-night stands."

"Um…" I glance at Byrd, who's eating homemade Pad Thai and smirking at me over his chopsticks. "One?"

"Oh my god, you're talking about Coen? *He's* your 'one'?" Now it's her turn to look horrified. Byrd appears to be trying not to laugh into his noodles, and I shoot him a dirty look.

"The guy you don't fuck on the first date but still go back for more? Yeah." I throw a chopstick at him. "Still waiting for that to pay off."

He snatches the chopstick out of the air and throws it back at me. Elke pokes me in the shoulder with hers.

"So you usually fuck on the first date, then?"

"Doesn't everyone?" Not that I've ever been the kind of guy to go on dates. Byrd is turning out to be a lot of firsts. Elke narrows her eyes.

"Exactly how many guys have you slept with?" she asks.

There's no way I'm answering that, but since I'm already failing whatever test this is, I give her my best degenerate smirk.

"At once? Or in total?"

She gapes at me while Byrd chokes on a bite of chicken.

"Elke," he says when he can breathe again. "How about we extend the whole no dick-talk thing to Echo for the rest of your trip?"

The next time, she asks about my family.

"*Tell me about your childhood.*"

"*Are your parents still together?*"

"*Do they have a good marriage?*"

"*Do you get along with them?*"

She gets as far as "*What about siblings?*" before Byrd steps in and rescues me.

My favorite nights are when the two of them get drunk and tell stories about growing up in Tilburg—mostly a young Elke getting into scrapes and a flustered teenage Byrd trying to navigate the repercussions. It makes me nostalgic for something I've never even had—not the memories, but the secret language of a shared past, saturated with laughter and stupid jokes. I wonder how long you have to love someone to get like that, and if I'll ever know the answer.

When she convinces Byrd to break out an old-school photo album, I almost forgive her for the rest of it. We sit shoulder to shoulder on the couch while Byrd lies on the floor, a throw pillow over his face, and pore over shiny fragments of his past, trapped in cellophane. Byrd with chubby, scabby knees and no front teeth. Byrd lanky and awkward with braces and a buzz cut. Teenage Byrd in a suit with a Zac Efron shag, leaning against one of those tiny European cars.

I steal the last one while Byrd is brushing his teeth after Elke's gone to bed and slip it behind the case on my phone.

I'm playing Elden Ring on the PS5 when Elke walks into the living room.

"How was Café Beaujolais?" I ask, glancing at her without pausing the game.

"Delicious. Coen brought you the sturgeon and some kind of chocolate torte." She throws herself down on the cushions next to me, and I set the controller aside.

"Is he in the kitchen?" Before I can go look, she stops me with a hand on my wrist.

"He's driving the trash bins down to the road. I wanted to talk to you."

"Okay." *What now?*

"Did Coen tell you I'm leaving tomorrow? He's driving me to catch the bus in Santa Rosa first thing in the morning."

"Yes." *Finally.* Even if it means I'll wake up alone on my birthday, it'll be worth it to have Byrd to myself for a few hours before the party at Big Top. My obvious relief brings a wry smile to her lips.

"Happy birthday."

"Thanks." I grin at her, not sorry.

"I know I've been a pain in the ass with all the questions."

"It's fine." *That's not why I can't wait for you to leave.* "I get what you were trying to do."

"You do?"

As if she isn't about as subtle as a train wreck.

"Sure. Prove to Byrd that I'm a bad idea. But only because you want to protect him, and you don't trust me yet." Even if she drives me crazy, I can appreciate her intentions. Neither of us wants to see Byrd hurt, and it creates a kind of kinship.

"You *are* a bad idea."

"Ouch." *So much for kinship.* "And also—not your call." *Thank fucking god.*

But I don't really want Byrd's sister to hate me, so I try again. "I'm not his ex, you know. I'm not going to ask him to give up his dreams."

"He hasn't had time to figure out his dreams. Not the ones he can have now that he's free of Lara. He's too busy trying to rebuild *yours*."

Mine? All my dreams are sweaty and naked and full of Byrd. *Now* dreams, obsessive and immediate. But that's not what she means.

Old Echo was so sure of his future, it was more like a movie—already written and released and waiting for the Oscars to start rolling in.

The kind of dreams she's talking about? I'm not sure I have those anymore. Future Echo is too intangible—a promise I'm afraid to look at except out of the corner of my eye.

"Maybe we're making new dreams together?" I like that idea. Naked dreams *and* future ones, where maybe I'll become solid again.

Real enough to matter.

But Elke shakes her head.

"You understand how much he's risking to give you what you want, right? His job, his friendship with Reggie, his trampled heart? I'm trying to figure out if you're worth it."

Oh.

This whole time, I've been pushing Byrd to be more selfish, but maybe I'm the selfish one, wanting him without considering the cost. Demanding things he keeps trying to convince me he isn't ready to give.

Did I lie when I said I wasn't like Lara?

Elke watches the uncertainty flood me with something like pity in her eyes.

"Has he told you about the guy who broke his heart in college?" she asks, and I shake my head, not trusting my voice. "I don't know that much about him—I was too young and self-absorbed when it happened—but I know Lara wasn't the first. Coen has a history of letting people in when he shouldn't."

I think about the Byrd in my stolen photo, unblemished by the expectations of others, and I want to find the faceless douchebag who took that innocence and fucking bury him. *But how many young Byrds have I ruined, without ever caring enough to count?*

"I do think you care about him," Elke continues, a bitter parody of my thoughts. "And I know he cares more about you than he'll admit. It doesn't make you good for each other."

I don't want to believe her. I've given up on finding my way back to my old self, and the only thing that makes it bearable is the nebulous feeling that this new version—*Byrd's version*—might actually be better.

But what she's really saying is *I'm* not good for *him*, and I don't know how to argue with that. Not when I'm just another asshole asking him to glue me back together with pieces of himself.

"I'm sorry, Echo." Maybe she even means it. "For what it's worth, I get what he sees in you. You're funny and charismatic and too gorgeous for your own good." She moves to touch me—to pat my shoulder or ruffle my hair—and I flinch away, shrugging her off.

"Lucky for me, I don't bat for your team." *I'm sorry. I can't help it. Please leave me alone.*

Her eyes go wide. "You little asshole."

"Don't you mean *manwhore*?"

She stares at me for a minute before she bursts out laughing, and even though I hate her right now, I can't help cracking a rueful smile.

"I'd tell him if he asked, you know," I say.

"Tell him what?"

"My body count."

"He'll never ask."

I know. You were the one who wanted to make it important.

"Then I guess it doesn't matter anyway." I shrug and go to unpause my game.

"Goodnight, Echo," she says. "Maybe I'll see you around Tilburg sometime."

"Goodbye, Elke. Maybe you will."

"You've been dead for five minutes."

I jolt at the sound of his voice, dropping the controller on the rug, and turn around. He's leaning against the wall at the base of the stairs, achingly beautiful in dark bootcut jeans and one of his Henleys. This one is the color of chocolate, making his hair glow warm in the lamplight—dark red and gold like the blurred edge of a flame where it turns to smoke.

"Are you hungry?" he asks, smiling.

I'm wondering if I can still be the new, better Echo on my own, or if I'll fall back to pieces without you holding me together.

"Not really." *When did this become so much more than simply wanting you to fuck me?*

"Are you coming to bed or taking another run at Godrick the Grafted?"

I wrench my eyes away and bend to pick up the fallen controller, straining to sort through the spiral riot of my thoughts—the things I want and the things I should protect him from. And underneath it all, the immense *inevitability* of him, and the spaces inside me he's begun to fill.

"I'm..." *Too weak to be the better man.*

I stand, switching off the TV as I pass, and follow him up the stairs.

In the dark, it's easier to be brave.

"Byrd? Are you going to lose your job because of me?" *Fuck.* I sound like a child, worried about getting in trouble. *Grow the fuck up, Echo.*

"This job? Almost certainly. But Reggie's pay is for shit, so I'll survive."

"I meant your real job." I don't want to say it, because he's giving me an out, and I love these rare flashes of his dry sense of humor, but Elke's words are too raw in my mind. And I'm trying to be a responsible adult.

He's quiet for a minute, and even though I also love that he never tries to bullshit me, I kind of wish this once, he would. When I start to pull away, his arm tightens around me.

"I don't think so," he says. "Not unless there's some public scandal, and I doubt we're important enough for that."

You feel important.

"You're not underage," he continues. "You're not audition-ing for Cirque. I'm on sabbatical. There's no real reason for them to care unless someone forces them to."

Some of the tension drains from my body.

"What brought this on?" he asks, dragging his knuckles up the back of my arm and sending shivers over my skin.

"I guess twenty-one is the magic age where I finally grow up," I say around the lingering ache in my throat. He chuckles softly.

"Elke get under your skin?"

"She didn't get under yours? I know she's been trying to talk you out of this. Me."

"She tried. I listened. And then I made my own choices."

"Are you sure you made the right ones?"

He lets people in when he shouldn't.

I don't think I could bear to be something he regrets.

"Yes." He says it without hesitation, and my heart gives one of those sudden, swooping throbs. "What about you? Is this still something you want?"

I think I want it forever. I can feel the words taking shape on my tongue, vast and terrifying. But I don't want to scare him, and I don't want him to start talking about August again, and if I open my mouth, I have no idea what might tumble out.

So I roll on top of him and answer with bold hands and languid kisses, and this time, he doesn't tell me to stop.

18

Echo

B yrd is late.

He texted me when he was leaving Santa Rosa, and the two hours it should have taken him to return have come and gone. I've thought about calling him, but it's not only the lack of cell service on the 128 that holds me back.

I've spent half the morning pacing the stairs between the kitchen and the living room, arguing with Elke in my head. Arguing with Byrd, too, although in those, I'm never sure if he's trying to get me to leave or to stay.

And arguing with the small, selfish part of myself that says *it's my birthday* and wants to stuff my pockets with condoms and lube.

By the time the 4-Runner pulls up the driveway, I've sweated through two tank tops. Giving up, I finally throw on a loose band tee—one of those cheesy eighties bands Byrd loves—that I've stolen and repurposed, with the sleeves cut off down past my ribs. I'm still sweating, but at least it doesn't cling to my skin.

Since it's a party, I've paired it with designer jeans—the ones with the artful tears across the thighs and the strategic holes above the pocket rivets at the back that Byrd can't resist sliding his fingers into.

It's possible selfish Echo won out where my wardrobe is concerned.

"Sorry it took so long," Byrd says when he finds me standing useless in the living room. "I had to drive back through Mendo to pick up this." He hands me a wrapped box about the size of a deck of cards.

"You got me a present?"

"Not the one you were hoping for, I know." He smirks.

My cheeks flush, which is apparently something I do now, although it's not for the reason he thinks.

I hold the box carefully in my hands, and it feels monumental. There's some meaning trapped inside the shiny paper, and I'm caught between hope and horror that it will be too much. Or not enough.

"Are you going to open it?" He's watching me, lips quirked in amusement.

"Okay." My hands are clumsy as I tear through the ribbon and the wrapping, and I should have done it sitting down, because the small box inside falls open in my rush, and something brown and glittering tumbles free.

Byrd catches it before it hits the ground and holds it out to me.

It's a key on a leather keychain stained the russet color of his hair.

"You already gave me a key to the house," I say, confused. And then, slightly breathless, "Are you asking me to move in?"

"Actually, it's for when you move out." His voice is so casual it hurts, but he cuts my legs out from under me when he continues, "The key is to my apartment in Tilburg."

When I still don't move to take it from him, he frowns slightly. "I bought the place years ago, to use when I visit. But I never do, and there's a pretty serious housing shortage in Tilburg, so I rent it out to students. Like you." He presses it into my palm. "It's not a big deal."

He's scanning my face now, embarrassment creeping across his features. "I'm sure you and your parents would have figured something out, but it's getting late in the summer, and this way, you won't need to have five roommates and—" He shoves his hands in his pockets and looks away. "Unless you want roommates, of course. I might be able to pull some strings with Reggie at one of the Cici houses if you'd rather..."

"And I'd pay rent and everything?"

A look I can't decipher flashes across his features.

"Sure. Of course. We can draw up a lease agreement to make it legitimate." He takes a deep breath, meeting my eyes. "I promise if I do make it over there in the next four years, I'll stay with Elke or my parents. I won't show up unannounced and expect anything." His voice softens. "But I want you to have a safe place to land."

I turn the key over in my palm and notice the shape of the leather for the first time.

"The keychain."

"Yeah." He clears his throat. "There's a guy in town who does leatherwork. I thought..." He trails off again while I run my finger over the tooling. It's a replica of my tattoo—the unbroken wings. Stamped in tiny perfect letters down the middle, it says: *Unlocked Dive 4-26-24.* "It's the day—"

"You kissed me." *Be still my fucking heart.*

He smiles, some of the tension leaving his frame.

"That too."

Meaning.

Enough to suck me under and spit me out weightless, like flotsam through one of those blowholes on the ragged coast.

"*Too much.*" It's barely a whisper, but he still hears it. Of course he does—we're breathing the same air. The air that carries everything between us—words and want and the weight of our collision.

"If your family has already made arrangements—" he starts, but I shake my head.

"No." I close my hand around the key and the kiss and the wings the color of his hair. "We had a place lined up last year, but we gave it up after...No."

I realize I want this helplessly. I want to live in his house, maybe surrounded by things he picked out, with a door that opens to the memory of his mouth on mine and his hand on my dick in the front seat of his car in the California sun. A way to keep him after he's let me go, no matter how it might hurt.

"Good." He smiles, then seems to notice my clothes for the first time, and his eyebrows go up. "Is that my shirt?"

"It was. It's mine now. Consider it another birthday present."

"I'm pretty sure it never looked that good on me anyway."

That's a lie. Byrd in a tight, ratty band tee is the stuff of schoolboy fantasy. He crowds me back until my ass hits the top of the couch and grazes his knuckles down my ribs through the loose holes in the sides. "'Hot for Teacher,' huh?"

"I like Van Halen." My head falls back as he steps between my thighs.

"Sure you do." He trails his fingertips down my neck. "Should I wear a tie and glasses to your party? Maybe one of those jackets with the elbow patches? Make you call me 'Mr. Baardwijk'?"

"Um, only if you want to be really, really late."

He steps back and crosses his arms. "Take off your pants."

"What?" I'm still picturing Byrd dressed like Indiana Jones climbing out his office window.

"I want to suck you off in nothing but that shirt and then go drink whiskey at Big Top with your taste on my tongue."

Happy birthday to me. I scramble out of my jeans.

"Yes, Mr. Baardwijk."

"Good boy."

19

Byrd

He's too quiet on the drive to the tent, turning his new keychain over in his fingers and staring out the window. I've grown so used to his eyes on me as I drive—the scorching look that makes me want to unbutton my pants and press his head into my lap.

I keep seeing his face when I gave him the key—confusion, surprise, hurt. *Too much.* I should have taken it back. Let him keep the keychain without the symbol of future obligation.

But he was wearing my shirt, mutilated into something so sublimely *Echo* that I couldn't think straight. And his cock in my mouth was as eager as ever, his incandescent skin pliant under my hands, and all the familiar, delectable little noises coming from his throat letting me believe I'd done something right.

What twenty-one-year-old guy doesn't like having his dick sucked, idiot?

He likes having his dick sucked by me.

Then why is he so quiet now?

I don't know.

Something's wrong. Ask him.

Something's wrong. I'm afraid.

I pull into the lot without saying a word.

Only a week until they leave for tour, and the Big Top clearing is packed with trucks and trailers, the full crew ready to roll out. They've left tearing down the tent until the last minute for rehearsals, but also for Echo's party, and tonight they've done it up with its crown of Edison bulbs, and someone—probably Milla—is blasting pop music from the sound system.

Josha greets us, leaning on an overturned barrel by the door.

"Are you the bouncer?" Echo teases. "Need to check my ID?"

Josha grins and punches Echo's shoulder, but his eyes stray to the steps of the ticket wagon, where a dark-haired young man in a leather jacket is smoking a joint with one of the hand balancers.

"Gem's home?" I ask, surprised. "I thought he was staying in Montreal this summer."

"He was," Josha says, "but Shilo talked him into coming back for opening week. He's only here until Sunday."

"She still hoping to coax him back to Big Top after all this time?"

"She keeps trying."

"Talking about me and my wayward prodigal?" Shilo appears, joining us in a wash of light and noise as she steps through the tent flap. "One year, that's all I'm asking. One year with my whole family together in this thing we built. Then Gem can go off and join Cirque if that's still what he wants."

"You can't keep him from following his own path, Shi," I admonish. *No matter how much it hurts to let them go.* "You know what it did to me."

She scowls and opens her mouth, but Echo, sensing the old argument, interrupts.

"Do I get to meet this prodigal son of yours, or are you worried I'll corrupt him?"

"Ha. Good luck with that." She waves Gem over, calling his name.

Josha grabs his ever-present flannel from the barrel and ducks inside the tent as Gem approaches.

"Hon," Shilo says, beaming up at her son. "This is Echo. He's the one working with Byrd on his NCC evaluation. Echo, this is my oldest, Gemiah."

The two give each other a classic alpha-pup once-over, and I can't hide my smile. Echo may have met his cocky match with this one. Another rock star accustomed to being adored and getting his own way. Whatever insecurities were birthed by the trauma of Echo's accident, I've yet to see them temper his brash mouth.

"Josha told me about you," Gemiah says by way of greeting, something curious and not quite friendly in his smile.

"He likes having another hot young gay guy on the lot." *Here we go.* "Byrd's too old, and anyway, he's terrible at flirting." He gives me a sidelong smirk, but I refuse to take the bait.

"And you're a master, I'm guessing?" Gem arches a brow, and Echo shrugs.

"Always happy to share my skills with a twink in need."

"Is that what you're doing now?" Gem asks. "Flirting?"

"Do you want me to be?" There's no mistaking the challenge in Echo's voice, but Gem shakes his head.

"Sorry, man," he says. "I like tits and ass."

Shilo smacks him. "Don't be crude."

Echo stares him down a second longer, then slides a hand down the back of my jeans and leans in. "Ass is the gateway drug," he says to me in a mock whisper, giving mine a squeeze.

"Brat," I reply in an actual whisper, tugging his hand free and swatting him with it. The man is shameless.

Shilo groans. "Play nice, children." Who she's talking to at this point is anyone's guess.

Unconcerned that it was recently shoved down my pants, Echo offers his hand. "Nice to meet you, Gemiah the prodigal." He grins. "I like your ink."

"Nice to meet you, Echo the flirt." He turns Echo's wrist over to study his broken wings. "Yours too." Despite the apparent sincerity, my hackles rise when his gaze lingers on the long scar beneath the black lines. Ignoring the unspoken question, Echo casually retrieves his hand before turning to Shilo.

"So where's my birthday shot?"

"Waiting for you inside. Ready for the gauntlet?"

"The what?"

"You didn't tell him?" She shoots me an accusing look as we move into the tent.

"You wanted him to come, didn't you?"

"Should I be worried?" Echo asks. His fingers find mine, and I give them a reassuring squeeze.

"It's a Big Top birthday tradition," Shilo explains. "You get one drink, and then you have to do a battle on your primary apparatus before you're allowed to let loose. It's a chance to show off and let us celebrate you."

"Who am I supposed to be battling?"

"Byrd, of course." Shilo pokes him in the ribs. "He's the only one who might actually give you a run for your money."

"And you knew about this?" he asks me. I can feel the nervous energy radiating from him, but there's an undercurrent of excitement running through it, and I relax a little.

"I did. I told them it would be okay."

It was a risk, letting Shilo go through with it and not warning Echo. But I'm hoping this might be the catalyst he needs to break through the last of his reservations. I want all these people to *see* him, and to give him a chance to bask in the recognition of his peers.

"You're ready," I murmur, wrapping my arms around his shoulders and hugging him close. And then, because I know it will push the right buttons, I bite down on his ear and whisper, "I'll go easy on you."

"Easy on me?" He tips his head back to look at my face and grinds his hips against mine, letting me feel his cock thicken against my thigh. "I think you should be worried about keeping up with me. *Mr. Baardwijk*." The last is a whisper full of dark promise that has my own dick twitching in response.

There he is.

The spark flaring to life, lambent blue fire in his eyes.

He got his haircut. It's no longer shaggy on the sides but is still long on top and freshly dyed to fall vivid along the sharp slope of his cheekbones. He's lost some of the anime/JRPG look—now a little older, more dangerous.

Still breathtaking.

Mine aren't the only eyes that follow him as he strips off his shirt and climbs the stage to the first of the two ropes. Shilo hands him his shot of whiskey, and he raises it to me in invitation.

"You coming, old man?"

Shilo arches an eyebrow at me and passes over my own shot. I knock it back and vault onto the stage, skipping the stairs. Adrenaline kindles at the base of my spine, eager as an old friend returning. Passing Echo, I peel off my own shirt and lean over to whisper "don't get distracted" as I pull the elastic from my topknot and shake my hair free with a wink.

"Totally cheating," he grumbles, but his eyes are dancing, and he sucks on his lower lip as he watches me take my place at the second rope.

"Your move, birthday boy. Gonna start us out slow?"

He should. One shot of whiskey is not a warm-up, and although Echo probably won't feel it, my body will punish me tomorrow if I hit it hard right off the bat. But I still hope he goes for it.

We stare at each other, surrounded by the chatter and occasional catcall from the gathered cast and crew. Milla is arguing loudly with someone—probably her brother—about the music, and Hals is asking anyone who will listen if they know where the tap for the keg ended up.

Under the lights, it's just us.

I'm thinking words I'll never say, and it's okay. His eyes are soft now, and when he says "unlocked dive," I let it mean the same thing.

On my turn, I choose ninja rolls, and even though he's too far for me to reach this time, it doesn't matter, because I'll never forget the taste of his elation.

After that, it devolves quickly as the audience gets into the game, calling out tricks—some of which aren't even possible on the rope and some of which have everyone arguing about what they mean. Circus is a wonderland, and although most of the moves are universal, every school has its own naming system, and not everything overlaps.

We do straddle-key roll ups and Crane rolls, saltos and wheel ups and bombs, and Echo never falters. We've had three shots apiece now, and we need to be done before it gets dangerous, but his cheeks are flushed and his eyes are wild, and he's so high, I never want to bring him down.

"Pirouettes." It's Milla who brings it all to a halt. I realize we've been lucky no one's called for them before now and wonder if Shilo laid some ground rules. But if she did, Milla never got the message.

Echo smiles at the girl, but when he looks at me, his face is tight with rising panic, and I know I should call it. If I forfeit now, we can end the battle and let the party move on.

But he's been fearless tonight, and if he crumbles at this last hurdle, it will taint the triumph of the last hour, and I might never get him to try again.

I hold his gaze and pour all my faith into the thread that stretches taut between us.

He's mine tonight. *My Echo*. And for another few hours, I'll protect him from the power of fear.

I *see* the moment he catches it—*feel* the shiver that ripples over his skin—as his head comes up and his shoulders settle and his phoenix will ignites in his eyes.

But he still doesn't reach for the rope.

"Do you want me to go first?" I ask, low enough to keep the crowd from hearing. I haven't done a pirouette in years. I'll probably blow it, and I don't know what it will do to him to watch me fall.

He shakes his head a fraction and blows out a heavy breath.

My heart pounds in time with his movements as he climbs. Three inverted straddles, and he's well past the midpoint—high enough to catch the trick without throwing off the swing. I'm expecting him to hesitate, bracing myself for the too-long pause and rising tension, but he beats right out of the third climb. Once to the right for momentum and then straight back into the release on the left.

It's perfect.

Effortless. And before I can start to breathe, he beats over and does it again on the right, exactly like the Echo in my dreams.

Shilo, who knows his whole story by now, lets out a piercing wolf whistle, and he descends amid whoops and laughter and cheers, straight into my arms.

I catch him up and kiss him under the lights in front of everyone.

He tastes like salt. And redemption. And wild things, once caged, set free.

20

Echo

Even if only Shilo and Byrd will ever understand why, it's already turning into my favorite birthday ever.

I'm pretty sure everyone else was cheering more for the kiss than for the pirouette switch, but between the two, I'm so giddy that I don't even need the beer that's pressed into my hands or the shots that follow. *Who needs tequila when I can be drunk on triumph and Byrd?* Of course, everyone still wants their turn at a drink with the birthday boy.

Apparently, parties at Big Top involve a lot of talented people mixing risk and alcohol, because the next game turns out to be knife throwing. Shilo and Hals have an act they do every year in the show, and they seem to think it's hilarious to coerce the other troupe members into joining the fun.

Hals invites me to give it a try, but I'm nursing a pretty solid buzz at this point and decide I've pushed my luck enough for one night with the switch. In the end, it's Shilo and Hals, the two jugglers, Josha, and *Byrd* dragging the large wooden target to the back of the stage.

"You can throw knives?" I ask, nibbling at his short beard and taking the plastic cup he hands me. "That's really hot."

"You wait," he says, turning his head to catch my mouth in a brief, searing kiss.

I've never seen him like this—oozing confidence and swagger. He's still Byrd—the core control never wavers—but there's an edge to it that borders on reckless, and the unexpected contrast has my cock at half-mast.

Watching the way he handles the knives, casual in his fingers, followed by the startling grace of the throw and the visceral *thunk* of inexorable contact, is doing seriously unholy things to my body. He's almost as good as Shilo and Hals.

Shockingly, Josha is even better. The quiet, steady redhead never misses a throw, his methodical competence turned to prowling finesse with the wicked-looking knives in his hands.

"They should put you in the show," I tell him when he joins me on my bench to take a swig of his beer. For the last round, they've pulled down one of the ropes still rigged above the stage and are taking turns trying to sink the target mid-swing. Josha grins and shakes his head.

"They've tried. I like my job offstage. Less chance of fucking up under a spotlight."

I tear my eyes away from Byrd—he's put his shirt back on, but his hair is still loose and tangled—to glance at my friend. Josha is staring past me, and if I turn to look, I know who I'll see.

"So that's Gemiah, huh?"

He blushes. "Have you met him yet?"

"Shilo introduced us outside after you bailed, remember?"

"Right. What did you think?" He asks it almost shyly, and I'm charmed that he gives a shit about my opinion.

"About as expected, based on what you've hinted. Cocky. Friendly in a snarky way. Hot as fuck." I punch him gently in the arm. "Not my type anymore." The look he gives me is unbearably grateful, so I change the subject. "Shilo seems pretty proud of him, even if she's not one hundred percent happy with his current choices."

"Studying at ENC, yeah. It was a total coup when he applied." His voice goes wistful. "But he doesn't have any interest in getting saddled with the family business and stuck in his hometown."

"Fair enough."

"I know." He still sounds so glum, I can't help feeling bad for him.

"Cirque hires riggers and engineers too, you know."

"Those people have professional training. I'm just a guy who's good at fixing things."

"And throwing knives."

"And throwing knives." He smiles slightly. "But I'm not gonna be the pathetic guy who follows his hopeless crush around."

"It could be a teen drama," I tease, trying to lighten his mood. "Secretly lusting after the boss's son."

"The boss's *straight* son."

I finally glance over at the guy in question and catch him watching us. As soon as he sees me looking, he turns back to the chick at his side.

"Maybe."

"I'm pretty sure."

"I bet I have better gaydar than you." That makes him laugh, but he still sounds defeated. Unrequited longing's a bitch. Thank fucking god I'm past that phase. *Actually*... "You know how I finally got Byrd to make a move?"

He raises his eyebrows. "How?"

"Flirting with you." *Well, and having an epic emotional meltdown*, but I don't share that part. Now he laughs for real.

"Too bad there's no one here for me to flirt with."

"That's not *entirely* true. Is he watching us right now?"

His eyes flick over my shoulder.

"Yes." Surprise coats his voice.

I glance at Byrd laughing with Hals while Shilo tries to coax Milla onstage. He's not looking my way, but I know he's aware of me, the way I'm always aware of him.

I am going to be in so much trouble. A shiver runs through me at the thought.

"Okay, I'm gonna kiss you now." I start to reach for Josha, pausing at his wide-eyed expression. "You have kissed a guy before, right? I don't want to...fuck it up if you want your first to be special or something."

He rolls his eyes.

"Fuck you. Yes, I've kissed a guy before. I'm not a total noob."

"Sure," I snicker. Josha has "virgin" written all over him. "He still watching?"

"Yeah..."

Let's see how straight you really are, Mr. "I like tits and ass."

Without warning Josha again, I cup the back of his neck and bring his mouth to mine. His lips are soft and tentative, and I brush my tongue across the seam between them until they part with a small rush of breath, before pulling back to find large, liquid brown eyes staring at me.

"Don't fall in love with me now," I warn, which makes him snort, *thank god*. "Did he see?"

"I think so."

"How does he look?"

Before he can answer, I catch Byrd watching me from the edge of the stage, lethal heat in his eyes.

Yup. So much trouble.

When I toss him a wink, he runs his tongue over his bottom lip, eyes narrowing.

"I gotta go." I stand abruptly, adjusting my thickening cock. "Good luck."

Josha glances from me to Byrd, and his lips twitch. "You too."

Byrd vaults off the stage and stalks toward me, not even a little unsteady, although I could swear he's had as much to drink as I have. I should probably meet him halfway, mitigate the damage, but watching him move through the small crowd like a hunting cat has me glued in place. With one last sympathetic look, Josha flees, rocking the iron bench in his haste to escape.

How Byrd can loom over me with only two extra inches of height, I have no idea, but he does, and I practically swoon. He's close enough to smell the whiskey on his breath and the clean tang of his sweat, and I sway into him, caught in his tether.

He curls his hand around the back of my neck and squeezes, the blunt bite of his nails along my pulse sending it skittering.

"What was that about?" he asks, voice deep and dangerous and oh so fucking hot. I slide my arms around his waist.

"An experiment."

"An experiment. Did it have the desired effect?"

"One of them." I bat my eyelashes as he brings his other hand up to cup my jaw, holding my head trapped between his rough fingers.

"Put your hands in my pockets," he commands, and I try to grin against his grip, slipping my fingers into the layers of denim hugging his ass.

They brush the unmistakable shape of a foil-wrapped ring, and all the strength leaves my body.

"You brought condoms," I breathe, heat rocketing through me.

He bends his head and runs his scruff along the shell of my ear.

"I think it's time for you to ride my cock until you paint my chest with your cum."

There's that swoon.

"That was only the first half of my fantasy," I manage to gasp out. His chuckle is a vibration I feel all the way to my toes.

"Don't press your luck, altar boy."

"Are you safe to drive?" I ask, fighting sudden panic. "I really don't want to die in a ditch right before I finally achieve my life's dream." I'm also not sure I'll survive the forty-minute drive back to the cabin without jumping his bones, but he shakes his head, grabbing my hand and tugging me toward the exit.

"I got a room in town."

Thank fucking god.

21

Byrd

I'm fucking nervous.

Despite a couple of short-lived hookups during my touring days, the last guy I did *this* with was Gabriel, and the last thing I can handle right now is his goddamn ghost in my head, taunting me with all the ways I fucked it up.

It helps that Echo is bouncing on his toes like a kid at Disney World and humming something I think is supposed to be "Hot for Teacher" under his breath while I fumble with the old-fashioned key to our tiny rented cottage. Gabriel was mocking, teasing—he could even be playful as long as he made the rules—but he was never *uninhibited* the way Echo is. Never so uncomplicated in his eagerness for me.

Giving up on the lock, I trap the man in front of me against the door and kiss him until I'm no longer haunted, drowning myself in the new texture of his shorter hair, the familiar glide of his tongue exploring all the corners of my mouth, and the hard immediacy of his rigid cock grinding rough against mine through two layers of denim.

Echo. More real for a few short months than Gabriel was for a year and a half.

"I'm down to go against the door for the first round," he teases, lips barely leaving mine, "but we are in the middle of town. It would suck to get arrested before we get off."

"I think I dropped the key," I admit, peeling reluctantly away from the eclipse of his body to scan the flower-lined stoop at our feet.

Echo retrieves it from the shadowed sill and lets us into the room. The queen bed, with its dark wood frame and white antique-looking quilt, takes up most of the space, and a couple of high windows look out into the dark garden courtyard.

"We're gonna tear this place apart," he says, grinning as he takes in the small, delicate nightstands and matching rocker.

He strips off his clothes and throws himself onto the bed, bouncing a few times and rocking it experimentally against the wall. I shake my head, wondering how drunk he is.

Drunk enough to kiss Josha and think it was a good idea.

But even though the image of his long fingers curled around Josha's neck stirs the primal, possessive part of me, I mostly feel sorry for the kid. I'm pretty sure awakening my inner caveman was only an added perk for my little brat. Gemiah was the real target. Manipulation with the best intentions, but still...

I toss our small overnight bag onto one of the nightstands but stay standing a few feet from the bed as my creeping demons claw at their flimsy chains. Echo finally goes still, sensing my shifting mood.

He's kneeling naked in the center of the mattress like an offering from my wildest dreams—ink and parchment and watercolor blue—his erection exquisitely flushed, curved against the cut of his abs. Something fragile flickers in his eyes.

"Am I okay?" he asks, and my heart staggers at the choice of pronoun.

"I don't want to hurt you," I blurt, and his taut features melt into a faint smile.

"With your massive cock? I promise I can take it."

I don't correct him, even though he's only touched on part of my fear. In the lingering silence, he crawls toward me and reaches out to hook his fingers in my jeans. He tugs me gently forward until my thighs hit the edge of the bed and starts undoing the buttons of my fly.

"You won't hurt me," he promises, and I want to believe him.

He slides my jeans and underwear down my thighs, and my cock springs free, obviously immune to my internal struggle. His warm fingers wrap around my base, firm and familiar. "I won't hurt you either," he says, then takes me in his mouth.

It's one of his indolent blow jobs, working me with his spit-slick hand and his ruthless, ravishing tongue without ever settling into a steady rhythm. The build is so slow and delirious that when he finally takes me to the back of his throat, slick muscle constricting around my crown, my orgasm catches me off guard, and my knees buckle, only his strong arms locked around my thighs keeping me afloat.

"Shit."

He pulls off with a soft *pop* and rests his chin in the short curls at the base of my softening cock, looking up at me with a lazy, self-satisfied smile.

"I have faith in your ability to rally."

My reaction to the sex-smeared look on his face is already proving him right.

I peel off my shirt and step out of my jeans, retrieving the condom from my pocket before crawling up to join him on the bed. I set it on the nightstand next to the bottle of lube Echo has liberated from the bag.

He's sprawled on his stomach, watching me over his shoulder with his head pillowed on his arms. Every contour of muscle and flesh is a path carved of desire. The athletic swell of his traps bleeding into the vulnerable shadow of his neck. The long grooves along his spine dipping to the decadent arc of his ass. The valleys behind his knees and the soft down on his inner thighs.

With lips and tongue and light, trailing fingertips, I draw a map of sighs and whimpers, of quivers and sweat and arching moans. A catalog of Echo burned into my soul.

For the rest of my life, I'll remember him like this, stripped to the raw bones of his arousal, unraveled by my touch.

By the time I spread his cheeks and flatten my tongue over his hole, he's cursing incoherently and I'm hard as a rock.

I've barely breached his entrance before he's rocking back, fucking himself on my tongue with his fists clawing at the quilt.

"Byrd," he begs, almost a sob. "*Please.*"

"Roll over." I sit back on my thighs, and he instantly obeys. His whole body is flushed, pupils blown to limitless black, his cock swollen and leaking on his belly.

He's ethereal, obscene, and achingly vulnerable, and I'm so far past the point of no return with him, I can feel the edges of my heart flying away.

"Condom," I say before my brain can follow. He fumbles the packet off the table, holding it out to me. "You do it," I tell him. "It's been a while."

He comes back to himself a little at that, smiling like a cat and tearing through the foil with his teeth and a practiced jerk that's so sexy, I have to squeeze the base of my cock so I don't lose it the second he touches me. Then he rolls the cool latex over my head and down my shaft, and I can't tear my gaze away from his dexterous fingers. It's new and nostalgic all at once, but even through my fatal fascination, I can't help wondering what it would feel like to take him bare.

Then he starts coating my cock with lube, and all my thoughts condense to the one vivid realization that this is *now*, and it's happening—here, with him.

I hold out my hand for the bottle, to coat my fingers and stretch him ready, but he tosses it away.

"No more," he says, a line drawn in a man's voice. "You've been prepping me for *weeks*. I want your cock inside me now. I'm done with teasing."

And I'd give him everything, anything he asked, so I hook an elbow under his thigh and line my trembling cock up with his waiting hole.

The first thrust is almost enough to destroy me—my cock-head trapped by the tight ring of muscle as he arches off the bed with a cry.

Fuck. Instinctively, I try to draw back, although I might die if we stop now.

His free leg comes around me, trapping my hips and obliterating my retreat.

"You said I wouldn't hurt you." I force the words through gritted teeth, fingers digging into his thigh and my other arm braced on the mattress, fighting the need to fall into him.

"I lied." But he bears down, drawing me deeper, and his hand comes up to tangle in my hair. "Not every pain is hurtful, Byrd. This pain—it's *always* part of it. It makes it real. Makes it *matter* when you let someone into your body." He tugs my head down until we're close enough to kiss. "Someday, I'll show you," he promises, "but right now, I need you to keep going. Please. Trust me."

I work my way in with short, careful thrusts, watching his face and soaking up his little moans. His eyes never leave mine, brimming with trust and lust in an intoxicating cocktail as he opens his body to my invasion.

When I'm fully seated, I rest my forehead on his shoulder, buried in his heat like a fever dream and clinging to the frayed wisps of my self-control.

It's so far beyond what I remember, so fucking tight along my entire length.

And so cripplingly, devastatingly intimate that I can't tell if I'm about to come or start crying.

"Byrd." His voice is low and breathless against my ear. "*Coen*. Look at me. You gotta move now, or I'm gonna go crazy." His hands stroke over my hair, my shoulders, and down my back to grip my ass. I'm supposed to be taking care of him, and here he is, asking me to let myself go.

I draw out, slowly, and rock back in with a smooth glide.

"More," he says, canting his hips to draw me deeper. "I need you to fuck me like you're breaking all the rules."

And I understand. Because Echo isn't the only one who's been living in a cage. And it's not only wild things that deserve to be free.

I push up off his chest, hooking his other knee and dragging him against me. This time when he arches off the bed, there's only pleasure in his cry, and I know I've found the right angle. The next stroke is a slow grind, and then my body takes over. With each thrust, I draw back almost to the tip and slide home a little bit harder, rolling my hips when I bottom out to drag my swollen head along the spot that makes him come apart.

His hand flies to his cock, but I snatch it away, leaning in to pin his wrist against the pillow.

"That's mine," I tell him. "I'm the one making you come tonight."

"*OhgodyesfuckinghellByrdplease*." He writhes beneath me.

"Hold on, baby. I've got you."

His knees are trapped against his ribs, and his hole is slick and spasms around me every time I peg his prostate. His curses dissolve into gasping whimpers, mixing with my own grunts, and I want it to go on forever—him, like this, under me and surrounding me.

But I'm taking him hard now, and I'm starting to lose the thread of our cadence. My release coils at the base of my spine, and I take his cock in my hand and jerk it without finesse, with nothing but the need to watch him spill hot over my fingers and feel him lock tight around my cock.

And even though I'm chasing it, *demanding* it, it still annihilates me when it happens. He detonates around me with a hoarse shout, fighting my grip, the fingers of his free hand clawing at my shoulder and his head thrown back into the pillows. With one last thrust, so far inside him that I might never find my way back, the world goes bright and liquid, and I belong only to Echo.

22

Echo

"You called me Coen."

"Yeah."

"Why?"

"I don't know. I felt like I was losing you, and I really, really didn't want you to stop."

"You weren't losing me. I might have been losing myself."

"Is that worse?"

"No. It's—it doesn't matter. You brought me back."

"Because I called you Coen?"

"Because you're *you*."

"What was all that shit about hurting me, anyway? You have done this before, right? You told me you had."

"I have. But it was a long time ago."

"The guy in college? Elke told me about him. Some asshole who broke your heart."

"Yes. Him. He liked telling me when I hurt him."

"That's fucked up. You know that's fucked up, right?"

"Is it?"

"You didn't hurt me, Coen. I've never come so hard in my life. Am I gonna be sore tomorrow? Yeah. Was it worth it? Hell yes. Do I want to do it again before we leave this room? At least twice."

"Savage. I've come twice tonight already. Have mercy on an old man."

"Fuck that. If my ass can take it, so can your cock. Let's do it in the shower."

"That was the last condom."

"Jesus. You only brought two? Next time, I'm in charge of packing."

"I might not survive that."

"You're too young to die by orgasm. And anyway, there are worse ways to go."

"Mmm. Echo?"

"Yeah?"

"What do we need to do to do it without the condom?"

I can't breathe.

"You want to fuck me bareback?"

"Well, yes. If it's safe. If you want to."

Form words, Echo.

"When was the last time you were tested?"

"About four years ago, when Lara and I were talking about having a kid."

"And you were clear?"

"We both were."

"I was tested right before I was supposed to leave for Tilburg. And I haven't been with anyone but you since." *Fuck. The stupid party.* "One guy." I don't know why I feel guilty. Byrd wasn't even on my radar back then.

"Did you use a condom?"

"Always." *Always.* "I can go to the clinic tomorrow."

"Okay."

"You like the idea, don't you?" *I sure as hell fucking do. What's happening to me?*

"Of taking you to the clinic?"

"Of fucking me raw and filling me up with your cum."

"Yes."

Fuck, his voice at that octave should be illegal.

"Who knew you had a breeding kink?"

"A what?"

"Oh my god, how are you such a baby bi and still so ridiculously phenomenal in bed?"

"I'm not phenomenal at anything. You're just easy to get off."

"Are you calling me a slut?"

"What? No!"

"Pretty sure you just called me 'easy.'"

"I meant easy for *me*. Shit. Echo, I like doing the things you like done to you, *so I pay attention*. I've always been paying attention. It's not magic, it's—"

Love.

"It feels like magic to me."

23

Echo

I burst through the sliding glass doors after running all the way up from the rig, only to find Byrd pacing the living room with his phone to his ear. He shoots me a warning look that wipes the shit-eating grin from my face.

"Yes. No. I appreciate the concern, but...I understand." He drops his arm to his side, staring at nothing.

"Who was that?"

The look on his face is so resigned, it sends a jolt of panic through me.

"Your father."

"Oh." *Oh shit.* "What did he want?"

I've talked to my parents a few times over the last two-and-a-half months. Mostly short texts to tell them I'm alive and training is going great, among other vague assurances. It's hard to share my progress when I never divulged how bad things were to begin with.

"To tell me he knows about our 'involvement.'"

"What? How?"

"I guess some business associate of his saw us together in town the other morning."

The morning after my birthday. When Byrd and I were all over each other at the local bakery. I remember the guy in the charcoal slacks and cashmere who'd stared at us over his cappuccino. He wasn't familiar—I'd figured he was either some bigot or a closeted perv—but I know my dad likes to show me off to his colleagues, so I could have been recognized from one of his videos. I've never really been good at blending in.

"Is he...mad?" My parents have always taken a "don't ask, don't tell" approach to my sex life, but if my dad *called* Byrd—yeah. Not good. Byrd sighs, scrubbing a hand down his face and shoving his phone into his pocket.

"I wouldn't say 'mad.' He wanted to make sure I know you don't have access to your trust fund until you're twenty-five." He shoots me a wry smile, and I snort.

"Did you tell him you're already worth seven figures?" I don't really know for sure, but owning houses in two of the most expensive areas of California provides a pretty good baseline.

"Well, slightly less since the divorce, but I'm sure he knows how much Cirque pays me. He seems like the kind of man who does his homework."

"So he was worried you were after my trust fund? That's not so bad."

Byrd raises his eyebrows, and I hurriedly add, "I mean, it's insulting, obviously, but also ridiculous and—" I tilt my head at him. "Do you care what my father thinks of you?" For some reason, the idea makes my stomach fill with warm butterflies.

"That wasn't all he wanted to tell me."

The butterflies die an abrupt, icy death.

"Is he—does he want me to come home?" He can't make me. I'm fucking twenty-one years old. But if he makes things ugly for Byrd, will Byrd want me to stay?

"He's concerned about your place at NCC. He was very adamant that if our behavior—*my* behavior—jeopardizes your evaluation in any way, he would be taking legal action."

"It's not illegal for you to fuck me."

"No, but it is unprofessional. Remember what I said about Cirque not caring unless someone makes them care? A sexual-misconduct lawsuit might get their attention."

"I'll call him back right now. I'll explain it wasn't your fault. It was me who pressured you. I'll tell him that I've decided not to go to NCC anyway, and he can keep his stupid money." I'm babbling, and Byrd is shaking his head.

"Echo. Echo, stop. That's the last thing he wants to hear, and it won't help anything."

"Then what do we do? Are you gonna make me leave? I—*please* don't send me away."

How can he make me feel like a man and a terrified child at the same time?

"Hush. I'm not sending you away. We still have some time."

"Do you need to get a lawyer?"

"Maybe eventually, but I'm hoping it won't come to that."

"You have a plan?" *Please have a plan.*

"I think it's time to call Reggie."

"But you said she'll fire you. That she'll find someone else to finish my evaluation." *I don't like this plan. This plan sucks.*

"Yes. Someone unbiased who will confirm that you are fully capable of starting classes in the fall at the level they expect of you. Reggie can assure your father that you still have a place at Cici, and he'll have no reason to make trouble."

"But I'll still have to leave. Go train with someone else."

"I think I can convince Reggie to put that off for a little while, but eventually, yes." His face is still, unreadable. "It's the best thing for you, Echo."

"Are you shitting me? *No.* The best thing for me is *you*." I'm trembling all over, dust falling from the mortar in the cracks in my soul. "I can't do this without you. I don't even *want* to." *How can he just stand there like it's already over?*

"Echo, I'm not Dumbo's magic feather."

"Fuck you, Byrd. Dumbo's feather was bullshit. You're *real*. I *love* you." The words fall out, and the room crystallizes, confession and indrawn breath coated in sunshine amber. Every gold fleck in the dark forest of his eyes shines, and the weight there is enough to bury me.

"You don't know what you're saying." A whisper neither of us believe.

"Don't do that." I start to move toward him, but he steps back, and I'm suddenly furious. "Goddammit, Byrd. You don't get to fuck me and then treat me like a child who doesn't know what it means."

"Do you?"

Another step. This time, he doesn't retreat.

"Lie and tell me you don't love me back."

Silence.

"Fine. Not brave enough to admit it? Then *show* me." I throw my phone at his chest, and he catches it in startled hands. "I got my results back," I tell him, then take the final step. "All clear."

I watch the words sink in, the heat pool in his eyes, and the struggle across his features as his infernal conscience tries to hold on.

Fuck this.

I'm done begging. I want him on his fucking knees.

Let him try to pretend once he's had me with nothing between us.

His hands fist white-knuckled at his sides.

"Don't break my phone." I back away, peeling my shirt off over my head and tossing it aside. His gaze tracks down my torso and over my abs, catching where my thumbs hook in the waistband of my sweats. My dick is already half-hard, outlined against my thigh by the gray cotton, and when he licks his tongue over his bottom lip, I know I have him.

I shove my pants and briefs down together and step free, retrieving the packet of lube from the pocket—I carry that shit everywhere now—before tossing them on top of my tee. He still hasn't moved, but his gaze is hungry on my naked body, and he palms himself unconsciously through his jeans.

I sink back into the couch, hooking one leg over the armrest so I'm spread out for him, and give my cock a slow stroke while I tear open the lube packet with my teeth.

A rough sound escapes him, his eyes flitting from my mouth to my hand on my cock, and when I pinch my tip and squeeze the lube over my fingers, it deepens to a growl.

"I know what you're doing," he grits out.

"Does it look like I'm trying to be subtle?" I arch a brow and let my other hand drag down over my erection to tease my hole.

He's straining against his zipper now, hands locked behind his neck to keep from touching himself. To keep from touch-ing *me*. I slump lower in the cushions to give him a better view and sink two fingers inside myself at once. "Fuck, that's tight."

"Echo." His eyes close, head falling back on his clasped hands.

Good luck with that.

I pump my fingers a few times, hard enough that the wet sound is audible even over my moans, and his eyes crack open. My other hand goes back to lazily stroking my cock while I fuck myself on my fingers, spreading myself open with every twisting pass. My ass is hanging half off the couch and my abs are clenched, but I don't take my eyes off his, daring him to deny me.

Fuck. I'm supposed to be taunting *him*, but the look on his face, the tense flex of his biceps, and the strip of exposed skin where his shirt has ridden up—I start to jack myself faster, chasing the orgasm building between my hands.

Precum leaks from my slit, and my breath gets jerky as I smear it roughly down my shaft. When I add a third finger to my ass, he snaps.

He's on me in two strides, dragging me up with a fist in my hair that would be painful if I wasn't so delirious with victory and lust.

"Turn around."

Instead of scrambling to obey, I give him an insolent smirk, sucking my fingers into my mouth.

He flips me around with a curse, tossing me against the back of the couch and crowding between my thighs with a rough shove of his jean-clad knee. His zipper rasps as he drags my head back with the hand still in my hair.

I'm flush against his chest, thrilling at the pornographic feel of his cotton shirt and the rough denim of his jeans chafing over my naked back and thighs—our only skin-to-skin contact the hot silk of his bare cock pressing into my crease.

It's filthy as fuck, and so is the kiss he claims, deep and possessive, with a vicious scrape of teeth as he withdraws.

"Tell me you love me," I say, licking the blood from my lip.

"Will it make it hurt less when you leave?"

"Yes."

He gives my head a jerk, my neck arched painfully back against his chest.

"Now who's lying?"

I can feel his helpless fury, and my cock throbs to the beat of the cut on my lip, but he's lining himself up at my entrance.

"I don't care."

He searches my face.

"You keep making me hurt you."

Yes.

"*I. Don't. Care.*"

He takes me all at once, merciless, the way we both need.

I arch into him with a strangled gasp, hands scrabbling at his hips to pull him closer, even as I struggle to adjust to his size.

A harsh groan escapes him, a drowning, surrendered sound, and I clench around his cock, drawing another string of curses.

"You like being hurt." It's not quite a question, and it's not quite the truth, but I give him the whole answer anyway.

"Only by you."

"*Fuck.*" He pushes my head away, so I fall forward, catching myself on the back of the couch.

And then he turns himself loose, hauling my hips back against his thighs and slamming into me, fingers tight enough to leave bruises on my hips.

This is punishment for daring to speak the forbidden words, and I bury my face in my arms and rock back into every thrust.

He leans over me, and my skin is so sensitive that even the brush of his worn cotton T-shirt is torture.

"What do you want?" he growls in my ear.

"Tell me you love me."

His rhythm slows and becomes a sadistic roll of his hips digging at my core.

"You think I'll give you what you want because you're letting me ride this tight ass of yours raw? That the wet heat of your pretty hole clamped around my bare cock is gonna make me come so hard that I'll forget all the reasons I can't keep you?"

I keep my mouth shut, swallowing my pleas. *I'm done begging.*

"I remember *everything*," he whispers. "Every single moment of you." And fuck if I can keep my hand from dropping to my cock—aching and so hard my abs are smeared with precum—at the devastation in his voice.

He fights me for it, tugging my hand away from my dick and capturing the one still locked on the back of the couch. When both my wrists are secured at the base of my spine, he leans back, pulling and pressing at once so my chest arches off the cushions, and *ohholyfuck,* at this angle, his thick head drives over my prostate with each brutal thrust, and I can't stay silent.

"Do you like this?" he asks over my wordless cries. "Being used by me? Knowing I'm about to fill you up and you can't touch yourself? That you're going to feel it, and take it all, and maybe I'll let you come, maybe I won't?" He hauls on my wrists, turning my wail to a gasp. "Is this what you think love feels like?"

"*Yes,*" I breathe. *Yes.*

Because this Byrd is *new*, and I know—from the burn in my ass to the ache in my shoulders to the hot, tight pressure in my balls—that this Byrd is also *mine*, and that no one else has ever had him this undone.

"Fucking hell," he grunts, and then makes good on his threat-promise. For the first time in my life, I feel the hot spill of cum deep inside me—*Byrd's* cum—and it seems to last forever. I'm flayed so fucking bare, so completely *owned*, that I'm amazed I don't blow with him.

He pulls out slowly, and his fingers brush my inner thigh, trailing up through the evidence of what he's done. Desperate to catch his expression, I crane my neck as he pushes two cum-coated fingers inside me like he can keep himself there.

"*Byrd.*" I swore I was done begging, but I'm about to break.

His eyes lift to my face, taking in the flush and the tears tracking down my cheeks with his hooded gaze. He tugs on my wrists, gently this time, and wraps his arm around my shoulders, hugging me to his chest.

"Ask me again," he says, husky in my ear, and brings his hand around to grip my cock. His fingers are slick with his cum and slide easily over my shaft.

"Do you love me?"

His hand tightens and strokes up and over my crown.

"Yes," he whispers, and I shudder in his arms and come all over his couch.

24

Byrd

I'm grateful Lara insisted on the extra-large tub, even though I'm sure she never expected I'd be sharing it with a twenty-one-year-old princeling who never learned the word "no." I'm drained, shaken—I've never unleashed myself on anyone like that before, and I keep expecting to feel guilty beneath the wonder.

"Don't poke at it," Echo says into my hair, trailing his fingers through the wet curls on my chest.

"Reading my mind now?" I close my eyes, resting my head on his shoulder.

"You're gearing yourself up to feel guilty. It's not mind reading. It's called paying attention." He nudges his hips into my lower back, a teasing reminder of when I said the same words to him in the Mac House cottage.

"Doesn't it scare you?" I ask. It scares me. Not the words, but the implications.

You're afraid he doesn't know what it means.

I'm afraid of what will happen if he does.

"Because I'm a fuckboy, I'm not allowed to fall in love?" His fingers tighten where they're clasped around mine, draped over the edge of the tub.

Reading my mind again. And missing the point entirely.

"You really are fearless, aren't you?" I tilt my head back to study his profile, the blue tips of his hair plastered to his forehead like the day we met.

"I've led a charmed life. Marked by one spectacular tragedy." He leans in to lay a kiss along the corner of my mouth. "Which turned out to be the best thing that ever happened to me."

He means it.

No, no, no.

At least I'll be gifting him the lesser tragedy.

How much more will it hurt when I have no one else to blame?

"And I *was* terrified," he continues, oblivious to the dark twists of my not-regret. "You saw how I was when I got here. I thought I'd never find my way back to myself. You took that fear away."

"So you love me because you think I saved you?" Simple. Understandable. Almost cliché. *Am I hurt or relieved?*

"No." This time, he shifts so he can see my face, water sloshing over the rim to splash on the tiled floor. "You were able to save me *because* I loved you."

Not simple.

"I loved you for kissing me when I was a total wreck. I loved you for being jealous of Josha. I loved you for seeing me broken and believing I *could* be saved."

I push up to meet his lips. All the lines I've drawn to protect him, to protect myself, have washed away, and he deserves to be kissed, at least once, with none of my fears between us. He melts into my mouth, releasing my fingers to draw his hand up my arm and tangle in my wet hair, pressing me closer, giving me more. As if he hasn't already given far more than I should have let him.

Could I have stopped it? Or was it already too late when he leaned through my window in the rain, smelling of smoke and wiping the image of Gabriel from the expectation of memory? The absolute novelty of his relentless, unashamed pursuit; my hollow resistance. How much of my fall was the catalyst for his recovery?

"*I'm not the Echo you want,*" he said, not understanding. There's only ever been one Echo. Brazen, flirtatious, broken, determined, *fearless* Echo, and I wanted it all. Something—*someone*—more than I'd ever allowed myself to claim.

"Besides," he says, smiling against my lips and going back to my original question. "You're scared enough for both of us."

Scared for both of us. Well, that's true enough.

"I know you think I was holding out to torture you, but I did have actual reasons for caution."

"Because you knew playing hard to get would turn me on?" He rolls his hips again, and I feel the thickening length of his cock along my spine.

"That was an unexpected consequence." I capture the hand wandering down from my chest and trap it against my abs before he can completely disarm me. "And probably tortured me more than it ever did you."

"Pretending it was about the condoms was a pretty good ploy. Although what we're gonna do with the lifetime supply I've hidden all over your house now..."

"A ploy?"

"Well, yeah. Considering you ditched them at the first possible opportunity. I could have gotten myself tested weeks ago and blown the whole thing up. You would have needed a new excuse." He tugs his hand free and continues his downward exploration.

"They weren't *excuses*." I'm mildly disgruntled at how easily he sees through me without ever stumbling on the deeper truth. "They were reasons. Legitimate ones, if you ever stopped thinking with your dick."

"Why? When, for once, my dick and my heart are in perfect alignment?"

"How about your brain?"

"My brain." He sighs but pulls his hand back to safer territory. "Reason one: You're too old for me. Obviously bullshit. You keep up with me on the rope and in the sack, and I'm clearly the more emotionally mature partner in this relationship."

"You are?"

"Sure. *I'm* not afraid of being in love."

"That's because you've never lived through it before. That's not maturity; it's naiveté."

"Jesus." He stills behind me. "Someday, you have to tell me how these exes of yours convinced you that you're only worthy of loving when you're on your knees."

"You seem to enjoy me on my knees."

Echo is not the only one who can distract with innuendo.

"Only when you want to be there." He traces the curve of my ear and rubs his chin in my hair.

"Reason two?" I prompt, caging the spreading warmth his fierce words leave in their wake.

"Reggie. The job." There's a hint of a grin in his voice. "That one's easy."

"Easy?"

"Yup. Reggie's only goal was getting me back to NCC in shape. That never would have happened without this." His hand has found its way back to my dick, and he gives it a squeeze.

"So really, she should be thanking you for a mission accomplished."

"Any coach Reggie sent you to was going to be good, Echo." But I'm only arguing on principle. I know what he means.

Love and fear, loss and desire; a perfect storm rearranging two lost souls in a redwood castle.

And he hasn't even guessed Reggie's second motive for sending him here—the lifeline she forced on me to take my mind off myself and my failed marriage. Even if me falling for her student wasn't exactly her plan, I think the part of her that loves me won't be as mad as she'll pretend.

As long as I keep my heartbreak to myself this time. Which brings us to...

"How about the third reason? Got an easy answer for that one too, my wise young twink?"

"Our expiration date," he grunts. "That one's on you, you know. I'm all in."

"Meaning what? You ditch your dreams and don't go to Tilburg?"

"There are other circus schools. Hell, there are other ways to have a circus career besides going to school. Just because you went there, and Gabe did..." He pauses, and I wonder with a flash of panic that feels like relief if he's finally put it together. "Well, Cici isn't a guarantee of a performing career, anyway."

"I made a mistake when I chose Lara over my career. You are not going to make the same one." *Please listen.* "And your brother..." *was never what you are.*

"You only want me to go because you're afraid of my dad." *Bitterness.* "But I could go somewhere else, somewhere just as good but closer. ACCA maybe. Or I could always take advantage of my new connection to Cirque. My dad wouldn't complain about that." He tugs painfully on my hair and laughs, but I'm afraid he's only half joking.

"So we're back to sucking my dick to get ahead?"

"I could suck your dick and stay here. Shilo won't give a shit about my dad. We could run away with Big Top."

Oh, Echo. Don't you see how small that dream is? Your dreams need to be unstoppable. Just like you are.

"I'm calling Reggie tonight."

He drops his face into my shoulder.

"Fuck me again first?"

One last time? I squash that thought.

No. Not yet.

25

Echo

Byrd kicks me out while he makes the call to Reggie.

"Run to the Navarro store, Echo. You can buy the beer now."

Going on a beer run softens the sting of being dismissed so the grown-ups can talk, but I'm still a wreck for the entire twenty-five minutes it takes to make the trip. For a moment, pulling out of the potholed parking lot of the country store, I fantasize about turning left and driving off the other way. If I disappeared, would he be sorry? Or secretly relieved?

He'd be worried.

And I'd be useless and devastated and come crawling back before the end of the night anyway. Plus, I can't steal his 4-Runner. He'd never forgive me for that.

So I sit in the driveway and chain-smoke, terrified to go inside and discover my fate. I know why Byrd sent me off on this bullshit errand, beyond preventing me from hearing him get chewed out and most likely fired. He's determined to salvage my commitment to NCC, and he didn't want me butting in.

I want to be angry at him, and at my dad, but I'm pretty sure that even without the latter's threats, Byrd would still be pushing me to go.

"You're not making the same mistake I did."

In my darker moments, I wonder if it's more than that—if he'd still want me if I didn't follow through on the potential he sees in me. *Why does being Byrd's Echo mean I have to give up Byrd?*

Our sex after the bath had an air of finality to it. One we both tried to fight—me with frantic need and him with extra care, which only ended up adding to the desolation. Now my ass is sore, I'm wrung out, and there's a burn behind my eyes that feeds off the ache in my chest.

He finds me in the driveway before I muster up the strength to go inside, leaning on the open window in a strange moment of reflected déjà vu.

Maybe he'll surprise me and climb into my lap.

Irrationally, I reach to slide the seat back, but he stops me with a hand on my neck.

"Two weeks," he says, and I blow out a slow breath. Better than tomorrow, but I feel a flash of bitter nostalgia for my hatred of August.

How many heartbeats in fourteen days?

"What happens in two weeks?" *Is there any answer I'm not dreading?*

"I take you to San Francisco. One of Reggie's contacts will be in town, and she'll meet us at Circus Center. Reggie will pull some strings so you can do the evaluation there."

"I'm not ready." *It's not enough time.*

"You are. You've been ready since your birthday."

I lean back into his hand and close my eyes. Another audition, and I'm out of excuses.

I'm not afraid of the rope anymore. I've remembered how to fly. The rest of the tricks—the double pirouette and the quad switches and the handful of others I haven't tried—will come back eventually. Especially once I'm training every day with the coaches at NCC. I'll learn new skills, meet new people to challenge me, make connections to launch me into the wider circus world. I can still have all the things I wanted for so long.

Assuming leaving Byrd doesn't tear a new hole in my soul.

But if I keep letting him prop me up, I'll turn into the thing Elke was afraid of. I'll disappoint him and force him to keep loving me anyway.

Byrd was right. Love *is* something to be afraid of, and it's time for me to grow up.

"What happens after the eval? Do I stay in SF and train with this new coach?" I ask, not opening my eyes. It's easier if I can't see his face, can't read the feelings there and risk being shattered by them.

"If you nail it, like I know you will, then that's it. You have your spot, and you can do whatever you want with the rest of your summer."

I open my eyes. He's smiling at me.

"I can come back here? Until—" I'm back to hating August, and the relief bursts out of me with a laugh.

"If that's what you want." His lips twitch in amusement as I scramble out the window and into his startled arms. He stumbles back a half step but regains his balance quickly, twisting to lean against the side of the truck as I lock my arms around his neck so I can kiss him breathless.

"What do I get when I crush the eval?" I ask, tilting my head so he can nibble down my neck.

"Besides a place at a top international circus school?" How dare he sound amused when I was three seconds from a complete breakdown?

"What do I get from *you*?" I clarify.

"Why do I feel like you're about to tell me?" He sinks his teeth into the muscle of my shoulder, and I arch into him.

"I want to top you."

His head lifts to study my face.

"Echo—"

"I'll make it good for you, I promise." I don't remind him how much practice I've had.

"That's not..." He shakes his head and runs his hands up my back. "You know my feelings for you aren't contingent on how you handle the evaluation or your performance on the rope, right?"

"I know." *Mostly*. This isn't about that. It's about something I'll be giving up to give him what he wants, even if, deep down, I know I want it too. It's about claiming another piece of him before I lose him, even if it makes it harder on us both. It's about closure I don't want but think I might desperately need. "Think about it?"

"I don't need to think about it. And I don't need to wait to parcel it out like a reward." His voice drops to that dangerous octave. "You're not the only one with those fantasies."

My dick is wide awake now, any residual guilt I might have felt at asking for another sacrifice gone in the rush of blood his words provoke. *Yesnowrightnowplease.*

"No." *What am I doing?* "You wouldn't be yourself if you didn't tease me with it as long as possible." I keep my voice light, but the truth is, I *need* him to hold out. I need a reason not to throw—*or fail*—the eval. Yes, I'd have to spend a few weeks in

SF faking it for a new coach, but then I'd be free to spend the rest of my life in Byrd's bed.

Most of me has already discarded the idea. Most of me knows I do still want to train in Tilburg. But the small, weak, *right now* needy part of me might still decide to sabotage the whole thing. My mortar is fragile, and I don't entirely trust it. I need an extra incentive.

Byrd will know if I throw the audition, and it will crush him. Yeah, but this incentive is way more fun.

I reluctantly peel myself away from his body and lean against the truck beside him.

"How did the rest of the conversation go?" I ask, changing the subject to one more likely to get my dick to behave. "Obviously you're fired, but is she really pissed?" I don't want to be the reason he loses his best friend.

He scrubs a hand down his face, but he's got one finger casually hooked in the waistband of my jeans, tracing the groove along my hip. *Not helping.*

"As my very temporary boss, she's livid, but mostly at having to cover her ass. As my friend, she's curious. And not as surprised as she's pretending to be." *Stroke.*

"Huh."

He gives me a sideways look at the nonresponse, then circles his finger lower with a smirk. "I've never known anyone better at reading people than Reggie."

"She's barely met me."

"She knows *me* very, very well."

"Does this mean—" I suck in a breath. My dick is still hard, and he just brushed across the head. "Does this mean she's actually on our side?" I was expecting a reaction like Elke's, skeptical and protective.

"She wants you at Cici."

Right. Preferably not dragging around the corpse of her best friend's heart, I'm sure.

Maybe Byrd and I don't have a side. Maybe all we have is a bubble of time to enjoy our miracle before it pops and spits us back out into the real world.

Byrd is on his knees on the rough blacktop of the driveway, unbuttoning my jeans.

And I know I'll take whatever I can get, for as long as I can get it.

26

Byrd

"F ucking *fuck*." Echo steps out of the handstand with less than his usual grace and collapses, flopping over onto his back at my feet. "I get why Reggie's pissed at *you*," he grumbles, "but why is she punishing me? She's the one who decided to trap me in an isolated mansion with a hot-as-fuck rope god. What did she think was gonna happen?"

"Feeling a little petulant?" I smirk down at him, admiring the sheen of sweat on his bare torso and the succulent pout of his lips. He's adorably bratty today, and it probably shouldn't turn me on as much as it does, but I've given up rational thought where he's concerned.

"I'm feeling *frustrated*." He squints up at me. "I haven't gotten laid in almost three days, and my hand is too sore and tired from these stupid handstands to jerk off."

Reggie sent the skill list for Echo's evaluation the morning after I came clean, and I've been running him through the requirements nonstop to make sure he's ready. I'm not worried about the rope portion—five compulsory skills he's going to nail with no problem and a list of ten recommended tricks to choose another five from. The list also includes some basic acro moves, which Echo says are all pulled from his original audition video and has been able to demonstrate with reasonable confidence out on the lawn. Once he's on the spring floor at the gym, he should be more than fine.

The last set Reggie's requesting is three handstands: a kick-up, a press, and a one-minute hold against the wall. All three should be in Echo's wheelhouse, based on his prior training, but handstands put a ton of pressure on his wrist and the small muscles that support the bones of his hand. It's a good way to measure his recovery, and I don't *think* it's meant as a punishment, but after watching him struggle all morning, it's starting to feel like one.

"We can take a break." I lower myself to the floor next to him and take his hand, massaging the sore muscles as I lean back against the couch. He moans in pleasure, snuggling closer to rest his head on my thigh. "Feel like getting out of the house for a bit?"

"I was thinking about a different kind of training." He turns his head and sinks his teeth into my jean-clad inner thigh. "Two hours of you hovering over my ass spotting me is giving me all kinds of dirty ideas." He raises his eyes to mine and bats his smoky lashes. "Three *days*, Byrd."

"Poor baby," I murmur, but not in protest. It's well-established at this point that being around Echo has destroyed any restraint maturity might have gained me over the years. As soon as I stopped fighting the inevitable, it became painfully obvious that I am completely gone over this man. My heart is a shipwreck waiting to happen, and I can't make myself care. "I'm not sure you need any more 'training' in that area, but I'm happy to put you through your paces if you're feeling deprived." I move one hand from his wrist to his hair, tugging in that way that exposes the pale line of his throat and leaves him gasping.

"The training part is for you," he pants, rolling up onto his knees and sucking my lower lip into his mouth.

"Mm-hmm?" I chase the kiss, tightening my grip at the base of his skull before he can pull away. His lips part and melt molten under my invading tongue. Yeah, three days is definitely pushing it. My heart is beating hard, its echo a heavy throb in my thickening cock. "What did you have in mind?" I ask, pulling back enough to breathe the words across his lips. Personally, I'm thinking how pretty he'll look with rug burns on his knees and my cum dripping out of his ravaged hole, but after that, I could be up for anything his deviant mind desires.

"How many times have you had my fingers inside you?" he asks, and despite the heat of the words, he's not teasing now.

"A few." Not that I don't enjoy it, but I can never hold myself back for long without taking over, turning the pleasure back on him and the way he lets me play his body like my favorite instrument.

"And never more than two at a time. What about on your own? Ever tried taking a dildo?"

"Um, a long time ago."

"In a galaxy far, far away." He rolls his eyes. "Before Lara, I'm guessing?"

I shrug. The more time I spend with Echo, the deeper I understand the tragedy of my formative sexual years under Gabriel's tutelage. Sex was about making *him* feel good—the teacher with the never-quite-explained assignment and the student who always fell shy of the perfect mark. It was brutal to brush the edge of rapture but never quite capture it, always wondering what more I could find to give. Over the years, I made myself very, very good at reading the language of pleasure in other people's bodies. As if by filling them all the way up, that rapture might spill over into me, but I never took much time to learn the language of my own.

I told Echo there was no magic in my bedroom skills, and it wasn't a lie, whatever he believes. But there is magic between us—magic that comes from *him* and the miracle of how he wakes to me. With his constant, fearless heart, and his body so wide *open,* his rapture fills me up a thousand times over every time we touch.

So yes, most of our encounters involve me turning him inside out and piecing him back together, all the while both knowing who's really in control.

"You need practice." He smirks at me, stroking his cock lazily and no doubt reading my last thoughts. "You think if I get three fingers inside you, that will prepare you for taking this cock?"

My eyes drop to the hand wrapped around his erection, thick and straining in his thin joggers, a wet circle of precum spreading from the tip.

"Maybe four?" I arch my eyebrows at him, and he rewards me with a wicked grin.

"Four?" He drags his tongue across his fingertips and brings them to my lips, forcing them inside until I'm sucking on all four long fingers. The calloused texture is so different from the silk of his cock, but when he twists deeper, the strain in my jaw is familiar, as is the brief flare of euphoric panic when he presses against the back of my tongue and I struggle to pull in air through my nose. Right before I choke, he pulls them back, glistening with my saliva, and uses them to coat his now exposed shaft, teasing over the thick head. "Practice," he says again, in a low tone that sends electricity straight to the spot behind my balls. "And it's my turn to play coach."

He sends me to my room with the slightly ominous promise of gathering "supplies." And I climb the steps slowly, trepidation and excitement beating feathered wings in concert behind my ribs.

Gabe never wanted to top me, and at the time, I never questioned it. Knowing him now through Echo's eyes, I think his bravado couldn't risk appearing less than perfect, or how it might have changed the way I looked at him to fall short of his own demands. The only guy who ever did ask—a two-week hookup on tour in Germany—I turned down, too unsure of what we meant to each other to offer up that vulnerability, even in my curiosity. But Echo...*Is this what love feels like when it's bound with trust?*

He enters the room already naked, because, *god,* this man was built to be bare before the angels that made him. He has a blue TheraBand—medium weight—dangling from the fingers of one hand.

I'm sitting on the edge of the bed, still in my jeans and T-shirt, hands fisted in the covers at my sides.

"Nervous?" he asks, amusement and something else, something predatory, alight in his cobalt eyes.

"A little." I give him every truth I can, poor penance for the one huge secret still hidden.

Soon.

After the evaluation. We can't hurt him until he's free to choose.

He moves to stand between my thighs, dropping the TheraBand on the mattress and slipping his fingers up under my shirt.

"Arms up." He strips me like a child. Like a lover. Slow and gentle, with his eyes locked on mine and his hands brushing lightly over each inch of newly exposed skin. I shiver under the weight of his attention, chills along my flesh warring with the mounting heat inside. When I'm fully exposed, he kisses me—a soft press of satin lips against my trembling mouth—and steps back with a smile.

"On your stomach," he commands, still in that gentle tone, so at odds with the blue flame of his eyes. "Arms over your head."

I obey. I don't think I'll ever say no to him again, my well of resistance drained dry in the futile battle against his fire. I press my face into the pillow and close my eyes as he climbs up my body to kneel astride my shoulders. When he leans forward and reaches for my hands, his dick drags through the loose tumble of my hair, and we both moan.

"Fuck," he whispers, losing himself for a moment to grind against the back of my head. The pillow smothers me under the pressure, but I don't fight it, my own hips rolling into the rough linen duvet, chasing friction over breath. When he releases me to begin binding my wrists in the thick elastic TheraBand, I turn my head, sucking in air and staring at the smooth slope of his inner thigh, inches from my head.

He uses a simple figure eight to capture both my wrists and then loops the slack through one of the slats in the headboard and ties it off. There's enough stretch in the band that I can pull my arms down about six inches before the loops on my wrists get tight enough to cut off my circulation, and the thick rubber is smooth and cool against my skin. It's improvised and barely restrictive—if I wanted, I could use one hand to free the other and be loose in seconds.

And yet, somehow, it changes everything.

My breath is coming quick and sharp as he slides back down my body, this time teasing every inch with his heat and hard muscle.

"You okay?" he asks, a low purr against my ear. His hands stroke along the undersides of my arms, soothing and barely shy of tickling with the slightest brush of his blunt nails.

I want to ask him to go easy on me.

I want to beg him to wreck my body like he's already wrecked my heart.

All I can manage is a nod.

"Need a safeword?" Now the amusement is clear in his voice.

"Do I?" *What the fuck is he planning?*

"Probably not. This is only *practice*, after all. But I should warn you, I'm gonna edge you until you can't think straight before I let you come around my *four* fingers. And that *is* punishment for depriving me these last couple of days."

"Oh fuck." I bury my face in the pillow again, and my cock leaks onto the linen.

"That's a terrible safeword," he teases. "It's supposed to be something you *don't* normally scream during sex."

"Brat," I grit out, but my shoulders shake with a suppressed chuckle.

"I can work with that." He sits up and smacks me on the ass, not quite hard enough to sting but enough to turn my mirth into a moan. "*Really?*"

I'm glad my face is hidden so he can't see me blush. The second spank is harder, leaving heat behind like a brand, and even as I flinch, I'm already arching back into the promise of his touch.

"Oh, Byrd." The next sensation is the soft rasp of his stubbled jaw along the pinkened flesh. "Maybe we really do need to get you a safeword."

I shake my head. *Too much.* He's barely started, and it's already too much. It's like the day he climbed into my lap in the truck and all my walls evaporated in half a second of blue hair and the pressure of his hand on my thigh. "*Break for me*," he whispered, and I did.

He's been inside me ever since.

I'm bracing for another slap when he spreads my cheeks and runs his tongue up my crack from the base of my balls to my rim. I come off the bed with a shuddered sigh, and he hums against the sensitive flesh.

"Oh *fuck*," I say again, and he bites into the inner slope of one cheek above the crease of my thigh so my balls go tight and I squirm away from him.

"Told you," he murmurs, and then sucks on the spot, soothing the marks left by his teeth with the heat of his mouth. He trails the tip of his tongue lightly across to the other side, dipping briefly to flutter against my hole, before repeating the whole bite-suck-flutter on the other side. The warring sensations have me alternately thrusting into the mattress and arching up to chase his mouth. The rough fabric of the duvet is soaked with my precum, a delicious chafe along my cock that borders on pain, and the unfamiliar feeling of being *toyed with* is wringing little growls of frustration from my chest.

When he hauls my hips up off the bed, I almost whine at the loss of sensation on my cock, but then he spears my entrance with his tongue, and it turns to a gasp. He threads one arm between my thighs, wrapping over my hip and splaying his long fingers over my ass, holding me still and spread open for his questing tongue. His other hand tugs lightly on my sac, rolling my balls gently in a warning grip.

And his mouth—*holy fuck, his fucking mouth*. With all the times I've had my dick inside it, I thought I knew the depth of that slick heat. Now I'm being invaded, and all the hot, wet, hard-soft textures are focused in one small place that feels like *everywhere*, lapping and sucking and plundering until *too much* becomes *not enough*. I'm pressing shamelessly back into him, trying to fuck myself on his tongue. My hands tug at their elastic restraints in a mindless, desperate bid to touch my weeping cock.

"Echo. *Baby*." I'm trying to growl, but my voice is a hoarse plea, ignored by the sadistic nymph with my balls in his hand. Right when I think I might actually tear the slat from the bed frame, he tightens his grip, and the sharp jolt of pain has me clenching on his tongue. Immediately, he pushes back, delving even deeper, and slides his dangerous hand up the length of my cock to squeeze the head.

I collapse on the bed, driving my cock into his palm as my knees give out with a shudder.

He lets me fall, trailing kisses up my spine as I rut into his hand, seconds from what is sure to be one of the most insane orgasms of my life. But as soon as I start to swell in his grip, he pulls away, leaving me bereft of sensation. When I grind against the bed, his hand comes down on my ass again, the hardest slap yet, and I grunt, jerking in my restraints.

"Ow," I complain, drunk on desire and ripped from the edge of release to the startle of pain.

"No coming yet," he chides, his fingers gliding over the hurt, cool this time and slippery with lube. *When did that happen?* "Four fingers, remember?" He leans in close and tugs my chin around, forcing me to meet his gaze. "I offered three, but you said four. Now you're gonna take everything you asked for."

I'm loose and heavy, almost drugged. His words wash over me, but I can't catch enough meaning to be afraid.

Only the fragments of his beauty taste real—a smear of blue like neon through mist, the midnight lust of bright eyes blown dreamless, the halo shine of white skin eclipsing lines of hieroglyphic ink along a curve of bicep. I blink, and he's kissing me, deep and thorough, the inexorable force of his tongue in my mouth creating an echo—*Echo*—of another invasion. Between one heartbeat and the next, I'm back on the brink, groaning into his mouth and fighting to keep still on the bed.

He pins me with his weight, settling the slick curve of his cock between my cheeks. With one hand tangled in my hair and the other firm on my hip, he rides me for his own pleasure, sliding roughly along my crease.

"Fuck, Byrd," he grunts. "It's gonna feel so fucking amazing when I finally bury myself in this perfect ass."

"Yes," I gasp, trying to arch into him, each drag of his thick head over my rim exquisite torture. The throb in my sac has climbed my spine, lodged now in my throat, escaping in rough grunts. He chases his orgasm, and I cry out the moment his hot cum spills over my lower back.

Did he come on my face?

No, those hot tracks are tears.

"Shhh," he whispers. "I've got you."

He smears his fingers through his cum and slips one down to tease my hole. "*One.*" He pushes gently past the first ring of muscle, and I'm too gone to resist. All I feel is eager. "Oh, *good boy.*" I can hear the smile in his voice as he sinks the rest of the way inside, curling slightly to brush against my prostate, and I forget my own name.

"*Echo.*" *His* name, I can remember.

"*Two.*" The second finger burns but melts almost immediately into that feeling of full, of *more.* This time, he scissors them, twisting and stretching, and my ass comes off the bed as my fists curl in the pillow.

"More. Please more." My voice is a low rasp, beyond pleading, dredged from the ache at the base of my dick. The rough pulse of Echo's breathing beats in my ears, matching my own.

"*Three.*"

I'm dying. This is what it feels like to fall into heaven.

There's pain. Pain like the fire of his palm on the curve of my ass. Pain like Echo on his knees, begging me to *take*.

Pain like falling in love when you least expect it.

He takes his time now, and his other hand comes around to stroke my neglected, sobbing cock, swirling the precum lazily over my crown. He pinches the tip and runs his tongue up through the mess on my spine, and I open with a sigh. Lapping me clean, he pumps his fingers to the rhythm of my heart until I'm rocking into his hands and my orgasm builds again in the space between each frantic beat.

I'm so close. I hear the words *"four, four, four"* and realize I'm chanting under my breath. His tongue is between my shoulder blades now, and he kisses each crest of my spine, a scrape of teeth and suction that echoes in my dick.

And then suddenly, he's gone, hands and teeth and weight lost to the weeping edges of my skin.

"Echo." I tug on the forgotten restraints and curl my toes against the duvet and wonder if I'm broken.

"Turn over," he says, and his voice does profane things to my overstimulated nerve endings.

Somehow, I manage to rally my trembling muscles and roll onto my back, squinting in the sun that streams through the skylight to paint Echo's image in green and gold.

"Still with me?" His smile is dreams and demons, and I have no answer but *please*.

He straddles my hips, a wild god with a wicked cock, and grasps the base of my erection in a vicious grip. "Show me that 'old man' stamina now," he taunts and starts to lower himself onto me.

It's rough and so, so tight—the only lubrication is what's left on his fingers and the precum coating my crown. If he's prepped himself at all, I missed it in the haze, and I hiss as he works himself lower with hypnotic little rocks of his hips.

"Jesus fucking *Christ*." My hands itch to touch him, to trace the smooth planes of his chest and wrap around the proud jut of his cock. "Let me go," I beg as his ass hits my pelvis and his head falls back with a sigh.

"Say it," he commands, clenching around the base of my cock.

"Brat," I groan. He shakes his head.

"Not that." He swirls his hips, adjusting to my size, and arches impossibly backward to fit the head of my dick into that perfect spot inside him. His cock leaks on his abs, and my whole body trembles at the blaze of his beauty. He sucks his fingers into his mouth, messy and obscene, before dropping his hand to trail them up the inside of my thigh. "Bend your knees," he purrs, "and *say it*."

"*Four*." I plant my feet and tilt my hips, giving him access even as I drive my cock deeper into his tight hole.

His eyes collide with mine, and his thumb braces on my taint, the tips of his fingers teasing my entrance. I continue to thrust up into him, a fractured, frantic rhythm, as he strokes himself and slips first one, then two fingers inside me. Right before I break, he beats me to it, spraying my chest with thick ropes of cum. As his ass clamps down and a hoarse shout escapes him, he pushes the last two fingers through my ring and curls all four hard against my prostate.

I come forever.

Blink.

His lips are pressing soft kisses to the inside of my knee.

Blink.

His hair is tickling my cheek while deft fingers free my wrists.

Blink.

A warm, wet cloth trails down my ribs, caresses my exhausted cock, and dips between my shaky thighs.

Darkness.

"I love you." A familiar body wrapped around my own.

"I love you too."

Don't leave me.

Fuck.

27

Byrd

"I'm sorry, Mr. Wash, but Ms. Blake's instructions were very clear. No one is allowed in the room during the evaluation. Not even his coach."

Griff is twenty-five, looks about seventeen, and is currently way out of his depth. Working reception at the San Francisco Circus Center is a cush job, handled in rotation by students looking for discounted classes. Angry men in dark suits are not usually part of the job description.

"*That man* is not his coach," tall, dark, and scary declares, "and that particular instruction came at my request. For the protection of my son. I'm quite certain Ms. Blake did not mean to include myself in the prohibition."

Griff's gaze shifts to mine, and his panic turns hopeful. "I'm sure if you talk to Coach Byrd..." He trails off when the man, Echo's father, rounds his fury my way.

I have a weird moment of dislocation as we study each other across the space. Echo's eyes in an older face with fine wrinkles at the corners. Gabe's curls tamed by a close, professional cut. The bravado of both sons matured into absolute confidence.

"Mr. Wash." I keep my voice carefully neutral.

"Byrd Baardwijk." His is cool and appraising, no trace of the frustration he was throwing at poor Griff. I think about offering a hand, but the look on his face stops me. "Where is my son?"

"Finishing his warm-ups." And trying to calm the raging hard-on I left him with.

Echo was a nervous disaster, bouncing around the studio room the Center had set aside for his eval. I ended up calming him down the only way I could think of—fucking into his hot mouth until he drank me down like he was starving at the end of the world. When I tried to return the favor, he pushed me away.

"If you make me come right now, I'll turn into a pile of spaghetti, and I need all my guns firing." He flexed one bicep with a smirk. "I just needed a shot of my favorite energy drink." One kiss, deep and hungry. "Now get out of here before I change my mind and blow the whole thing off."

I don't think Mr. Wash wants to hear any of that, though, and I have no idea how Echo would react to seeing his dad right now. From everything he's told me, he has a pretty decent relationship with his parents. Not close, exactly, but they've definitely contributed to his "charmed life." On the other hand, Echo was pretty freaked out after that phone call.

"I'd like to see him." The words are polite enough, but there's no mistaking the command in his voice.

"I'm not sure—"

He cuts me off. "Mr. Baardwijk. While I appreciate all you've done to get Echo here—" His mouth twists, obviously fighting the urge to lay me out and charge past me. "Do not discount the sacrifices *I've* made to support him. In fifteen years, I have never missed an audition or performance. I have no intention of breaking that commitment now, and you would be wise not to get in my way."

Okay. So he's a domineering asshole, but maybe his heart is in the right place. In-person auditions for NCC are always closed, which Wash knows if he's telling the truth, but I can't blame him for wanting the chance to wish Echo luck. To let him know his father is here pulling for him. I'm also not sure I have any right to be the person standing in his way.

You've loved him for a few weeks. This man has loved him his whole life. He'll be around long after...

"Give us five minutes," I say to Griff, then head back down the hallway, gesturing for Echo's father to follow.

At first, Echo is wary, and I wonder if I made a mistake. The look he throws my way is trepidatious—a look that does not go unnoticed by Mr. Wash.

"He came to wish you luck," I say, answering the unspoken question, and some of the tension leaves Echo's body. He climbs slowly to his feet as I cross to him, standing as close as I dare under his father's watchful gaze. I'm not sure if it's for Echo's comfort or mine, only that I'm ready to shield him in whatever way he needs.

"Hi, Dad." A slight smile quirks the corner of his mouth. "Wasn't sure you'd make this one."

Wash's answering smile is a mirror. "You should know better by now."

I step back as they embrace, giving them room and letting the relief breathe through me.

"I'm sorry I can't watch the evaluation," Wash says as they pull apart.

Echo shrugs. "I know. They won't let Byrd in either."

"Need me to kick some ass?" his father asks. "Regina is pretty tough, but that kid at the front desk was two seconds from folding." He winks. "I think I could take him."

I'm starting to see where Echo gets some of his attitude.

"I'm okay, Dad. When have I ever fucked up an audition?" He says it without hesitation, cocky grin firmly in place. If I hadn't seen him twenty minutes ago, trembling on his knees and begging me to distract him, I'd even believe it. His father claps him on the back.

"Your mother sends her love. She wanted to be here."

"Let me guess. One of her 'appointments' with Dr. Nip-tuck?"

"You know *Dr. Tucker* books six months out, or she would have rescheduled." They share another smile, wry and fond at the same time.

"I'm glad you're here, Dad," he says sincerely, and my heart swells in sudden gratitude for the man who helped shape Echo's ability to love. And then he spoils it with a devious glance in my direction. "Maybe you can keep Byrd from climbing the walls while I'm in here."

Mr. Wash cocks an eyebrow at me, a familiar gesture in an older face. I can see Echo at fifty, those same fine lines winking from—

Echo at fifty.

Not Gabe.

My relief bubbles up like laughter as Echo steps shamelessly into the waiting circle of my arms, pressing his forehead to mine. I don't tell him he's got this, or that he's ready, or that I believe in him. I've told him all of those things a thousand times over the last two weeks. I don't ask if he's okay, because I know the answer better than he does.

"Be Echo," I say instead, soft and fierce, with my hands locked at the back of his neck.

"Your Echo?" His heart beats staccato wings against my chest.

"*Your* Echo." I press a kiss to the offer of his mouth and whisper against all the vulnerability there: "You'll always be mine."

In this moment, it doesn't feel like a lie, and I'm rewarded with that lightning flash in his eyes and the slow smile that stops my heart.

"See you after," he whispers back. "I'm gonna change your life tonight."

You already have.

It's hard to look someone in the eye when their son just promised to wreck your ass with his cock, but I'm a fucking adult, so I manage. To my surprised relief, the look on the man's face is thoughtful rather than suspicious.

"Graham Wash," he says, holding out his hand. "You can call me Graham."

"Byrd." I shake, resisting the absurd impulse to thank him, and I don't fight it when he exerts a little extra pressure.

"Just don't call him 'Mr. Baardwijk,'" Echo murmurs behind me, and I stifle a shocked snort. Guess my boy's feeling better. Graham's eyes flit between us, but other than a slight tightening of his lips, he wisely doesn't react. *Jesus. Is he trying not to smile?* I drop my hand and clear my throat, fighting a blush.

I'm saved further embarrassment by the arrival of Reggie's surrogate coach. I make the introductions, since Claire and I spoke earlier while Echo was getting changed, and then she shoos Graham and me toward the door.

"We'll be right outside," I promise, while Echo gives his father one last hug, and I wonder if I'm about to have the most awkward conversation of my life.

28

Byrd

I don't climb the walls.

If I was alone, I might distract myself with one of the ropes in the main gym, but instead, I sit with Graham Wash on a backless metal bench outside the audition studio and breathe into the stilted silence. A teenage girl in bright shorts jogs by on her way to the bathroom, muted curiosity in her adolescent gaze. My lips twitch imagining the picture we make: Me with my messy topknot and ripped jeans, him in his pinstripes and thousand-dollar haircut, staring at youth troupe posters and stick-figure safety notices like the world's unlikeliest pair of miscreants outside the principal's office.

Or nervous parents waiting on the fate of the prodigal child.

Not that Wash looks nervous. He leans against the wall with his hands in the pockets of his dark designer slacks and his long legs stretched into the hallway, ankles crossed, casually taking up space with his boardroom bravado. If he feels out of place in this land of sweat and bruises and acrobatic dreams, he doesn't show it.

He catches me studying him, glancing at my white-knuckled grip on the edge of the bench, and breaks the silence.

"You did the right thing, calling Regina."

"I know." As peace offerings go, we could both use some practice.

"I wasn't sure you would." He chuckles. "To be honest, I wasn't sure he would let you. Jericho can be very stubborn. But I appreciate it."

I force my fingers to relax and meet his gaze. "I didn't do it for you."

His laugh is rich and almost honest.

"I believe you." He quirks an eyebrow. "I can't imagine Regina was any happier with you than I was."

I shrug. Her exact words were "*Please tell me you did not risk my professional reputation—and your heart—on another Wash man-child. That is* not *what I meant when I told you to find yourself a hot rebound fuck.*"

"We've known each other a long time."

"You inspire loyalty." It almost sounds like a compliment, and he's got that thoughtful look on his face again. "Echo has never kissed anyone in front of me before." The implication is clear, despite his casual tone, and my already tortured heart stutters in my chest.

"He cares for you," he continues, not even trying to mask his surprise, "and you care for him. Enough to put his future before..." His vague gesture takes in the length of my body.

My heart?

My dick?

I decide not to be offended.

"He deserves this. He's worked hard for it."

Wash looks away, and I take in the tight line of his mouth and the too-casual set of his shoulders. Maybe he's not as nonchalant as he's trying to look.

"He's not going to disappoint you," I say. His eyes flit to mine.

"He never has."

There's something dismissive in his tone, an edge of condescension that has me sitting up straighter, hackles prickling. *And here I was almost starting to like him.*

"If that was true, I'd think you'd trust him by now," I challenge, and I don't back down from his appraising look.

"Are we still talking about his career?"

"We're talking about Echo."

He studies me for a moment.

"Do you have any children, Mr. Baardwijk?"

So much for first names.

"You know I don't." Reggie told me when I took the job there'd be a "basic background check," and this guy isn't the type to slack on his homework.

"Mmm." He tilts his head against the wall, closing his eyes. "When they're little, they're always begging for your attention. *Daddy, watch this. Daddy, look at me. Daddy, can I show you something?* And you watch, because you're terrified that if you look away, you'll miss something. Or worse, that they'll be taken from you. That all that fearless fragility will shatter against the cruel edges of the unfeeling world." The words are polished, but they carry genuine nostalgia. An image of Echo, bright with childish innocence and insistent joy, sparks behind my eyes.

I wonder if I was ever like that, before Elke. Before "*Take care of your sister, Coen*" and the exhaustion of parents who never quite knew what to do with their wild daughter and their quiet, invisible son.

I don't have to wonder if Gabriel begged for his father's attention too.

"Then one day it changes," Wash continues, his tone going wry. "They kick you out of their life, all ferocious independence and invincible ego, and you find a whole new set of fears. Now they're driving, experimenting with substances, having sex." He cuts his gaze to mine, but I don't look away from the not-so-subtle jab. We both know I wasn't even close to Echo's first foray into *that* department.

"Now imagine raising an athlete, an aerialist. It should be even worse. Every day, risking their body in extreme ways. All their hopes pinned on an elusive future so few can achieve.

"But then imagine that child is *Echo*. That he's incredible. He never falters, never disappoints you, and he's so fearless that, over time, you also stop being afraid. All you feel is awe that something so perfect came from you." He smiles, his pride evident, and even though I know how it feels to marvel at Echo's magic, I almost choke on the sudden swell of anger that threatens to swamp me.

"That Echo? He ruined my fucking life." How much blame for Echo's collapse can be placed at the feet of this man? On the internalized expectation of perfection Echo carried onto the rope that day? Would he still have tried to prove himself flawless to Gabriel if he'd ever been allowed to be human?

"Sounds like a lot of pressure for a young man." I can't keep the judgment from creeping into my voice. Wash throws me a sharp look.

"He'd been training in that studio alone since he was twelve years old. I knew he wasn't careful—what teenage boy knows the meaning of caution? But he was *smart*. He never made mistakes."

"Until he fell." *And you left him alone to rot in* that studio, *with his broken wings and his fear.*

"That wasn't a *mistake.*" He glares at me, and I suck in a startled breath at his vehemence. "That was—" He cuts himself off with an angry slash of his hand.

"An accident?" *One spectacular tragedy.*

"An unfortunate accident, yes."

I barely catch the flicker of hesitation. He's a successful lawyer. He's not supposed to have tells. But Echo is his son, and one whose every nuance of expression I've been obsessing over for months.

My thoughts spiral, Echo's voice in my memory tugging at a dreadful epiphany. "*It was a big crash-style mat. Four by eight and six inches thick. My parents wouldn't let me train at home without it. I shouldn't have been that far off-center, even with the bad swing.*"

"He wasn't alone that day." It's not a question.

"He told you about it?" His voice is resigned.

"He told me his brother was there." Slow horror creeps over my chest.

"Gabriel." He closes his eyes, and the muscles clench beneath his clean-shaven jaw.

Gabriel.

"Echo said there was a video," I say, carefully.

He looks up at the door, where the son he loves fights for his future, and the last of his arrogance leaks away.

Why couldn't he have loved them both the same?

As if I don't know the answer.

"Gabriel deleted the video. He said it would be too traumatizing for Echo or his mother to see, and too tempting for Echo." His eyes meet mine, and he looks a hundred years old. "He called the paramedics. He called me."

"But you still think he could have had something to do with the fall. Something more than taunting him into an unstable trick." Bitterness leaks from my tongue. "You think he moved the mat."

I can picture it, stark behind my unwilling eyes. In my vision, Gabe is still young, darkly jealous of the lucent boy he named Echo in a shabby bid to dim his light. I remember his baffling fragility and the cut of his cruelty.

Wash straightens in his seat, shaking off the edge of his decay in the face of my accusation.

"I don't think anything." He sighs, giving away the lie. "I know there was envy and resentment when they were younger. I know I failed Gabriel when his mother and I divorced, and that Echo suffered for it. But Gabe is a grown man, successful now in his own way. Surely he's outgrown his petty rivalry."

A broken laugh escapes me. "You don't know either of your sons nearly as well as you think you do."

He frowns at me, insulted. "And you do?"

I freeze.

"I know Echo."

"And Gabriel?"

I don't owe him anything, but the air is already heavy with confession, and my throat is hollow with the ache of grief. I slump on the bench and let my head fall back against the wall.

"I knew him in college."

"In Tilburg?"

"He never mentioned me?" His ignorance shouldn't surprise me. Byrd Baardwijk isn't exactly a common name, and I can't imagine Wash letting Reggie hire me if he'd known the connection. But *Christ*, Gabriel and I were together for over a year before I broke his rules and he broke my heart. And he talked about his father all the time in school.

He doesn't deserve your pity.

"We were...not close during that time." Wash shakes his head, dismissing his fatherly flaws. "You were friends?"

A bitter laugh escapes me. "Something like that."

Calculation stirs in the haunted shadows of his eyes. "You were lovers."

"Yes." I blow out a breath and let the word hang, eyes fixed on the door across the hall.

For a long moment, his eyes burn into the side of my head.

"Does Jericho know?"

"Not yet." I wait for his condemnation, but he surprises me again.

"Good. Keep it that way."

"I'm tired of lying to him."

"You've kept the secret for this long. What's another few weeks?"

"If I tell him, he might spend those weeks in LA. Isn't that what you want?" I tilt my head to meet his eyes. "This could be the thing to break him free of me so he never looks back."

"Or it might just break him. And this time, he won't have you to put him back together."

"Echo put himself back together."

But that's not the whole truth, and I can tell by Wash's face that he's not buying it.

"I'm not an idiot, Byrd." First names again, now that he wants something from me.

Or maybe we've bared too many painful truths to hide behind formality now.

"I saw the way he was with you. I've watched a lot of young men come and go in Jericho's life, and I wasn't lying when I told you I've never seen him kiss one before. Whatever you've made him feel for you, he believes it's real."

"So do I."

He waves a dismissive hand. "He's going to Tilburg. That is not up for negotiation. You've done the job you were paid for—barely—and I thank you for that." He leans in. "But I will not let you hurt him again when he's so close to achieving his dreams."

I think his dreams have changed lately.

The thought is guilty. Exultant.

I don't need this man to tell me who Echo is or what he's capable of. I'm certainly not about to let him discredit everything Echo has done this summer.

"You know what, *Graham*?" I straighten, forcing him out of my space. His eyes narrow, but he shifts back. "I'm not an idiot either. I know what we look like, Echo and I. We look like a mistake. Something desperate or convenient. Or predatory." I shake my head and push to my feet, pacing the three long strides to the door and back. "You're not the first person in our lives to try and protect us from each other. Hell, *I* tried to protect us from each other." Wash softens a bit at that, and I give him a rueful smile.

"But not Echo." My voice is full of wonder. "Echo never saw us together as something to be protected from. Since the very beginning, he chased it without fear. Who are you and I to say he hasn't known exactly what he needed every step of the way?"

Wash opens his mouth, but I cut him off. He had his turn.

"What we have *is* real, and Echo deserves the truth. If he forgives me, I'm taking him back to Mendo until it's time for him to leave for school. If he doesn't..." I reach out and press my palm to the door to the audition room. "Then you take him home." I let my hand fall and turn back to pin him with my gaze. "And you keep him the hell away from his brother while he's there."

Wash flinches, but I don't let up.

"Whatever happens, it will hurt, but he won't break." *I won't let him.*

I'll break for both of us.

29

Echo

I am fearless, flawless, and I can still fly.

The handstands are a bitch, but the coach lets me do them first, and then I have the rope in my hands. If her eyes are blue and impersonal, I know now what it's like to be in the air under Byrd's warm hazel gaze, and the adrenaline is an old friend welcoming me home. I flow through first the mandatory and then the elective skills without hesitation. My limbs are strong and exultant as a part of myself, once withered and dead, wakes to the familiar challenge.

Beyond the fear that paralyzed my brain, my hand was pieced back together from a serious trauma. The bones might be reinforced with surgical steel, but muscles and tendons take time to strengthen. I'd neglected my grip while running pathetic circles around my studio last winter. But none of that matters now because Byrd had me conditioning the basics even before he coaxed me from my panic with kisses and dirty words.

I'm probably imagining the surprise on the coach's face when I complete all five of the required one-arm straddle-ups, but a flush of pride that has nothing to do with my burning muscles warms me anyway. Even if it's only half as many as I pulled off at my original audition.

My beats are weightless, and I show off my flexibility by landing the last one in a perfect scorpion. And I finish with my double pirouette—even though Byrd assured me the single would be enough—because fuck it, I feel like a badass, and I know as soon as my hands leave the rope for the first rotation that I'm gonna nail it.

When it's over, I'm so giddy with relief, I can barely make myself thank the woman.

"I'll let you break the good news to your family," she says, shaking my hand with a smile. "It was a pleasure to meet you, Jericho."

Family. My heart leaps in my chest. I *want* Byrd to be my family. Flush with victory and high on endorphins, anything seems possible. He could come with me to Tilburg. We could get married. I could spend the rest of my life being his Echo and have it all.

Rein it in, idiot. You don't even know if he wants those things. Smothering my shit-eating grin, I step into the hall.

As soon as I appear, Byrd stops his obvious pacing and turns toward me, shaking out his fisted hands. My dad looks up from his seat on the metal bench, pocketing his phone as I lean against the door with a slow smile. He throws Byrd a quick look I can't read and gets to his feet.

"Getting along with your future son-in-law?" I blurt. So much for reining it in. Jesus. Byrd comes to an abrupt halt and my dad scowls.

"Very funny," he says, shifting his narrowed eyes to Byrd.

"I *just* got divorced," Byrd chokes out, but his eyes are hot and possessive on mine, and a thrill runs up my spine. Or rather *down* my spine and straight to my dick.

"First wives don't count. Right, dad?"

"*Echo*," Byrd growls.

"Enough." My father rolls his eyes, but he's more amused than angry after Byrd's obvious shock. To be fair, he's been dealing with my mouth a lot longer than Byrd has. "Clearly, you weren't spanked enough as a child."

"Oh!" I bounce away from the door. "Byrd likes—"

He's on me in two strides, clapping a hand over my mouth and pinning me against the wall. Never say my man's not a fast learner.

"How. Did. The. Evaluation. Go?" he grits out, then grimaces when I stick my tongue out and lick his palm. "*Someone's* getting spanked tonight," he hisses. But he lowers his hand. Cautiously.

"I nailed it." I grin. "So that *someone* won't be me."

He throws up his arms and leans against the wall next to me with a groan. In spite of our shenanigans, my dad's smile is proud—once he's dragged his eyes from the ceiling.

"I knew you would," he says. Byrd drops his hand from where it's covering his face and grips mine, hard.

"I'm ready to celebrate," I declare, bouncing on my toes again and squeezing back.

"I made reservations at Angler," my father says, glancing at his Rolex. I cut my eyes to Byrd.

"We kind of have plans."

Byrd got us VIP tickets to the Cirque show in town, and the gates open at six. Which gives us just enough time at the hotel for me to rock his world before we have to get dressed and head to the tent.

"Go to lunch with your dad," he says, leaning in to press a kiss to my temple. "I have an errand to run anyway."

"An errand?"

What errand could be more important than my dick in his ass? He winks at my obvious incredulity. "It's a surprise."

His eyes shimmer with illicit promise, and I sway into him, caught. *Nope. Not actually helping.* As much as the idea of a surprise—especially one that sparks *that* look—intrigues me, I'm all about instant gratification when it comes to Byrd. Call it conditioning after the weeks of torturous teasing he put me through.

"You're getting me a present? I wanna come." I'm definitely not whining.

"It's a *surprise*," he repeats, and actually has the audacity to push me gently toward my dad with his fingers on my chest. "I'll see you back at the hotel after your lunch."

Fine. He's gonna pay for that later, though.

30

Echo

"**Y**ou seem better."

"I am better." I'm still in my tank and joggers, but my dad is known at Angler and probably slipped the host a fifty, so no one complains. We have the window table, of course, and the Bay Bridge glitters iconically in the weak afternoon sunlight. I'm sipping the same beer I always order and am feeling only slightly disgruntled that the waitress didn't card me now that I actually have a legal ID.

"It was worth it, then?" He studies me over his own beer, and I bristle.

"Worth it? You mean, worth letting Byrd fuck me if it means I can still perform?"

"I *mean*, I'm happy to see you have your confidence back. I've never cared who you fucked."

It's true, but I don't miss the subtext. He's never cared because it's never been serious before. He likes that I remind him of his own fuckboy glory days.

Thanks to Gabe paving the way, my dad didn't even bat an eye when I came out to him at fourteen. And my mom relaxed the grandkids bullshit when she realized after three days of researching adoption that California is hyper-liberal and doesn't give a fuck if the couple is queer. She can keep dreaming. I'm not sharing Byrd with some rug rat any time soon.

"It's more than that this time. I love him." The words fill me with blue skies and butterflies, but my dad frowns, unimpressed.

"It might feel like that now—"

"Don't do that. Don't start treating me like a child after all these years because I finally want something you don't approve of."

"You're twenty-one years old, and you have your whole career ahead of you."

Jesus, he's a fucking cliché. I squash the niggling voice that reminds me Byrd's made the same point on more than one occasion.

"And Byrd knows all about that career. He had the same one." *Until his bitch ex-wife made him give it up.*

As if he can read the rancorous thought, my dad continues, "He's also barely out of his marriage. To a woman."

"He's bi. So what? And how long were you and Detta separated when you hooked up with Mom? Five minutes?" I can't believe he's trying to give me serious relationship advice.

"This isn't about me. It's not even about Byrd. It's about you and your future."

"I want *him* to be my future. I wouldn't even have one if it weren't for him."

That stops him, and he leans back in his chair, frustration dissolving into concern as he shuffles his silverware and studies me.

"How bad was it?" he asks quietly.

"Bad." Ignoring his flinch, I lay my hand on the table and curl my fingers into a fist. The muscles flex as easily as memory, rippling under my tattoo, but the scars are still there beneath the ink. "Not only the hand—that sucked, but it wasn't the pain that broke me. It was the fear." Guilt flashes across his face, but I barrel on. "I know you don't want to hear it, Dad, but after the fall, I was scared of everything. The rope. My body. That I'd never be Echo again." *The son you wanted.*

"We never meant...*I* never meant to abandon you." He stumbles over the admission. Admitting his own failings has never been my dad's forte. "Or to make you feel like you weren't loved for more than your talent."

"It wasn't your fault." *Not entirely.* "You weren't the only one attached to that perfect version of me. I built that identity for myself too." *Made myself the star of our perfect, fucked-up family and fooled myself into thinking it meant I was grown up.*

"And now?" The caution in his voice doesn't hurt the way it would have a few months ago.

"Now I think maybe I can be something better. Something grounded. Something real." *The Echo that Byrd sees.*

"Because of *him*?"

Before I can answer, his phone vibrates on the tablecloth, and my brother's name flashes across the screen.

"What's up with Gabe?"

"Nothing." He flips the phone over without looking at it, hiding the incoming call.

"Then why is he calling you?"

"*Nothing*" is a load of bullshit. Gabe and my dad rarely speak to each other, and there's no reason he'd be calling instead of texting unless it was important.

"Your brother is in the city and is asking to see me. I'll call him back later."

"Gabe's in SF? Today?" Holy shit, I'd love to see the look on his face if I introduced him to Byrd. Bringing Byrd home to LA is probably out of the question at this point, given my dad's current attitude, but meeting up with Gabe and casually showing my man off a little?

"Tell him to come by the hotel when you drop me off."

"No."

"What? Why not? I wanna rub Byrd in his face."

"Absolutely not."

"Aw, c'mon. You've seen Byrd. He's exactly Gabe's type—all chiseled and stoic." Maybe it's petty little-brother bullshit, but making Gabe envious is one of my favorite skills.

It's not like I've ever been able to make him proud.

"Jericho. Stop."

Jericho. Shit, he's breaking out the big guns. Of course, all it does is make me more curious. Especially when the next thing out of his mouth is "Byrd has no interest in meeting Gabriel."

"Because I told him what a dick Gabe can be?" I scoff.

"You told him—?" He hides a snort in his napkin.

"Of course. But Byrd's a gentleman. He's nice to everybody. He won't let Gabe get under his skin."

My dad sobers, eyes flashing a warning I still don't understand. "Stay away from your brother this weekend," he says. "And keep Byrd away from him too. Please trust me on this."

"But why? I know your relationship with him is complicated, but you've never tried to keep us apart before." That was always my mom's job.

"Because I don't trust him with you. Now leave it alone."

"Are you shitting me?" No way I'm letting that declaration slide. "What the fuck are you talking about, you don't trust him with me?"

He leans back, pinching the bridge of his nose like he can stem the authority draining from his posture. A cold rush of apprehension washes through me at the sudden exhaustion on his face.

"Dad. What are you talking about?" I push my half-eaten bluefin away and lean toward him, the meal turning sour in my stomach when he won't meet my eyes. My fists clench in the white linen, and he looks up in time to catch my beer before it topples.

"How much do you remember about your accident?"

"I—" It's dark behind my eyelids, but pain is a red tide under my skin. "What does that have to do with Gabe?"

Are you scared, little brother? Let's see this famous trick.

The same eyes I see in the mirror every day hold mine, and in a burst of cruel insight, I recognize the stark awareness buried in the blue depths before he speaks.

"Maybe nothing. But it's possible that Gabriel...adjusted the mat the day you fell. I can't be sure, since he was the only one with you in the studio, but he's always been jealous of you. And the circumstances are suspicious enough that..." He trails off as I shake my head, struggling to draw breath through the horror blooming bitter in my chest. "You *never* fall."

I never fall. Until I did.

"So you understand why Byrd won't want to meet him. And why we both think you should take care around him in the future."

"Wait. You're saying you told *Byrd,* five minutes after meeting him, that you think my own brother tried to destroy me? But you couldn't tell *me* sometime in the last, I don't know, nine months? Gabe was at the fucking hospital, for Christ's sake. And at the house over the holidays. If you had all these suspicions, why didn't you say something then?"

"Immediately after the accident, I wasn't thinking clearly about anything but you. And later...Maybe I thought you'd been through enough. Maybe I didn't want to believe one of my sons could be capable of such a thing."

"But you were fine letting me think it was my own fault? That I'd fucked up and this"—I slam my hand down on the table between us, palm up so the broken wings are visible—"was some kind of punishment?"

"I had no idea you blamed yourself." He reaches for my hand, but I snatch it back and bury my fist in my lap. "You wouldn't *talk* to us. You hid yourself in the studio and told us you were fine."

"I wasn't *fine*."

"I realize that now. I'm sorry. I should have pushed harder to make you talk." He shrugs, the apology lacking his usual lawyerly aplomb. He *looks* sorry—older and more defeated than I've ever seen him—but I'm too upset to mourn the crumbling pedestal he's falling from. *I guess neither of us is as perfect as we thought, Dad.*

"You should have told me the truth. If Gabe hadn't called, if I hadn't wanted to see him, would you even have said anything today? Or would you have kept letting me think I had a brother?"

"I'm trying to protect you, Jericho. That's why I'm telling you all of this now. I will handle Gabriel, and in another month, you'll be at school where he can't touch you."

Where Byrd can't touch me either.

Is this what loneliness feels like?

His phone vibrates again, and I lunge for it, but he slides it from my reach and brings it to his ear with a warning shake of his head.

"Gabriel. I'm with your brother. You and I will speak later."
He disconnects before I can shout accusations across the table,
probably knowing as well as I do that his cool dismissal will hurt
Gabe far more than anything I could throw at him.

"Lying doesn't protect me, Dad. And Byrd would've told me
tonight anyway."

"Perhaps."

"*He* doesn't keep secrets," I spit, going for blood. "*He's* a good
man."

My dad studies me, but I don't look away.

"If I had said something last winter, would it have changed
anything?"

"It would have pissed me off," I cry, startling the blue-haired
ladies at the next table. "Angry is better than broken. Maybe it
would have given me a reason to fight back."

*But maybe if I wasn't broken, Byrd wouldn't have fallen for
me.*

I shove that thought away. "Take me back to the hotel."

"Finish your lunch. Please. You worked hard today, and you
need the calories."

His concern only infuriates me further, and I push away from
the table, wrapping my arms around my chest as I stand like I
can hold the rage inside with muscle and grip.

"I need *Byrd*," I tell him. "Take me back, or I'm calling a ride."

Fuck my pathetic brother and my too-late protective dad.

Byrd is the only family I want now.

The heavy door to our hotel room slams with a satisfying crash when I enter, and Byrd gives me a quick scan, searching for the crisis. He's already half-dressed in his tux for the evening, and all thoughts of Gabe's assholery fade to the background at the sight of Byrd's perfect ass in the tailored pants and his tan skin against the starched white of his dress shirt.

Home. I lean against the door with a low whistle.

"You clean up nice, Mr. Baardwijk."

Gold glints at his wrist as he fastens a cufflink with deft fingers, heat and amusement lighting his hazel eyes. This is so much better than arguing with my dad or reliving the tragedy of my fall.

I'm okay. I'm better than ever. Gabe didn't break me more than the man in front of me could fix. I lean against the door and take deep breaths, willing the tension from my muscles as I appreciate the view.

"How was your errand?" I ask.

"How was your lunch with Graham?" he counters with a hint of a smirk. Ooooh, mischievous Byrd. I push off the door and drift toward him.

"Eventful," I admit. His hands go still on the second cufflink, and his eyes turn serious as he watches me approach.

"Echo," he says, "I need to tell you something."

Relief settles over my skin like one of those Mendocino mists, easing the hectic jitter of my dad's revelations and sapping the last of my lingering rage. *No secrets. Not with us.* I shake my head.

"You don't have to say anything. My dad already told me about Gabe."

31

Byrd

The muffled thud of my cufflink hitting the carpet is bizarrely loud in the hollow silence following his words.

Wash begged me not to tell Echo the truth. Was it all a ruse to drive a wedge between us? And Echo...

He should be angry, not looking at me like he wants to devour me. Why isn't he angry?

My mouth opens, but my voice is mired in the acrid taste of panic-laced regret, and before I can force an explanation, he continues.

"Yep. Apparently, my brother's a psycho scumbag, and my dad's a fucking coward who didn't think I could handle the truth. I can't fucking *believe* he waited this long to tell me." His hands come to rest on my forearms. *Can he feel the muscles vibrating under the bite of his grip?* Each bitter accusation rings uncomfortably close to home, even as pathetic relief douses my dismay.

The fall. He's talking about the injury.

Remnants of my own anger with Wash prick my conscience. Wasn't I just arguing that Echo was strong enough to handle the truth—all the truths—about his brother? Wasn't I seconds away from a confession? Why, then, this numbing sense of re-lief?

Tell him.

"Echo, I—"

"Gabe was at our house for New Year's, for fuck's sake. Prob-ably gloating over his handiwork when I couldn't even...*Fuck.* I'm such an idiot." He drops his forehead to my chest.

"You're not an idiot." The words come on autopilot as relief and guilt continue to war in my thundering heart. "Your broth-er is—"

"A narcissistic piece of shit?"

"Something like that."

"See? You've never even met him, and you figured it out."

This is your chance. Do it now.

"Actually, that's—"

"I want to kill him. You'd help me hide the body, right?"

My lips twitch despite the nausea crawling up my throat.

"I do know a secluded piece of land up North." *Fuck, fuck, fuck.*

"*God*, I love you. I'm so fucking glad I don't have to go home with my dad tomorrow." He offers a crooked smile. "I told him you'd tell me the truth. I knew you wouldn't try to keep it a secret." My heart stutters at the raw faith in his words, even as it shrivels in shame. His lips brush mine with all the weight of the final nail in my coffin.

I can't do it. I've learned to be selfish after all, and I can't lose him. Not yet.

Not when he deserves one perfect night of triumph without his brother casting further shadows on his dreams and desires.

He pushes away and swipes angrily at the unshed tears turn-ing his eyes to pebbled pools of lapis, oblivious to my inner disintegration. "I need a shower. Wanna join me?"

Always. But he catches my hesitation and reads it as reluctance.

"You're already dressed. Never mind. I'll be faster alone anyway." He slips away before I can decide to snare him and leaves me torn and shaken in the wake of his sudden storm.

I'm sitting on the foot of the king-sized bed, toying with my rescued cufflink, when he emerges fifteen minutes later with one towel wrapped around his slim hips and another turbaned on his head. My shameful heart lurches at the sight of him, all sin and seduction like a harem boy out of some Arabian Nights fantasy.

"Are you okay?" I ask, defeated once again by his ruthless beauty.

"Stop," he says, shaking his head. The towel turban tumbles loose, and he tosses it on the bed beside me, raking his other hand through his dripping hair. "Stop looking at me like I'm something fragile. I'm not fucking broken anymore."

"You were never broken." *You were always perfect.* "But I'd understand if you want to stay in tonight. We don't have to go to the show if you're not up for it." *I'm not sure* I'm *up for it*.

"I said *stop*." He stalks toward me. "I'm not missing out on a chance to see you in your Cirque-boss element. Competence porn is a thing, you know, and I'm pretty sure it looks like you in a tux."

"Don't do that."

"Do what? Tell you how I'm fantasizing about peeling you out of those clothes one slow piece at a time after I've edged myself all night ogling you?" He cocks his head, but I'm not buying the act.

"Bury your shit under the flirting. We're past that phase of this relationship." *I'm such a fucking hypocrite.*

He flinches but doesn't retreat, running a hand down his inked abdomen to fiddle with the knot in the towel at his waist.

"I thought you loved my cocky mouth."

"I do." *It's the ruin of me.* I grab his wrist before he can loose the towel. "But you don't need to pretend you're not hurt. Not ever with me."

He wrenches his hand from my grip, eyes flashing fury even as his mouth trembles with heartbreaking vulnerability.

"I'm not *hurt*. I'm pissed. *I fucking hate him.*"

"I know." My own rage swims to the surface. The Gabriel in my head is forever nineteen, but I can see him all too clearly—wicked and vengeful above the broken body of the brother who taught me what it is to love without condition or restraint. *If I could go back in time, I'd destroy him before he ever had the chance to fuck with Echo.*

"I get it. He's *supposed* to be your brother. You have every right to feel betrayed." I reach for him, wanting to soothe away the pain—wanting to nurture his righteous anger until it's an impenetrable shield around the scarred and sacred spirit I can never be the one to fully shelter.

For one breathtaking moment, he leans into my touch, damp and ephemeral beneath my fingertips, and I think he's going to fall into my arms and let me try.

Then he lets out a ragged laugh and runs a thumb over my mouth.

"I don't want to talk about Gabe anymore. I'm pretty sure I could die happy if I never heard his name again." Defiance screams from every syllable. "And you owe me a blowjob."

I can't deny him anything, and hell can have my soul.

I curl my fingers in the thick terry cloth and unwrap him, tugging him into the space between my thighs.

"He can't hurt you anymore," I murmur into the hollow of his hip, and then take him in my mouth to smother the lie.

32

Echo

The blowjob helps. So does the look on Byrd's face when I emerge from the bathroom in my own tight, tailored slacks and a black Versace shirt that shows flashes of ink and skin through the devore pattern.

He kisses me stupid in the elevator on the ride down to the parking garage, then drives us to the sprawling big-top lot under the Bay Bridge with a hand on my thigh. He's also one hundred percent as hot as I imagined leading me past the lines to the backstage area and chatting up the chick who lets us in through the staff entrance.

I've been to a dozen Cirque du Soleil shows before, both with my parents when I was younger and later with Asha—including a whirlwind tour of every Vegas casino show my bestie and I could fit into a three-day graduation trip the summer after we finished high school.

Being backstage is different. Byrd knows at least a third of the performers by name, and their respect for him is obvious in the way they break from their warm-ups to say hi and ask him questions as we move through the impressive space. Even here behind the scenes, everything glitters in royal blue and gold, with costume racks and spotting blocks and insane professional rigging everywhere.

There's no rope act in the show we're seeing, but the guy who does the solo Chinese Pole grins when Byrd introduces me and launches into an excited explanation of his rope background and how he adapted a few of "our" classic moves for the pole.

No one notices my scars—in fact, half of the people I meet seem to assume I'm one of Byrd's new recruits, which is flattering as hell. And still, Byrd doesn't bat an eye when I slip my hand into his warm, calloused one and lean into him like the cheeky twink arm candy I'm perfectly happy to be tonight. He leads me through the dark wings and presses me up against the taut canvas wall to claim my mouth and palm my dick before dragging me half-hard and breathless to our front-row balcony seats.

The spectacle never gets old. Nor does the thrill of recognizing moves I've executed on the silks or the tumbling floor performed by real professionals under dazzling lights. It's a wild combination of elation—*I can do that*—and awe for the jugglers, contortionists, and fliers doing the kind of skills I've never attempted.

Byrd holds my hand through the whole first act, running his thumb along the ridge of my scars with casual ownership. Like they're a piece of me worth cherishing.

At intermission, we weave our way through the hyped-up crowd to the VIP lounge, where he leaves me with a glass of champagne and a wink before heading off to find a restroom.

The crowd is thinner here, and no one is paying attention to me. Shooting off a quick text to Byrd, I wander past the roped-off entrance in search of a place to smoke and end up outside general admission by a row of port-a-johns separated from the parking lot by a chest-high chain-link fence. Even in

July, the Bay Area nights are soaked with the Pacific's damp chill, so I tuck myself into a corner by a dark trailer out of the wind and rest my elbows on the fence, wishing I'd thought to borrow Byrd's jacket so I could wrap myself in his lingering heat.

"I hear congratulations are in order, baby brother."

The familiar voice sends a shock of rage through me, banishing the cold in an instant. I turn slowly to face him and marvel that he can look the same after everything I've learned. Slim and arrogant in his charcoal suit, with a wraith-like smile tugging at his stupid, pouty lips and too much product in his dark curls.

"Are you disappointed?" I ask, matching his mocking tone. "Sorry, not sorry."

"Why would I be disappointed? I think it's cute that you want to follow in my Cici footsteps."

Would it be too dramatic to throw my drink in his condescending face? Instead, I take a sip, forcing my fingers not to crush the plastic flute.

"I know what you did," I tell him.

He doesn't even flinch, amusement crinkling the corners of his eyes. *Careful those wrinkles don't become permanent, big brother.*

"What is it I'm supposed to have done this time?"

"Dad's the one who told me." That wipes the casual smirk off his face.

"Dad doesn't know shit," he asserts, but my words etch cracks in his poise. "He's loved nothing better than to imagine the worst of me ever since his perfect little trophy wife gave him his perfect little trophy son."

Fuck him and his *little*. I push off the fence, straightening to my full height, and almost grin when he takes a step back. *That's right, Gabe. The little trophy son is taller, stronger, younger, and hotter than you'll ever be.* "I can't help it if he's always seen through your bullshit."

"*My* bullshit. Sure. Nothing to do with the fact that he's coddled and pampered you since you were born. Of course his precious Jericho couldn't possibly have made a mistake. So much easier to blame it on the son he never wanted."

I refuse to feel sorry for him. "Maybe the reason Dad doesn't love you enough has nothing to do with me. Maybe he's always known you're a *fucking psychopath.*"

"Am I the bogeyman in all your nightmares, baby brother?"

"Am I the bogeyman in yours? How threatened and petty do you have to be to try to break me to prove—what? That you're better than me? That I'm as worthless as you are? Did you think Dad would actually forget what a disaster you are because I have pins in my arm?" My voice is starting to draw alarmed glances from the other showgoers, and I wrestle it back under control. "It didn't work, *big brother*," I hiss. "I'm stronger than ever, and everyone knows the truth about you now."

It's a good last line. I should leave him and go back to Byrd in the VIP lounge. Drink another glass of mediocre champagne and tease him about all the things I'm gonna do to him later. But Gabe is still glaring at me, leaking cold fury and jealousy like cyanide, and I'm suddenly shaking with something sadder than righteous contempt.

"I'm not afraid of you, Gabe," I say, tossing the last inch of my drink into a nearby trash can and slumping back against the fence. "I never have been. I just thought it would've been cool to have a brother once upon a time. I didn't know you hated me so much."

"I don't hate you," he lies. "I'd have to give a shit to hate you."

"You gave enough of a shit to try to ruin my life."

"And is it? Ruined? Or are you here, 'stronger than ever,' the same daddy's golden boy you've always been?"

He's the broken one. Small and helpless under the weight of his resentment. How could I have been so fucking naive? I close my eyes, but he keeps going.

"Why don't you come talk to me about ruined lives after you've been on your own for a few years. Oh, wait. That'll never happen. You've got your trust fund waiting to keep you swaddled in never-never land forever."

Got a thing for lost boys?

I'm fucking done.

"Fuck off, Gabe. I really want to punch you right now, but I don't want to waste two good surgeries on your face." I study the fingers on my right hand and swear I can feel the screws beneath the flesh and tendons. "But I can't promise Byrd will show the same restraint, so you might want to disappear before he finds me."

"*Baardwijk?*" He bursts out laughing. "*He's* your rehab coach?"

I narrow my eyes at him. "And my boyfriend."

"Oh, baby brother. You really can't help yourself, can you?"

"What's that supposed to mean?"

"Poor Jericho. Have you ever had anything that wasn't mine first?"

What?

33

Echo

Byrd's fist comes out of nowhere. Or maybe I conjured it with my wishful warning.

"Stay. The *fuck*. Away from him."

Gabe's head snaps to the side, and he stumbles, catching himself with a hand in the fence right before he hits the ground. The susurration of the thinning crowd washes against the periphery as my awareness tunnels, sharpens, coalescing on the sight of the berserker in the James Bond tux glowering down at my brother.

"Hi, Byrdie. Nice to see you again too." Gabe spits blood on the concrete and pulls himself back to his feet.

Byrdie? Maybe I say it out loud because Byrd's gaze hits mine, swimming with familiar remorse. I fucking hate that look. The look that means his doubts are winning. That he thinks he *took* something from me that I'm too young, too demanding, too *broken* to give.

But I'm scared that this time he might be right.

He ignores Gabe, who's now dabbing at his mouth and examining the blood on his fingers with wicked delight. My heart pounds in my chest, a cavern of chaos between each lurching beat:

Euphoria—Byrd swinging at Gabe like an avenging hero from my boyhood comic book fantasies.

Calamity—Gabe's eyes dancing between me and *my* Byrd with savage glee, while his voice says words like, "*You didn't tell him about us?*" and "*I was his first.*"

Byrd finally tears his eyes from mine.

"Stop it, Gabriel," he says, and his weary frustration torpedoes my last clinging remnants of disbelief. "How many of the people who've loved you have you hurt for having something you wanted?"

"Don't flatter yourself, Byrdie. You haven't been something I wanted for a very long time."

They know each other.

"I'm talking about Echo, you fucking piece of shit. Haven't you already done enough damage? What could you possibly gain by hurting him more?"

"How am I hurting him now? By telling him the truth? He called you his boyfriend. Shouldn't he already know you were my boyfriend first?"

They *fucked* each other.

Byrd's shoulders slump, his aggressive posture fading into something helpless and defeated. He shifts his gaze back to mine, his eyes an ocean of regret, and my breath strangles in my throat.

"Yes," he admits. "He should."

"Did he tell you about the guy who broke his heart in college?"

Byrd loved *him* before he ever loved me.

He moves as if to reach for me, and I flinch back, dimly aware of Gabe's caustic laughter beneath the roaring in my ears. My voice comes out small and pathetic.

"Why did it have to be him?"

But even as he shakes his head, the bitter symmetry clicks into place, cracking my heart in two. Why shouldn't it be Gabe who shattered him? And here we are now, two splintered souls trying to pull each other from the wreckage, one eternally apologizing and the other...

Furious.

Not at Byrd—not yet, although sparks of it flicker in the pit of my stomach—but at the absolute asshole who thinks he can trample through his pathetic life over the hearts and dreams of anyone who offers him an ounce of care.

Two Cirque lot security guards approach. One, built like a bruiser, ushers Byrd a few yards away, arguing in low, insistent tones. The other, a woman who looks almost as young as me, murmurs nervously to Gabe about cops and charges and whether he needs to see the on-site doctor.

"He doesn't need a doctor," I interrupt. "And no one is pressing charges."

Gabe arches a brow at me, a mocking mirror of the expression I've thrown a hundred times. But he doesn't argue, sending the guard away with a reassuring smile and a rueful shake of his head. His anger is gone, replaced by a cruel satisfaction that slices into my skin like retribution. *Like a surgical scalpel.*

He couldn't take my wings, but now he wants to take my anchor.

Like hell I'm giving him the satisfaction. Whatever past claim he had, Byrd is mine now, to punish and forgive. *I've only just begun to coax him free.*

"I know what you did to him."

"What *I* did to *him*?" He feigns hurt, but his lips curl with sadistic mirth. "He was the one fucking me, little brother. And then he fucked my career over too."

There's a story here. *Another* one Byrd never told me. Or maybe it's all the same story, and I know both of them well enough to guess the ending.

"Bullshit. If you're talking about that big showcase you didn't get in sophomore year, don't forget I've seen you on the silks. And I've seen him on the rope. If he's the one you whined about beating you out for that spot, it just means the judges knew what they were doing." Tears burn behind my eyes, but I clench my fists against the ache and cling to my disdain.

"We all got into the same school, you know." Gabe scowls. "Me, Byrd. *You*. Don't try to pretend you deserve it more than I did because Dad's been blowing smoke up your ass. Or that Byrd is some unrivaled god because you've discovered you like taking it as much as sticking it in."

"Back to that shit?" I run my tongue over my own un-bloodied lip and flip him off. "Get out of here, Gabe, or I'll be the next one to lay you out. You wanna call the cops if I break your nose with my bionic hand and watch how fast our rich daddy bails me out?"

"Looks like it's two rich daddies now." He smirks. "Byrd always was a sucker for a pretty little asshole."

Before I dissolve into pure, unhinged violence, my snarky mouth comes to my rescue. *I can hit where it hurts, too,* brother.

"Yep. Two men who love me more than they ever loved you." *Please, god, let it be true.* "One is a lawyer who could probably get me off even if I put you in the hospital, and the other is waiting to take me back to our hotel so we can get each other off and forget you ever existed."

Unfortunately, Gabe's mouth comes from the same stock as mine.

"You sure about that last?" he asks, glancing at where Byrd is arguing quietly with the burly security guard, his fists shoved in his pockets, looking anywhere but at me.

"Yes," I lie. "Byrd chose me."

"He chose me first."

It's a knife in the ribs, but I got good at faking functional after the last time he wrecked me.

"And look where that got him. He's spent his whole adult life afraid to reach for what he wants because *you* taught him he's not worth it when he does. But he is worth it. He's worth *everything*, so you can fuck all the way off now and leave us the hell alone." I keep my gaze steady and my trembling hands shoved in my pockets and pray he doesn't call my bluff.

"Sure thing, baby brother. Have fun with my leftovers." He pushes off the fence and finally saunters away, leaving me alone in the ashes of my trust.

Byrd, now free of looming authority figures in uniform, watches him go and sighs when I step up beside him.

"I'm so sorry, Echo. I never wanted you to find out that way."

It's too many revelations for one day, and weary exhaustion laps at the frenetic tension keeping me afloat. I've barely had time to process the first betrayal, and now I'm caught in this tenuous space between sympathy and rage, the urge to lick his wounds warring with the need to inflict them.

"Can we go back to the hotel?" I ask. His gaze snaps to mine, surprise and relief written in the widening of his eyes and softening of his jaw.

What would he be like now if I'd found him first?

"Yes." His hand hovers at my back as I lead him toward the nearest exit, but he never actually touches me, and I keep my own hands to myself.

For the first time since he found me in the rain at the Santa Rosa airport, I don't obsessively ogle him while he drives. The streetlights are just starting to come on, winking bravely against the deepening shadows of the sunken streets.

"Have I ever actually been Echo to you? Or have I always only been Gabe's little brother?" I think it comes out pretty casual, but the 4-Runner lurches as Byrd's foot hits the brake a little too hard, and he lets out a heavy breath before easing out of the parking lot.

"Jesus, Echo. How can you ask me that?"

"Seems like a fair question." There are a million more on the tip of my tongue, but I force myself to wait and pretend my patchwork soul doesn't hang on his answer.

"Both," he admits, after enough time has passed that I'm seriously considering abandoning him here while we sit at a stoplight. "You were Gabriel's brother, and then you were Echo. And then you were everything." He rests his forehead on the steering wheel as we wait for the light to change. "I was going to tell you."

"Sure. When? I wanted to think maybe you didn't know I was his brother, at first. But Wash isn't that common of a last name, and I talked about him the first night while you were making puttanesca..." And a dozen times after. So many chances to tell me the truth. *If I'm really your everything.*

"Yesterday. This afternoon. I meant to come clean a hundred times over the last few months."

"But you didn't."

"No."

"Because I'm leaving in three weeks anyway." The last time I broke, it was blurred, drugged edges. Denial and the ache of loss and slow-mending bones. This breaking is sharp with the glass edge of betrayal. Agony rushing in after the smooth parting of skin.

He turns his head without raising it from the wheel, and a lock of hair that's escaped from his topknot falls over his cheek. My fingers twitch with the urge to brush it away, but I refuse to let myself be lured.

"At first, I told myself it didn't matter," he says. "Because I wasn't going to let myself keep you. And then I didn't say anything because I'm a coward, and I didn't want you to leave."

"How uncharacteristically selfish of you."

He's no less beautiful, but it hurts to look at him, and I still can't help wondering how much of Gabe he sees when he looks back. I lean my head against the cold window and watch the moon rise over the skyscrapers like a ghost in the lavender sky.

I taught Byrd to be selfish, and he taught me to be afraid of being in love.

What an ironic fucking coup.

It doesn't make it stop, though—the loving part. After ten minutes of pretending I don't notice him shifting miserably in his seat as he navigates the early evening traffic, my runaway mouth can't take it anymore.

"You better be squirming like a guilty toddler because you kept the mother of all secrets from me and not because you punched my asshole brother."

He throws me a startled look, and even in the halogen glow of the city sunset, I can see the flush creep up his neck.

"That's not—umm...neither. I..." He shifts again. "I'm wearing a plug." The last comes out a rushed and almost apologetic whisper, and all of my tortured thoughts stutter to a halt beneath the onslaught of blood racing south. My stupid dick doesn't care that he fucked Gabe or that my heart is in shreds. It wants me to tug that toy out of Byrd's virgin ass with my teeth.

This is not a healthy way to handle my shit.

Byrd's called me out a million times for chasing my body's distraction when I don't want to face the cracks it hides, and even I can't fool myself into thinking sex is gonna fix anything this time.

But he's supposed to be the fucking grown-up, and he's been keeping secrets the whole time. Why should I try to be mature when it would be so much easier—and feel so much better—to punish him with my cock?

Because that's the whole point of a relationship, asshole. You're supposed to be making each other stronger, not enabling the same old crap.

We've almost reached the hotel, and the silence is thick with edgy tension and laced with treacherous lust.

Maybe for a little while, we can pretend the rest of this day never happened—that I never went to lunch with my dad or stumbled onto the mother-of-all-assholes on the lot.

Fuck all these revelations. Fuck being strong.

I'll take denial and Byrd's perfect ass, please.

"I can't believe you hit Gabe while wearing a plug to prep your ass to take my dick," I say as we climb from the truck in the shadowed parking garage. "Have you been wearing it all night?"

"Only since intermission. And I wasn't planning on punching anyone tonight."

"The punching part was actually really hot," I confess. "Assuming it was a knight-in-shining-armor thing and not a shut-up-before-you-out-me-as-a-lying-bastard thing."

"Echo." His fingers brush my arm, but I keep walking. "It was a blind rage, get-the-fuck-away-from-the-man-I-love thing," he finishes, so soft I might be dreaming.

Goddamn fucking butterflies.

He doesn't get to be romantic right now.

"So you seriously inserted a butt plug in a Cirque lot port-a-john? That doesn't sound very sexy. Or sanitary." The snort that escapes me is halfway between derisive and hysterical, and he gives me a guarded glance, holding the elevator door so I can slide past.

"Jean let me use one of the trailers. And no, I didn't tell her what I was doing."

"How does it feel?" Even in the harsh fluorescents of the elevator, he's stunning—loose tendrils of his chestnut hair framing the lines of his jaw and tickling his throat. His jacket is slung over one forearm, and he leans against the wall, watching me with his hands in his pockets, a study in wary affection tinged with tentative relief.

"Better now that I'm not driving. Or dealing with lot security."

I step across the enclosed space and grip the handrail at his hips, caging him in.

"Don't think this lets you off the hook," I tell him. He shakes his head.

"I don't expect that. I don't *want* it. You deserve—"

"He was the last guy you fucked, wasn't he? Before me?"

"Yes."

"But you never let him top you." I don't even think Gabe is vers, and Byrd said he'd never bottomed, but I have to be sure.

"No."

"And you did this"—I slide my hand around to cup his ass and press lightly on the end of the plug with my middle finger—"for me. Because you didn't want me to hurt you?"

"I didn't want you to have to be careful. I wanted to make it good for you."

"Fuck you, Byrd. You know that's my job tonight, right?"

"Are you sure you still want to?"

The elevator dings, sliding open on the executive level before I can answer. I let him go and walk out first, because *of course* I still fucking want to. But I also want to hurt him right now—at least a little—and it's making me reckless.

"It's probably a bad idea," I confess, leaning against the wall while he uses the electronic key card to open the door to our suite. He nods, his Adam's apple bobbing, and doesn't look at me. "But I'm gonna do it anyway."

I can forgive him. That's what love is, right?

"Okay."

34

Echo

*F*orgiveness *is fucking* hard.

I'm halfway across the living room of our suite when I realize he's still leaning against the door, watching me miserably, and the regret painted on his features brings all my old frustrations rushing back.

"I'm sorry," he says, for what feels like the millionth time. My least favorite words from his mouth, even if, this time, I know I should want them.

I take a breath, forcing the words out calmly through the spike of rage. "Why are you always apologizing for giving me your truth? I never asked you to fucking coddle me. I *want* your truth. Even if that truth is that you fucked my shit-stain brother and let him break your heart."

"I'm not apologizing for lo—fucking Gabe. I'm apologizing for keeping it from you for so long."

He's afraid. *Again*. Does he think I'll leave him now? No—that would be vindication, not fear—fulfillment of the prophecy he's been so sure of all along.

Does he think I'll hurt him, here tonight, taking what he promised?

God, I want to. I want to throw him up against that door and drive into him until the only name he knows is mine, and it bursts begging from his lips.

I close the distance, and something darkly eager blooms in his eyes alongside the fear. And yes, when I turn him to face the door, I'm not gentle. A sigh escapes him, laced with gratitude. He's expecting punishment—for me to soothe his guilt by giving it life.

His body vibrates with tension as I strip him with rough hands, all the cracks he tries so hard to control as sharp and clear as ley lines on his skin. When he's naked, I trace my fingers around the base of the plug, drawing a shuddering gasp from his throat. It's small, too small to have really prepped him properly, and I press my thumb against the top, stretching his rim, before giving it an experimental tug.

"You shouldn't have done this without me," I admonish. "Now I'm going to make you tell me everything you did and everything you were thinking while you were alone in that trailer."

He shakes his head and drops a hand to grasp his swelling cock.

"Were you thinking about me?"

"Of course," he whispers, hoarse with the remnants of his fear.

"Did it make you hard? Did you stroke that thick cock of yours like that while you fingered yourself open? Did you suck on this"—I tap the base lightly with a finger—"to get it all warm and slick before you slipped it in?"

"*Jesus.*"

"Or did you just lube it up and go for it?" I tap it again, harder, and he groans into the door. "Tell me."

"I—yes. *Christ*. I lubed it up after I fingered myself. I pretended it was you entering me, and I almost came all over my tux."

The clink of my belt buckle makes him shiver, and I breathe out one last sadistic flare of pleasure before pressing my lips to the nape of his neck.

"I'm not your sister, trying to protect you from your own desires while you make yourself small in my shadow."

I trail my tongue down the valley of muscle along his spine and let my fingertips drift over his hips.

"I'm not your ex-wife, needing you to hide your passions behind false reassurances of my importance."

His forehead thumps against the door and his knuckles whiten where his hands press into the wood at his shoulders. I drop to my knees and dip my tongue into his crease, tasting the fear and the want on his skin.

"I'm not your shitty ex-boyfriend—" *God, it fucking* hurts. "—Threatened by your power, doling out affection like a reward every time you put me above you." I trail my mouth down his crack and sink my teeth into the sensitive flesh of his taint, hard enough to make him jolt against the door.

Not nearly as hard as I want to.

"I *crave* your truth," I tell him, spreading his cheeks with my palms. "All of it and always. The way I've given you mine." The last is whispered into the dark heat between his thighs, a breath across his quivering balls. He makes a broken sound and tries to turn around, but I keep him spread and press his hips into the door.

"Echo, I *know*." One hand drops as if to reach for me but hesitates, curling into a fist at his side. "I'm so—"

Maybe it's not another useless apology about to fall from his lips, but I don't wait for him to finish the thought.

I stop admiring the way he stretches around the base of the plug and cover his entrance with my open mouth, teasing my tongue around the circle of warm metal and turning his words into a gasping groan. Then I make my earlier fantasy a reality by drawing the toy from his body with my teeth.

He clenches gorgeously around the sudden emptiness, and it's my turn to groan at the sight. Letting the plug fall, I squeeze my dick through my briefs and fumble through the pockets of his discarded jacket for the lube I know is there, before returning to devour his hole with wet, sucking kisses.

When I spear him with my tongue, he opens easily, drawing me in and drowning me in the silky taste of his hidden flesh, even as he fights the sensation.

He doesn't want me making him feel good right now.

Too bad.

Short, aborted moans escape through his clenched jaw, and when I add the first finger, he says my name like a curse.

I stand abruptly, fisting a hand in the loose bun at the back of his skull and adding a second finger.

"Say it again," I command.

"Please," he mumbles. "I can't—"

"No." I give his head a shake and shove both fingers deeper, twisting to press against his inner walls. "*Who am I?*"

"Echo." A whisper, defeated. But defeat leads to surrender, and that's my favorite sound from him. Surrender means *my* Byrd is coming out to play.

I brush his prostate until his knees buckle and he arches back against my palm.

"Are you ready for me?"

He's not, not really. But he's craving punishment and I'm chasing revenge, and this is how we both get what we want. When he hesitates, I pull my fingers free and step outside the heat of his body, leaving him open and empty. "Give me the truth."

"No," he admits, then shudders at the sound of me slicking my cock with lube. He tilts his head as if to look back at me, but his eyes are still closed. "And yes. *Give it to me.*"

There it is.

I slide the tip of my cock through his crack and nudge at his hole. He's gone tense and shaky again, but I'm done with foreplay.

"Remember what I told you about the pain? Make it matter. Let me in, *Coen.*"

He tries, but I still have to force my way through the first ring of muscle. As I breach him, he sucks in a breath, squeezing the head of my dick almost hard enough to bring me into his pain.

But *holy fucking shit, I'm inside Byrd Baardwijk.*

Well, barely.

"That's it." I catch his hands and lace his fingers with mine, drawing them up above his head. "Strangle my cock with your tight virgin ass. You can't stop me. You've never been able to stop me, *and you don't want to now.* You want me to fuck all that worthless guilt right out of you."

He nods, a short jerk of his jaw, and I feed him the rest of my cock in one hard thrust, covering the line of his body with my own as his eyes finally fly open, a whirlpool of panic and need.

"I'm not *Gabe,*" I say, low and ruthless, letting the name tear through us both. He goes rigid with shock, but it's too late—I'm inside him, and he's never getting rid of me now. "I'm *Echo*, and this ass is *mine.*"

And then he melts for me, and it hits me *everywhere*. His head falls back onto my shoulder as the last tension leaves his muscles and his tight, hot channel stops strangling my cock enough for me to start to move.

My anger is a distant, buried thing, drowned out by the sheer wonder of finally having him like this. Each stroke is rough and deep, and each time I bottom out, I grind my hips, straining to get even closer.

My name rumbles in his throat, an unending prayer, and I know I should slow down—make him come first and take care of him the way I promised. Instead, I release his hands to yank his hips toward me and punish his prostate, using him ruthlessly until my knees buckle and the sweat on his back turns into stars.

"*Mine*," I growl again as I explode, filling him, the heat and slick of my cum coating his walls and my pulsing cock. I give him a few more lazy thrusts, reveling in the new sensation. *Holy fuck.*

No wonder he fucking loves this.

He turns to look at me over his shoulder, flushed and panting, and I lean in to capture his mouth.

Is this the first truly honest kiss between us? I can taste the desperation on his tongue, and I slide my hand around to grip his neglected cock. He moans into my mouth, bruising my knuckles against the door as he ruts into my fist.

Reluctantly, I slide free, and he rotates to face me, hurt and hungry.

"Don't worry," I tell him, backing toward the bedroom as I unbutton my shirt. "That was only the first round."

His eyes drop to my dick.

"You're still hard."

I give myself a squeeze. "I'm twenty-one, and my cock was made for this. It was made for *you*. I'm not gonna be done until

I've fucked away the memory of every other cock you've ever tasted."

35

Byrd

Where is the line between penance and salvation?

Somewhere in the middle of his ruthless thrusts, I crossed over into absolution, pain melting under the raw onslaught of desire. There's a freedom in being used for his pleasure that gives my own a sharper edge. I couldn't fight him even if I wanted to, and it drives my arousal higher in acute spikes, peaking in some kind of savage satisfaction beyond orgasm when he comes hard inside me for the first time.

But if this is atonement, surely my dick shouldn't be this hard.

Echo appraises me in the aftermath, righteous and effortlessly erotic. His shirt hangs open and his dress slacks are falling off his slim hips, rendering him debauched and decadently deviant, his impossible erection flushed and dripping with the evidence of his brutal claiming.

I'm too far gone to do anything but humble myself in worship. My knees hit the carpet, and I crawl to him until I can capture the firm slope of his calves in my hands and press my face into his groin.

A soft sigh escapes him when I brush my mouth over the head of his cock, my tongue flicking out to taste his triumph. And then his hands are in my hair, and I'm sucking him clean as murmured words of praise sing in my ears.

"Fuck, baby. You're killing me. How can I stay mad at you when you feel so fucking good?" And then, "Okay. Okay, Coen." He pulls free and tugs me to my feet. "It's your turn now. Come to bed with me."

He sits me down on the foot of the bed and strips out of his clothes, holding me hostage with his bright gaze. If he was demanding before, now he's nothing but seduction, feathering his fingers over his pebbled nipples and down the black script decorating his torso.

"Close your mouth. Unless you want me to fill it again."

It's hardly a threat, but I do as he commands, leaning back on my hands so he can measure my reaction to his naked body.

With flashing eyes and a cocky smirk, he straddles my hips, lacing his fingers behind my neck.

"Do you know how long I've been fantasizing about getting my cock inside you like that?" he asks, grinding his slick length against my own.

"Since I told you I'd never done it and jacked you off in the front seat of my car?"

"Mmm. That was fun. But no. Since before I even met you. There's this video on YouTube. The song was some slow piano thing, and you were..." He runs his tongue up the side of my throat and sinks his teeth into my earlobe. "You were so fucking beautiful. I was terrified of meeting you, of letting you see me broken, and I still couldn't stop myself from jerking off to that video every night."

My hands find his hips as a shiver runs down my spine. "'Glitter in the Air' by Pink. I remember that act. Pretty romantic for a horny twink."

"What about you?" He pulls back to study my face but doesn't stop the slow roll of his hips. "When did you first let yourself think about fucking my tight ass?"

It's a test, despite the filthy words and teasing tone, and I'm pretty sure there are no right answers. So in the continuing spirit of the night, I go with honesty.

"Since you leaned through my window, nicotine scented and rain soaked, looking nothing like your brother."

His eyes flash electric fire and his blunt nails dig into the back of my neck, but he doesn't retreat. Instead, he spits into his palm and uses it to coat my cock, smearing the saliva into our combined precum.

"I'm *nothing* like him," he declares, raising up on his knees and slotting my eager dick against his entrance. "*Nothing*."

"You're not prepped," I protest, but he sinks himself down on my shaft, and his body opens for me like it always does. Like he was made for me as I was made for him.

"Ever heard of a flip-fuck?" he asks. "I know *he* never taught you." And then he squeezes around me, obscenely tight, and I struggle to form words.

"Slow," I warn as he begins to rock his hips. "Or I won't last."

"You'll last," he promises. Or maybe it's a threat. "You want to be *good* for me tonight, remember?"

"Fuck," I groan, torn between letting him take whatever he wants and flipping him over to fuck him hard into the sheets.

"No more talking," he whispers against my lips, and then he's kissing me deep, flooding my tongue with his smoky, sylvan taste as he carves away the last of my secrets.

It's me who snaps first, crazy with the need to come and desperate not to disappoint him, chasing his mouth when he arches away from me and cants his hips to give me access to that perfect spot inside him. I plant my feet to leverage my frantic thrusts, and only my fingers painting bruises on his hips and the velvet vise of his channel keep him from falling backward off my lap and spilling onto the rug.

When I'm about to lose it, when I start to swell inside him, he stops me with a hand wrapped around my throat.

"Enough." His other hand grips his leaking cock, staving off his own release. "My turn again," he says with a smile both wicked and angelic. My chest heaves, and I stare at him blankly until he pushes me down on my back and climbs off my cock to stand between my dangling legs. I lie panting, trying to claw the lust-drunk pieces of my brain back together while he coats himself with a fresh layer of lube. "Feet up."

My legs are jelly, but with his help, I comply, bringing my heels to the edge of the bed by my hips.

"Look at you," he marvels, dragging two fingers through the mess of lube and cum between my cheeks and pressing them into my hole. "Still all fucked out and open for me."

I shudder but don't deny it. It feels right, being vulnerable and exposed to him. He deserves so much more than the cautious, fearful version of myself I've been willing to share in the past.

This time, I get to watch his face while he enters me—the way his eyes reflect my own wonder and the lines of his throat go taut as his head falls back.

This time, he presses in slowly, letting me adjust to the strange and splendid fullness with none of the pain.

I almost miss it.

"Fuck," he hisses, mesmerized by the sight of himself disappearing inside me. "You know what you feel like?"

All the times I've taken him, captured his confidence and made it taste like my own, coalesce in this moment of vital union.

I know exactly what he's feeling.

"It feels like coming home."

At my words, he annihilates the last space between us, hooking his elbows under my knees and folding me in half to reach my mouth. I catch his face in my hands and surge to meet him, pillaging the sinful sounds he makes in his throat. His hips rock with each swirl of my tongue against his, and the hard heat of his stomach slides over my cock, making it weep.

A ravenous rumble rises from my chest, and he peels back, flushed and gasping.

"Gonna come if we keep that up."

I slide my hands from his neck and trail my fingers over the luxurious luster of his skin to tug on his nipples. "Isn't that the idea?"

"Mmm." He rolls his hips again, this time with a deliberate precision that has me arching off the bed with a hoarse cry. The corner of his mouth—deliciously swollen from our fevered kiss—quirks with satisfaction. "You first this time." Another devastating thrust, accompanied by a toss of his head. "Wait until you feel what it's like to come around a cock in your ass."

"*Your* cock in my ass. Only yours."

His nighttime neon eyes blow black, and the next surge buries him so deep that the threads holding me together begin to unravel. My hands scrabble at the sheets and my eyes flutter closed as he begins to move, building the euphoria in slow, shivering pulses.

"Watch me," he commands, and I do, tethered to his gaze as he strips me to the raw core of sensation.

If that first question was a test, *this is a lesson.*

This is *give* and *take* like the tide—Echo the incandescent moon, his inexorable gravity drawing rapture from my flesh like surf upon the shore.

He doesn't need to be cajoled into fucking without restraint, and he doesn't need to hold himself back to fuck with intimate delight.

He can take me hard and selfish.

He can take me slow and deep.

And all of it is love.

And him.

And *us.*

Somewhere in the spiral of desire, he's kissing me again, his thighs under my hips and his fingers tangled with mine above my head.

"Come with me now, baby," he whispers against my lips, slipping a hand between our bodies to stroke my aching cock with his exquisite grip. I'm already lit up everywhere, every nerve ending ignited, a writhing mess of love and lust and regret. I drink the words from his tongue like the holiest communion and spill into his fingers as the hot pulse of his release fills me up for the second time.

Penance.

Atonement.

Salvation.

He collapses on my chest, peppering my jaw with languid kisses, a breathless laugh rumbling in his throat.

"God, I could forgive you for anything if you let me do that, like, once a week."

Instead of replying, I turn my head to capture his mouth, threading my fingers through his sweat-damp hair.

I could kiss him forever, and it would never be enough.

By the time he rolls off me, he's half-hard again, the little demon, but he lets me drag him into the glass-walled shower, and his hands are gentle when he pushes me under the hot spray and washes me clean.

"Are you sore?" His fingers graze my hole as he presses against my back, resting his chin on my shoulder.

"A little. But it's a good sore."

His chuckle tickles my ear. "I knew you'd like it. I'm glad I got to be your first."

"I am too." It would be so easy to stay like this, warm and drowsy in the half-space between sated and aroused. Echo pleased and playful, even if I know it's partly a mask. If I close my eyes, I can pretend Gabe never happened to either of us, and our futures aren't half a world apart. "I'm sorry I made you wait so long."

"Everything with you is always worth the wait." He sucks the water from my pulse and slips his arms around my chest.

"Even the truth about my relationship with Gabriel?"

He goes still, then pushes away and turns to grab the hotel-sized shampoo bottle from the shelf.

"I don't want to talk about that."

"We have to talk about it sometime. If not tonight—"

"Why? I don't make you listen to me talk about my exes. You want a list of all the guys I've fucked?"

"None of your exes are related to me. None of them tried to destroy my body and my career. We can't keep acting like it doesn't matter, just because this"—I wave a hand between the two of us—"feels good."

"Like *you've* been doing for months?" He runs angry hands through his sudsy hair, eyes narrowed and accusing.

"Exactly," I sigh. "Look where that got us."

"I didn't hear you complaining ten minutes ago when you were coming all over my cock."

"I'm not *complaining*, I—"

He shoves me out of the way and steps under the spray, tilting his head back and closing his eyes. Shutting me out.

"Echo," I try again. "Please talk to me."

"Fine." He shakes the water from his hair and reaches for the door. "But not here. I can't do this naked."

The words are clipped, but the raw admission chills the last of my lingering afterglow.

The man who's taunted me with his nakedness since the first week I met him.

But I think we might be out of weeks.

36

Echo

B yrd sits on the edge of the bed in a pair of gray sleep pants that should be illegal, watching me pace the bedroom with his hands folded in his lap. Even pulled into one of its casual knots, his damp hair spills the occasional droplet onto his bare shoulders, and *why the fuck does he have to look so good when he's about to break my fucking heart?*

I know he thinks he needs to tell me everything, even if I don't want to hear it. Maybe I'm the pervy priest and he's the altar boy, and my punishment for his seduction is to hear his confession and absolve him of his sins.

But I'm not a priest; I'm *Echo*.

And it *hurts*.

More so because Byrd has never really hurt me before today. He's always been the one filling the cracks.

I stalk the plush room, resenting the romantic glow of the gilded lamps as the story spills out in his low voice and sparing words. Gabe as the new guy at Cici and Reggie's warnings. The slow seduction and Byrd's naiveté. And then the inevitable decay, colored in shades of narcissism I know regrettably well. A showcase Gabe wanted. A teacher who convinced Byrd to audition against him. Jealousy and gaslighting and vindictive betrayal, ultimately leaving Gabe pettily unscathed and Byrd a cautious, ever-careful supplicant when he should have been a god.

"I hope Reggie busted you with the biggest 'I told you so,'" I mutter when he finally runs dry, turning from the city skyscape at the massive window.

"Not until later," he admits. "At first, she was too busy picking up the pieces."

"You loved him." *I hate this.*

"I was infatuated with him. At the time, it felt like the same thing. Now I know better." His eyes beg understanding, even as his shoulders slump with the expectation of rejection. My feet carry me across the room until my fingers can tangle in his hair and tilt his face to meet my gaze.

"Ask me anything," he says. "I'll tell you whatever you want to know."

I already know too much.

"How could you fall for his shit?" The question bursts out of me, layered with the roots of betrayal and the creeping sprouts of my own self-doubts. "How could you let *him*, of all people, hurt you like that?"

He circles my wrist with one hand and rubs a thumb over my fallen angel's wings.

"How could you?" he asks softly.

The question sinks into my scars and clogs my throat with bitter irony.

"I was twenty-one," he sighs, relenting. "Like I said, I didn't know any better."

Fucking ouch.

I release his head with more force than probably necessary and stalk back to the window.

"Right. Because twenty-one-year-olds don't know shit about their own feelings." I round on him, tendrils of fury spiraling over my skin. "That's why you didn't believe *me* when I said I loved you. Why you kept trying to reject me for my 'own good.' Because I'm just a fucking *child* to you. No wonder you felt so guilty about wanting to stick your dick in me."

"I never thought of you as a child." He stands and moves as if to come to me but stops when I shake my head in warning. "Understand something, Echo. I wasn't like you at your age. I wasn't out and confident in my sexuality. I didn't draw attention as effortlessly as breathing. I was barely figuring out what my attraction to men meant."

My heart lurches at the unexpected compliment buried in the confession, but he barrels on. "Gabriel was the first man to ever return that attraction. It was addictive, overwhelming. And he was..." He trails off, scrubbing a hand through his hair, and a bitter sound escapes him as his fingers tangle in the hair tie.

"What? What was he?" *Why am I asking*? Do I really want to hear about Gabe's fucking charms?

"He was magnetic. Needy and unattainable in this contradictory way. You couldn't not want his attention. And when you had it..." He pulls the elastic from his ruined bun with an impatient shake of his head. "He made me feel special."

I'm crumbling, a devastating slide into shattered pieces that ache for the fragile dream of lost potential.

"You *are* special."

This time, when he closes the space between us, I don't retreat, letting his arms come around me and resting my forehead in the crook of his neck. He smells like floral hotel shampoo and starlit skies.

He smells like Byrd.

"I'm not perfect, Echo. I never was. You put me on a pedestal I couldn't possibly live up to."

"Fuck you," I mumble into his skin. "I never put you on a pedestal, and I never asked you to be perfect." My hands come up to push him away but curl into his waistband instead. "You were always perfect for *me*."

But I did expect perfection from him—when I asked him to fix me. When I dumped all my useless, broken pieces in his lap and used them to blackmail him into loving me back. I made him want *me*, when all he really wanted was to help.

"*You're* the perfect one," he murmurs. "You let me explore my own power without ever giving up any of your own, and it showed me a kind of love I never knew was possible." He buries his face in my hair and clutches me desperately tight. "But I lose myself in you. I can't think straight when we're in bed together, and—"

"I don't want you thinking when we're in bed together. Especially not *straight*."

He laughs, a breathless, hopeless rush of air across my skin.

"I never wanted to be another person who disappointed you," he whispers, tracing subtle patterns along my spine. "Everyone you've ever looked up to has let you down. Including me."

Not him. Not really.

Not yet.

"So that's why you didn't tell me about Gabe? You didn't want to let me down?"

"I tried to tell you this afternoon, but you were already so hurt and angry, and I..." He shifts back when I stiffen, creating reluctant space between us. "I wanted to pretend I was the man you saw in me for one more night."

"So you decided to let me fuck you as what, some kind of favor because you felt sorry for me? Or to appease your fucking guilt?" This time, I do push him, with all my strength, until he staggers and the distance between us crystallizes into something real.

"No. God, no. I *wanted* this. For you, yes, but also for me. It was..."

"Stupid of us." Denial is a flimsy shield. Foolish of me to rely on it, when he's never let me hide behind any of my other defenses.

"*Important.*" His voice rasps over the raw edges of our anguish.

"Important. Because it was the first time or because it was the last?"

He covers his face with his hands, and I sink to my knees beneath the sudden weight of awful understanding. I can't even pretend it's not my fault we ended up here.

How many lines have I forced him to cross while convincing myself it was what he wanted?

Take, I told him, eroding his resolve and his choices with the torrent of my need.

How am I any different from his other lovers—despite my grand declarations—when I make him compromise himself again and again? I was so sure I was better than them, but I've been the selfish one, endangering his career and his relationships to mend my own fractured soul.

Selfish enough that I still don't want to let him go.

"Look at me," I beg. "I crushed the most important audition of my life today because of you. I found out my own brother tried to ruin my life *and* he had you first, and it fucking sucked, but I didn't let it break me. *I defended you.* And then you let me have you the way no one else ever has and think everything was gonna be okay. That we'd get through this, because we're *Echo and Byrd*. And now, after all of that, you're breaking up with me?"

"That's not what I'm doing," he says, dropping to join me on the carpet. His hair is curling along his jaw as it dries, and I could reach out and touch him if he wasn't so fucking far away.

"It feels like you are."

"I may have held back the truth about Gabriel, but I never lied about anything else. I wasn't lying when I said I love you."

"Then what is this shit? Why are you looking at me like you're saying goodbye?"

"Everything that happened today—with your father, with Gabe, and with me—it's all been there the whole time, underneath the rest. Just because we've been pretending—"

"*Who was fucking pretending*? I never was. Don't try and tell me you were either. I fucking know you, Byrd Baardwijk. You don't do anything you don't mean. You would have fucked me the first week without giving a shit if you were that kind of guy."

"I wasn't pretending to love you. I was pretending I could keep you."

"Why can't you?"

"Because I *can't*. And you know this. Think about it, Echo. Think about your future and what you really want."

"I want you more than I want school."

"*Don't say that*. You know where that choice got me. Seven years drowning in a resentful marriage that was never going to work. I won't do that to you."

"I'd never resent you." But I can tell I'm losing the battle. He's been warning me the whole time that this has to end. Did I really think I could change our fate by offering to give up my own future? So that every time he looks at me, he's haunted by the ghosts of his past failings.

Or worse, by asking him to follow me across the world the way Lara did?

"Don't you understand?" he begs, cupping my face to brush away my tears. "If you don't do something incredible with your life, Gabriel wins. We can't let him win."

I crumple forward and smear my useless misery into his lap. His hands are achingly gentle in my hair.

I need this day to be over. I need it to never end.

"Take me to bed, Coen. Please?"

37

Byrd

"**B**yrd."

I know that voice.

What the fuck is James doing in our bedroom? Echo better be under the covers and not flashing his ass, or I might have to kill my friend despite the pounding in my head. And why is my face wet?

I open my eyes. A dimly lit room that is definitely not my cabin swims blearily into view, framing the bulky shoulders and brunette head of my ex-brother-in-law.

"What the fuck are you doing here?"

"Clancey called me." James jerks his head at the graying bartender, who gives me a wry smile and a shrug. Traitor. "The question is, what are *you* doing back in the old neighborhood getting plastered by yourself on a Sunday night?"

Fuck. Everything hurts, but when I try to close my eyes again, all I see is an empty pillow with an Echo-shaped imprint marring the 1600 thread-count cotton like a bitter haunting.

Reality isn't much better, though. James's coffee-colored eyes are rich with concern, and I'm pretty sure the puddle under my cheek is whiskey. At least it smells like the good stuff. I lift my head from my arms and squeeze the bridge of my nose in a futile attempt to stem the throb settling in behind my eyes.

"What time is it?" If I'm already halfway to hungover, it's probably too late to make the drive back to Mendo, even if I was in any condition to navigate the dark and twisty deathtrap of the 128.

"Ten past seven."

"You've been camped on that stool since noon," Clancey adds, oh so helpfully, and exchanges a significant look with my friend. Assuming we're still friends. I haven't talked to him since the semi-disastrous visit when Echo—

"Give me another shot of Basil, Clance." If I'm stuck in the city for another night, I might as well see if I can crawl back into oblivion. Thinking is clearly a terrible idea. "Please."

"I think you're all good, buddy," James says, laying a hand on my back. "Why don't you come crash at my place and let me get some food into you."

"Not afraid the guy who likes dick might try something if you bring him home drunk?" *Shit*. I'm not usually this good at being an asshole. The lines around James's mouth tighten under his short beard, but he only shakes his head and gently tries to pry me off the barstool.

"I think I can handle you."

I let him drag me to my feet but only make it as far as the first empty high-top table. The surface is blessedly whiskey-free, and I slump wearily into the matching chair before burying my face in my hands.

"I'm sorry," I mumble through my fingers. "I'm a shitty boyfriend."

"You're not my boyfriend. And for what it's worth, I don't think you were a shitty husband to Lara, either."

"Lara? I'm talking about Echo."

He sighs and slides into the tall chair across from me, signaling Clancey over my shoulder. "The kid? Sorry." He lifts his hands in apology when I level a glare at him. "The *guy* you were..."

"Fucking. We were fucking each other."

"Okay, man. It's cool."

Clancey appears and sets a glass of ice water in front of me and a pint of dark beer in front of James.

"No." I shake my head. "That's wrong. We weren't just fucking. I...he was—Goddammit." Ice clinks and water sloshes over my fingers as I shove the glass away.

"You were in a relationship?"

"I'm fucking in love with him." I slam both hands down hard enough that the table tilts alarmingly as the matchbooks holding it level shoot out from under the leg to skitter across the floor. James grabs both glasses before they topple.

"Jesus, Byrd."

"Don't call me that."

"What the hell, man? Fucking talk to me. Tell me what happened."

"I fucked everything up." *I lost him*.

"How?" He eyes me skeptically. "He ask for something you weren't willing to give?"

"Fuck you." I stagger from the table back to the bar. "Whiskey, Clancey. Fucking *please*."

The bastard has the nerve to look at James again. "How about a beer?"

"Fine. IPA."

"You get a Busch Light for passing out at my bar and being a dick to the guy who's trying to help you." Before I can argue, he cracks the tab on a cold can and slides it over. I swig half in one go and instantly regret it. Fucking piss water does nothing for my head. Or the gaping hole in my chest.

"Brother." James is at my elbow again, steering me back to the table. "Sorry if I touched a nerve. I didn't mean anything by it other than...I know how much you gave up to try and make my sister happy. And I know it wasn't your fault it didn't work. But Christ, I haven't seen you like this since before the divorce, and I thought maybe..."

"Echo didn't ask for anything."

"*I'm telling you to take.*"

Fucking hell, I couldn't even do that right.

"Except for me to be honest with him. And with myself. Turns out, I failed at both."

"You lied to him? That doesn't sound like you. What about?"

"I dated his brother in college." How easily the words come out now that they don't matter.

"Oh. Oh shit."

"The same brother who broke his wrist and almost ruined his career."

"What? His brother broke his arm?"

"Maybe. Probably. In a roundabout way. Gabriel's a sadistic fucking asshole, and I wouldn't put it past him." The memory of his face breaking under my knuckles pulls a dark grin to my face. I wish I'd pounded him into the ground when I'd had the chance.

"That's...seriously fucked up. Does Echo know?"

"His dad told him."

"And I'm guessing he also found out about the college thing?"

"Gabriel told him."

"Gabriel the brother? Shit. No wonder you're a mess. Where's Echo now?"

"He went back to LA with his dad this morning." *Because I pushed him away with my guilt and my misplaced savior complex.*

Because I thought he'd fight me like he always does, only this time, he slipped out of my grasp like a wraith in the middle of the night. And I woke up alone for the first time in months with nothing left but a single message on my phone.

Do you miss me yet?

I suck down the second half of my crappy beer and contemplate how pissed Clancey would be if I climbed over the bar and swiped the bottle of Basil Hayden. Maybe if I went for a cheaper one, he'd let it slide.

James sighs, reading my intent, and takes pity on me. "Bring him one more, Clance. And I'll take a double."

"Don't you have somewhere better to be?" I ask. "I don't need a babysitter. There's a motel around the corner."

"Fuck off." He grins. "I'm taking you home to sleep it off. If you keep acting so pathetic, I might even let you snuggle me."

"You're not my type."

"Let me guess. Your type is young, blue-haired, and tattooed, with a smart mouth and a bubble butt."

Bubble butt?

He throws his head back with a genuine laugh.

"I work tech in the Bay Area, remember? I pick up a few things."

"I don't care. Never say those words in my presence again."

"Hey, I'm only trying to bond with you." The place is starting to fill up with the evening crowd, so he walks back to the bar to retrieve our shots. "Now," he says, after I knock mine back and he takes a respectable swallow. "Tell me why you're drowning your broken heart with Clancey instead of chasing that boy of yours down and getting him back." For once, I don't argue with the "boy" comment. It hits a little too close to home.

"He's leaving for college in a month. His whole life is about to start, and he doesn't need me holding him back."

"Why would you try to hold him back?"

"I wouldn't *try* to, asshole. I just would. Did you hear the part about how he's leaving? No way I'd ask him to give up the prime years of his career to hole up with me in Mendocino."

"So why couldn't you go with him? The school's in Tilburg, right? Your hometown?"

Is he fucking kidding me? I snag the glass in front of him and drain the last inch of his whiskey before he can protest.

"Because. He didn't ask me to."

"Jesus fucking Christ, Byrd. Of course he didn't ask you to."

"Exactly." Maybe if I'd stuck to the beer, he'd be making sense?

"Get your head out of your ass, old man. This kid, *Echo*—I'm assuming he knows about your history with Lara? You didn't hide *that* from him, or you never would've let him meet me and Elke."

"He knows everything." *Now.* "What does it matter?"

The mirth fades, replaced with compassion.

"It matters, you idiot, because that's exactly what my sister did to you. She asked you to give up your life for her. And Echo knows it destroyed your marriage. If he loves you as much as you obviously love him, he'd never do that to you again. It doesn't mean he wouldn't say yes if you offered."

"I can't keep chasing the people I love across the world, James. Echo is the one who drove that home for me."

"It's not the chasing that's the issue. It's what you leave behind." He slaps me on the shoulder and stands up from his chair. "Try to figure that one out while I go get my car."

38

Byrd

Monday

My ass is still sore.

I let James think I'm walking gingerly because I spent the night hugging the porcelain throne and that it's the hangover and not the heartbreak keeping me buried in his guest bed all day. I'm not sure he's fooled.

He leaves me with some high-end Whole Foods electrolyte bullshit and a bottle of Advil and heads to work with an unsympathetic chuckle. I ignore the offerings and retreat into the oblivion of sleep.

I wake up midafternoon, cotton-mouthed and sticky with sweat and half-remembered dreams—Echo at my back like a righteous god, driving me to the brink of madness with his tongue and fingers and elegant, ruthless cock. The pain has faded to a vaporous ache, and I slip a hand between my legs to coax it back to urgent life. If I let my body forget him, I'll have nothing left.

Wednesday

"Go home, Byrd. Get your shit together. Self-pity never looked good on you."

"I still have nine seasons of *Supernatural* to finish."

James glances at the TV and shakes his head.

"I'll save you the trouble. The show peaked in season five, and Dean and Cas never fuck. Also, you have Netflix in Mendo."

"Your TV is bigger."

And a ghost haunts my once-sanctuary.

I'm not ready to face it. When the future I pushed him toward subsumes the past that drowns me—when I can close my eyes and see him walking the halls of Cici instead of sprawled wanton in my bed—then maybe I can move on with my own.

"Fine. But you gotta take a shower, man. The whole apartment is starting to smell like a midlife crisis, and we're both too young for that shit."

Friday

The heat baking off the 101 flickers over my skin, burning away the memory of blue rain, blue eyes, blue hair. I leave the window down and crank the AC and *fuck the carbon footprint* because I find half a pack of Spirit golds in the cupholder and smoke them all the way past the drought-bleached hills and checkerboard vineyards of Sonoma county, until my stomach curdles and my fingers stain.

When Reggie's name lights up my phone, I pull off onto a gravel road bracketed by the scorched-earth scabs of last year's wildfires and climb out into the sun to answer.

"About fucking time. I was starting to get worried about you."

"I'm alive." Sort of.

"Barely, by the sound of it. Keeping up with the twenty-one-year-old taking more out of you than you expected, old man?"

Something like that. I drop my head back onto the roof of the 4-Runner and close my eyes, letting the hot metal sear into the back of my neck.

"Never mind, don't answer that," she barrels on with a laugh. "I talked to Claire, and she said he killed the eval, so that means he's officially my student again. I don't want to think about the two of you holed up in some swanky hotel room celebrating all week."

"That's not—"

"Seriously, though. Claire said he was amazing. I'm almost sorry I gave you so much shit. You pulled it off in spite of everything."

"It was all Echo." *It was always Echo.*

"So how did you celebrate?"

"*You're so fucking tight. I'm gonna come so hard inside you, baby.*"

"I took him to see Aluré." Regret is bitter on my tongue. "I punched Gabriel."

"You *what*? Not that that doesn't sound like a celebration, but how?"

"He was at the show. He hurt Echo, and he told him everything, and…" It's too fucking complicated, and I'm too fucking exhausted to explain. "So I sent Echo back to LA." It sounds better that way. Like a choice instead of a tragedy. It's almost true.

She's quiet for so long that I open my eyes to make sure my phone didn't drop the call.

"Reg?"

"Why?"

"Because I'm a fucking coward. I don't deserve him anyway. He's all yours now."

"For fuck's sake. Will you just come home already?"

Why does everyone keep talking about home like I still have one?

"I could blame you, you know," I say. "You threw him at me. I could have had a nice, quiet, lonely summer. But you told me to be selfish. *He* told me to be selfish." *I want to be selfish again.* To glut myself at the banquet of tangled limbs and decadent mouths and—"I've gotta go. I'm gonna lose service." A wave of déjà vu rolls through me at the lie, setting my guts adrift. Any minute, and she's going to tease me about paperwork and tell me he's Gabriel Wash's little brother.

I disconnect while she's still talking and stumble over to heave nicotine-laced bile into the weeds.

The cabin mocks me with layers of memory like secrets tucked between the pages of my ordinary life. Pieces of him like petals that crumble at my touch.

The clothes we left in the dryer. AirPods on the nightstand and a stray sock under the bed. The rosin bag still on the mat in the living room because he could never be bothered to return it to its drawer in the sideboard. Dried shaving cream like confetti on the bathroom mirror—I can see him shouldering me out of the way in the mornings, laughter in his lapis eyes as he shakes out the razor.

The bed is full of his scent, and when I finally force myself to change the sheets out of pure hygienic necessity, I pull one of his T-shirts from the hamper to cover my pillow in the perilous hope that he'll grace my elusive dreams.

Reggie texts me daily, and only after she threatens to send Elke to make sure I'm still alive do I reluctantly reply. I've become a recluse, a shell, as if the last four months never happened, and all of my wallowing plans have covered up the interlude. Only, Lara never hurt like this—like something snatched away on the threshold of becoming real.

I spend hours on the rig under the redwoods, driving my muscles to the brink of breakdown in the pursuit of the exhaustion that lets me collapse into sleep. I stop marking the days on my calendar because the little circles look wrong without his cheeky little pornographic additions, and I can't bring myself to add my own. It's the fifth of August before I finally resurrect the strength to flip the page.

Echo was here.

Truth and mischief splashed across the photograph at the top in his prep-school penmanship.

He was here.

I *had* him.

He was mine.

I'm on the floor of the kitchen, cool tile under my ass and the brushed chrome of the refrigerator against my cheek. My phone is glacially heavy in my hands as my fingers fumble at the screen, opening his final text.

Echo: Do you miss me yet?

With shaking thumbs, I drag three letters from my sorry, screaming soul.

Me: Yes.

39

Byrd

*E*cho: *Hi.*

    Me: How are you?

Echo: (laughing emoji)

Echo: That's how you're gonna play it?

Echo: I'm fine, Mr. Baardwijk. How are you?

Me: I've been better.

Echo: Because you miss me.

Echo: I knew you'd cave eventually.

Me: You did?

Echo: We have a track record.

Me: True...

Me: So how are you really?

Me: Are you as ruined as I am?

Message deleted

Echo: You know I saw that, right?

Me: Shit. Ignore me. I'm sorry.

Echo: More apologies? Is that why you texted me? To say you're sorry for the millionth time?

    Me: If I say yes, will you actually listen?

Echo: Depends on what you're apologizing for this time.

Me: How about for making you wait? Again.

Echo: I'll accept that.

Me: And I do miss you.

Echo: I miss you too.

Echo: What have you been up to?

Me: Catching up on all the wallowing I forgot to do while I had a siren in my house.

Echo: A siren, huh? Sounds dangerous.

Me: It was. But he was worth it.

Echo: I'm glad you finally texted.

Me: I'm glad you answered.

Echo: Always.

Echo: And Byrd?

Me: Yeah?

Echo: I'm only a little bit ruined.

Echo: I went back to the gym with Asha today.

Me: That's amazing. How was it?

Echo: Epic. I got three offers to suck my dick.

Me: Are you trying to make me jealous?

Echo: Is it working?

Me: You know the answer to that.

Echo: (Winky face emoji)
Me: ...
Me: ...
Me: But it's okay if you want to...
Echo: Fuck. Stop.
Echo: I didn't do it.
Me: I'm glad.

"I need a job."

"I gave you a job. You fucked it up by fucking my student."

"Not a coaching job. I want to get back on the rope. I need another month to get my chops back, but then I want in on a show. Something small to start. I know you have connections."

"You have connections too. Cirque is all over the world."

"And I'll be calling them. But I want something based in Amsterdam. I'm coming home."

"Are you going to steal my student?"

"I'm not going to *steal* him. Although I do plan on fucking his brains out when he's not at school. If he'll let me."

"As his director, I'm going to pretend I didn't hear that. As your best friend, I expect details. Over wine. That you're buying."

"I don't kiss and tell."

"Bullshit. I had to hear all about Gabriel back in the day."

"We're adults now, Reggie. And Echo is nothing like his brother."

"I know, babe. I met him, remember? You think I would have pushed so hard to get him here if he was anything like that whiny prick? Or dumped him in your lap?"

"No. You've always had my back. Speaking of which, don't tell him I'm coming when he gets there, please."

"You're not going to tell him?"

"No."

"Why the hell not?"

"I want him to focus on school and have time to get settled in."

"Really. So you're just gonna show up at his door and surprise him?"

"Technically, it's my door. And I...What if he tells me not to come? I can't risk it, Reg."

When she's done laughing her ass off, Reggie connects me with a friend of hers directing a six-week gig in Amsterdam. I have a month to pull an act together before I need to be on-site for rehearsals. Luckily, it's a cabaret-style show, so I won't have to learn a bunch of group numbers when I get there.

Packing up the cabin would take too much time I don't want to spend, so I call a realtor about leasing the place furnished and send an email to Cirque HR, letting them know my sabbatical is now an official resignation. After making me promise to catch one of their shows before I leave, Shilo tells me I can store the 4-Runner and the rig at Big Top, and that she'll send Josha to drive me to the airport in San Francisco when I'm ready.

No one tells me I'm making a mistake except Elke, who lays into me with all her scathing sisterly fury. It's only after I figure out what James meant with his final cryptic comment at Clancey's that I'm able to shut her up.

"I'm not leaving anything behind this time, Elke. Everything I want for my life is already over there."

Echo: I said goodbye to Asha and Audrey today.

Echo: Audrey gave me a new tattoo.

Me: Sounds like a good way to commemorate your departure. What does this one say?

Echo: Hot for teacher.

Echo: On my ass.

Me: It does not.

Echo: (Laughing face emoji)

Me: Are you packed and ready for your move?

Echo: Ha. I left all my favorite stuff at the cabin.

Echo: I had to make Asha take me shopping for a whole new workout wardrobe.

Me: I should have sent you your clothes. Shit. I'm sorry.

Me: I can send them to Tilburg. You're taking the apartment, right?

Echo: Yeah.

Echo: Is that still okay?

Me: Yes, of course.

Echo: Thank fuck. My parents would freak if I had to find a new place to live.

Echo: I think they're getting sick of me.

Me: I doubt that.

Echo: They weren't too happy when my therapist made them come in for a family session.

Me: You're seeing a therapist?

Echo: A couple of times, yeah. It was Asha's idea. She thought I should talk to someone about all the Gabe stuff. Probably had something to do with the hole I punched in her wall.

Me: Is it helping? The therapy?

Echo: I think so.

Me: Am I allowed to be proud of you?

Echo: Always.

Echo: I'm kinda proud of myself.

Me: How are you liking the apartment?

Echo: You should have warned me it doesn't have air conditioning.

Me: There are fans in the back hallway closet.

Echo: I know. Reggie already showed me.

Me: Shouldn't you be calling her Ms. Blake or something?

Echo: She also showed me the David Bowie video.

Me: I'm not sure I like this new friendship between you two.

Echo: I didn't know you were into karaoke. ;P

Me: It was Halloween. In Amsterdam. There might have also been tequila.

Echo: And a bathroom blowie, apparently. With a tongue ring.

Me: Have you ever had an appropriate relationship with an authority figure in your life?

Echo: What are you wearing?

Me: Sweats and a band tee. And you're proving my point.

Echo: You don't have any authority over me anymore. Tell me about the sweatpants. Are they gray?

Me: ;)

Echo: Send me a pic.

Me: I'm not taking a selfie of my dick outline in the grocery store.

Echo: Mendoza's or Big Harvest?

Me: Mendoza's.

Echo: Ask Julie to do it. Tell her it's for me, and she'll get the framing just right.

Me: Absolutely not.

Echo: Spoilsport.

Me: Brat.

Echo: You love it.

"*It.*"

My heart trips over the word. I imagine him hesitating, thumbs suspended over his phone as he chooses the two little letters. For all his brash, familiar flirtation, he hasn't said he loves me since the night he left.

I haven't said it either.

I don't want to assume or pressure him into a declaration he might regret. Ironic, considering how he baited me with his first confession.

Underneath the caution, I'm also terrified it might not still be true. That my altruistic determination to give him this time to move on will actually work, and he'll choose someone else to claim the chaos of his affection.

Maybe he never hesitated. Maybe he'll start to slip away, and these texts will become perfunctory before fading into a distant memory I'll cherish alone.

Or maybe it's my turn to say it first.

Echo: I've started taking straps classes.

Me: Straps are fun. Great cross-training for flares and roll ups, too. It never hurts to widen your skill base.

Echo: And the coach is hot.

Me: You do know I recruited Gale Shepard?

Echo: I don't think he likes me much, though. Probably because I hit on him at a party during auditions last year.

Me: Isn't he married?

Echo: Something like that.

Echo: His husband is hot too.

Little shit. Two can play at that game.

Me: So is his wife.

Echo: Gross.

Echo: Are you awake?

Me: I am now. What's going on?

His schedule and the time change between Tilburg and California mean a lot more of our texts go hours between answers these days, but I still sleep with my phone on his pillow and jolt awake at the first vibration. Even in sleep, even eight thousand miles away, my heart is attuned to him.

Echo: We have a day off for some administrative bullshit, and the gym is closed. I need something to do with myself.

Me: Don't you have friends?

I know he has friends. I spend half of every day trying not to be envious of the time they get to spend with him.

Echo: Fuck off. It's 10 a.m. Everyone's still sleeping off their hangovers.

Me: Except you?

Echo: I came home early.

That shouldn't make me as happy as it does, but I can't help the smile that breaks across my face.

Me: So you're not hungover?

Echo: I'm horny.

My sleep-addled brain is no match for the images the message conjures, and one hand drifts to my dick as the other taps out an instant response.

Me: Show me.

The picture comes through half a second later, like he was anticipating the request. Tangled sheets in morning shadow, Echo's long fingers wrapped around the arc of his erection, one toned thigh displayed in the background.

Fuck. Me.

I've been so good, so careful, trying to give him his space. Walking the treacherous tightrope of his flirtation without letting myself consume his fledgling life. But my thumb finds the video call icon without any direction from my rational brain, and after a single ring, I'm looking at his face, haloed in the light of a sun half a world away and so *immediate,* my breath stalls in my chest.

"Hi."

His voice is husky with sleep, and he's cut his hair again. The blue tips are gone, only raven strands falling across his forehead to kiss the dark wings of his brows.

"No fair," he pouts. "I can barely see you."

He's so fucking beautiful, it hurts.

"Turn your camera around." Before I break down completely.

"Turn your light on."

"Turn your camera around, Echo." This time, it's a command rather than a plea. He huffs, half-pained, half-amused, and the image of his hand idly stroking his silken cock rips a growl from my throat.

"*Oh.*" His fingers tighten, then quicken their pace. "I missed that sound. Do it again."

"Kick the sheet off and plant your feet on the bed," I say instead. The camera jostles with his sharp intake of breath.

"Mmm. Bossy Byrd. You know how hard that makes me."
His thumb swipes over his crown as he follows my instructions, and I free my own leaking dick from my briefs.

"I missed that sexy cock of yours," I confess.

"It missed you too. Look at how it weeps for you."

"I see it. What are you imagining right now, dirty boy? Tell me what you missed. Am I tonguing the precum from your slit and teasing that thick vein running down your cock? Or am I taking you straight to the back of my throat?"

"*Jesus.*" He arches into his hand, hips thrusting off the mattress, and pumps furiously, breath ragged in my ears.

"Do you miss the way my hair spills over all that sensitive skin while I swallow you whole?"

"Unggh. Shit. *Yesfuckgodyes.*" His toes curl in the sheets, and the camera trembles as spurts of cum jet over his rippling abs. "Fucking holy fuck." A breathless laugh escapes him, and I squeeze the base of my cock with a rough grunt, unwilling to let this dream end by following him into his climax.

"Sorry," he gasps. "I told you it missed you."

Like watching him come after ten seconds of my voice isn't the hottest fucking thing I've ever seen.

"Show me that beautiful mess you made, baby."

With the lingering tremors of his orgasm spurring me on, I fumble for the bottle of lube in the nightstand while he drags his fingers over his torso and holds them up to the phone.

"I bet you wish you could taste it."

"I want you to pretend it's mine and rub it all over your hot little hole. I bet it's clenching gorgeously for me right now, all aching and empty."

The screen goes dark, and he curses.

"Shit. You made me drop the phone."

"I'm gonna make you do a lot more before I'm finished with you." I snap the cap on the lube and squeeze a generous dollop over my cock.

"Was that *lube*? This is totally unfair, you know. You're getting a show, and I can't see shit."

"You get to listen to me get myself off while I think about stretching your pretty hole around my cock. And I know you can give me one more with that famous college-boy stamina. Now show me what I'm fucking, Echo. I need to see you come again with your fingers in your ass."

Christ, I've missed turning myself loose on him. I was an idiot to think I could give this up. The wasted weeks condense to nothing as my greedy gaze devours him, and I tell myself I won't regret it in the morning.

He flips himself over, and I get an intoxicating kaleidoscope of sinful skin and blue-black ink as he shoves the phone between his legs.

"That's it. Ass in the air for me." Delicious shivers race up my spine, and my own ass curls off the bed, chasing his phantom heat.

"Yes, Mr. Baard—*Oh shit*." His bed creaks, and with another dizzying flash of flesh, I'm left staring at his ceiling with my dick protesting in my palm. "Someone's at the door."

"Don't answer it," I growl.

"I didn't lock it last night and—*fuck*."

A dresser drawer slams as he scrambles around the room, and I bite back a whine, squeezing my balls to vent my frustration.

"Echo..."

He snatches the phone up, eyes wide with mischievous mirth and not nearly enough remorse. "I'm so sorry. It's Gia and PB. I completely forgot I promised I'd hit the climbing gym with them this morning."

"Seriously?" I flip my phone around to show him the state of me, ruddy and swollen and slick. His answering groan sends another drop of precum pulsing from my slit. "Tell them to fuck off."

What am I saying?

This is exactly what I've been trying to avoid—muscling my way into his life in Tilburg before he's ready. Filthy midnight video sex is not part of my plan. *Make a new plan*, my body begs. Heaving a sigh, I release my poor erection and scrub a hand through my hair. Unfortunately, it's the one currently coated in lube. I guess I'm finishing this in the shower.

"Who the hell is PB?" I thought I knew the names of all his friends.

"He's—*I'll be right there*—It's what Gia and Shepard call Lyot. They won't tell me what it stands for, but they all think it's hilarious when I use it, so..."

The manic image on my screen goes still as he sucks in a steadying breath. One side of his loose tank top is twisted, clinging to his muscled shoulder, and I want to bury my face in the naked slope of his neck and suck my claim to the surface of the pale skin.

Soon. I can be patient a while longer.

"Coen." The ache in his voice tugs on all of my carefully packed dreams. "That was...we can do it again, right? I mean, now that we've started, we don't need to...Fuck." A rueful smile plays at the corners of his mouth. "It's the middle of the night for you. Go back to sleep."

"You know I'm going to finish jacking off first." The thought of letting him go with that uncertain look on his face has my chest burning.

He breaks into a breathtaking grin. "Will you film it and send it to me later?" He darts a glance over his shoulder. "In, like, three hours?"

My time is up.

"I'll even turn the light on first. Go have fun with your friends."

40

Byrd

"Holy shit. It's you." The young woman with spiky orange hair and a riot of color on her amber skin gawks at me as the door of the tattoo parlor swings shut to the chime of bells.

"Um, hi?" I take in the vivid mural on one wall and the clutter of images crowding the others. It feels clean, at least, the faint odor of sanitizer wafting from a curtain at the back.

"You're Echo's Byrd." Her elbows hit the display counter with a thud, and a crooked smile tugs at the piercings in her purple-painted lower lip.

Echo's Byrd. Every time he called himself *my Echo,* it turns out he had it backward, and it takes a girl I've never met to call it out.

"He wasn't kidding about the hair."

I drag a self-conscious hand through the waves I've left loose today. "You must be Audrey."

"Yep." Her smile fades at the edges. "You know he's not here, right? He left for that school in Europe a month ago."

"I know. I'm here to see you."

"You want ink? And you couldn't find anyone to do it in the Bay? I know a shit-ton of sick artists up there. You could've saved yourself a long-ass drive."

"How do you know I drove?"

She jerks her head toward the glass door behind me where the 4-Runner shimmers in the Southern California sun. "That's not an airport rental."

"I like driving the coast," I admit, crossing the room to rest my elbows on the counter.

"Everyone likes PCH until they're stuck behind some geezer tourist in an RV. Or are you one of those pseudo-locals who still goes apeshit over the scenery?"

"I had a lot of thinking to do."

"About a tattoo?" Her grin is infectious, and I find myself returning it. I can see why Echo likes her. He'd still win in the sass department, though.

"Well, c'mon, then," she says, snagging a sketchbook from the counter and vacating her stool. "You must have some good ideas after, what, nine hours on the road? Let's go make them better."

"More like twelve. There were a lot of RVs." And I follow her laughter through the curtain to place my heart in her hands.

It turns out tattoos are fucking painful. By the end of my grueling session under the needle, I have a whole new appreciation for Echo's commitment to his body as a canvas, and I'm convinced Audrey has to be a sadist to do what she does.

It's also a strangely intimate experience. Maybe because of the piece I chose and how close she is to Echo. Maybe because the whole time, I was thinking about how her hands and her tools have been on his skin too.

Or maybe because I seem to have a knack for surrounding myself with women who have no filter and find it infinitely amusing to lecture me about my life.

"Are you going to tell him I was here?" I ask as she snaps pictures of the finished tattoo—first with her phone and then with an ancient Polaroid for her portfolio.

"Are *you* going to go show it to him?" She shakes the Polaroid in one hand while flipping through the album with the other.

"I plan to."

She huffs in satisfaction—at my response or possibly because she's found the page she's looking for. "Then why would I ruin the surprise?"

Peeking over her shoulder, I find a collage of a dozen shirtless Echos. Even in the ones without his face, I recognize the words and familiar contours of his skin. The ink in each is fresh and vibrant black, the edges lined with the same red protest my own skin has recently discovered. Unthinking, I trace a finger over the cellophane shielding the image of his broken wing. She slides the new photo into an empty sleeve beneath it and tosses me a sympathetic look.

"Sit down so I can get you wrapped up before you run off after him."

I sink obediently back onto her chair, balling my discarded shirt in my hands.

"I wasn't trying to break his heart, you know."

Her deft fingers stall in the process of taping the bandage to my chest, and she pins me with amused eyes.

"Don't give yourself too much credit. I'm pretty sure he knew you'd come around."

"Why do you say that?"

She smirks. "Hot for teacher."

"He was *not* serious about that."

"Don't worry. It's very tasteful for a tramp stamp. I have standards, even if he obviously doesn't."

"Jesus. Thanks a lot."

"You're welcome. You can put your shirt on now."

With my blush hidden in the ratty cotton, I find the courage to ask, "How was he doing? When you saw him."

She waits until I emerge from my dubious armor to reply.

"He was sad. And beautiful. And *better*."

"That's...good." My fingers trace the bandage over my heart. "Thank you." This time, I mean it.

"Thanks for driving all this way. I'm glad I got to meet you." She offers her hand, and when I clasp it, she doesn't let go. "You know, it is possible to be more than whole together without being less than whole apart."

Wisdom from the vantage of youth. I guess it's past time I start listening.

The smart thing—the *responsible* thing—would be to get a hotel room, but I'm too wired to subject myself to a whole night of staying still. So instead, I grab a quick dinner from a roadside taco shack and hit the road as the sun sinks into the Pacific.

I call as soon as I clear the city, hoping to catch him before he heads to classes for the day.

Hope is an unlocked dive.

"An actual phone call. You're showing your age, old man."

"I'm driving. This seemed like the safest option."

"Where are you going? Isn't it late out there?"

I'm chasing you.

"I'm headed home."

"From a hot date?"

"What? No. Why would you say that?"

"I don't know. I don't know what to think anymore. I haven't heard from you since you turned me the fuck out the other morning. I thought maybe I pissed you off by leaving. Or that you regretted it."

"I sent you the video. Did that look like me regretting anything?"

"No," he admits. "But then where have you been for the last three days?"

"I've been doing some thinking."

"Sounds ominous. Good thinking or bad thinking?"

"Hard thinking. About stuff I should have told you weeks ago."

"I'm not sure I can handle any more of your confessions."

"Too bad. You're gonna listen to this one."

"I'm almost to campus. Do I need to turn around?"

"Just give me five minutes, and then I'll let you go, I promise."

"I hate it when you let me go."

"Fuck, baby. I *know*. That's why I need to say this, okay?"

"Okay."

Now that he's listening, my hands are shaking on the wheel, and the smear of oncoming traffic sets off a pike of panic behind my eyes.

"Coen?"

I fucking love it when he calls me that, the syllables somehow softer and more vivid from his tongue. I love that he's resurrected something from my life before Gabriel, and how he's claimed it as his own.

"I never knew I could want something the way I wanted you," I blurt, unable to hold back any longer. "It made me stupid when I should have been brave, and reckless when I should have been strong. It made me want to keep pieces of you for myself when I've only ever been good at giving things away.

"I didn't know what to do with those feelings, Echo, so I decided the only way to have you and still leave you intact was to make you temporary. For your sake even more than mine. I convinced myself that if you were *temporary*, then my past didn't matter. My *secrets* didn't matter. Because I was afraid that if you found them out, you'd disappear before I was ready to let you go."

"I—"

"But then you found out, and you not only *stayed*, you kept right on loving me. And even though it was what I hoped for, it scared the fucking shit out of me. I realized if you'd let me hurt you that much and still forgive me, then you might *never* leave. And how badly I wanted *that* paralyzed me." I press a palm to my chest, breathing hard, as the taillights in front of me run together like blood on still water. "I couldn't let myself be that man."

"I *know*, Coen," he says, tinged with frustration, and I blink back to warm leather sticky at my back and the hum of the 4-Runner's AC.

"You know?"

"You think I fell in love with you without learning who you are? You think I would have let you drive me away if I could have stayed without destroying you?" The helpless urgency in his voice threatens to unravel me. "But none of those things are excuses. You should have known me just as well. You should have trusted me to make my own decisions, even if they scared you. Why did you assume I'd make the wrong ones? You might have been clueless at my age, but we've already established I'm the emotionally mature one in this relationship. Situation. Whatever." He sighs, uncertainty oozing from the pause that follows. "*Is* this still a relationship, Coen?"

The most important one I've ever had. But his opinion is the one that matters.

"Do you want it to be?" I definitely shouldn't be driving. I can hardly feel the pedal under my foot, and the highway is a blur through the windshield. Rolling down the window, I suck in brine and diesel and wish I could see his face.

"Send me another video and I'll decide."

Something tenuous stretches its fragile wings behind my ribcage.

"And you wonder why I question your decision-making process." I'm grinning like a lunatic, alone in the dark. "That's not going to help you think with the right head."

"You don't know that. My dick and my brain have always been on the same page when it comes to you."

"Lucky boy." *My* brain is finally catching up to what my dick—and my heart—have known all along.

"Coen? Do *you* still want this to be a relationship?"

"I'm hoping you'll let me try."

Echo

*B*yrd: *What are you doing right now?*

    Missing you.

I'm always missing you. Every second of every day. In my sleep, at school on the rope or the straps or the trampoline. Even when I'm reading your texts, I'm wishing I was hearing your voice.

One fucking FaceTime in eight weeks, and I could barely see your face. It's not enough, and I'm slowly starving on the scraps.

I don't send any of that. I'm trying to prove he didn't make a mistake reaching out and giving us another chance. That I'm *strong* and *independent* and *totally fine* with him a million miles away. That the scraps are enough.

And I am fine. Sort of.

Because, yeah, NCC is pretty awesome. I've made friends, people who challenge and inspire me and make me laugh. I'm learning new skills and expanding the limits of my creative process—taking modern dance and contemporary theater and even performance art. I'm muddling through the culture shock and picking up pieces of Dutch and German and figuring out how to navigate a new city on a fucking bicycle, for fuck's sake, because that's how everyone gets around over here.

It's everything I dreamed of when I decided to audition—except for the part where I'm not getting laid. I mean, I *could*—there are plenty of guys in Tilburg who would love to fawn over my dick—but none of them have chestnut hair or eyes like sunlight through redwood needles. And none of them look at me like they want to put me back together after they take me apart.

So I can wait for an eventual future with Byrd.

But it doesn't stop the gaping pit of loneliness that cracks my heart open every time I get one of his stupidly casual, frustratingly adorable texts.

I roll over in search of a cool spot on my sheets and try to decide how to respond to the latest.

I could be honest, but mopey, needy Echo is unlikely to get me what I really want—another video call to tide me over. One where I actually get to stick around for the stunning Coen cock finale.

Immature and sassy it is, then.

Me: Hanging out with Thor.

Byrd: Is that a real person? Or are you talking about the Avenger?

Me: Real people can be named Thor. Especially this close to Norway.

Imagining him thinking that over, I bite my lip to stifle a grin.

Byrd: Is he a new friend? You haven't mentioned him before.

Me: He's my new roommate.

Byrd: ...

Byrd: It's a one-bedroom apartment.

Me: So? It's bigger than a dorm room. Isn't sharing a room one of those classic college experiences I'm supposed to be having?

Five minutes later, he still hasn't answered, and I'm starting to sweat from more than just the lack of air conditioning.

Me: jk.

Still nothing. He hasn't even read the text.

Fuck. Why did I think it was a good idea to taunt him? I jump out of bed and almost trip over the box fan in the doorway. Fucking things are all over the apartment, and they barely do shit.

Me: Ignore me.

Me: I'm an idiot.

Me: There's no roommate.

I pace the living room, eyes glued to my screen. Should I call him? Should I hop on a plane back to California and climb naked into his bed and refuse to let him make me leave ever again?

I should calm the fuck down.

Yeah, that's not happening.

The phone is halfway to my ear when the front door flies open, and I'm suddenly staring at a very large, very pissed off, very *beautiful* man.

"Where. The fuck. Is he?"

Thank fucking god.

And also, *oh no.*

Because that's not just heat in his eyes, that's rage. An inferno of green lit by lightning gold.

"You're here," I say. Rather stupidly. His hair is unbound and he's wearing jeans and one of those threadbare T-shirts that make me want to lick him, and *is that my duffel bag slung over his chest?*

"Obviously. Stop fucking around and let me in."

Fucking around? Is he serious?

Actually, I probably deserve that.

"It's your apartment."

"Good point." He pushes past me and scans the living room, eyes narrowing on the half-open bedroom door when he sees I'm alone.

"Is he in my bedroom?"

His bedroom?

"Byrd. There's no one else here."

Turning to look at me—*finally*—he frowns.

"You pierced your nipples." A menacing step closer. "Did you do that for him?"

Okay. This is getting ridiculous.

"*Coen.* There is no Thor. Well, there is, but he's not my roommate. I mean..." I shake my head. "Thor is a dildo."

Some of the tightly wound tension leaves his body, replaced by wary suspicion.

"A dildo."

"A vibrator, actually. And it does this other swirly thing—"

I stop talking because his fist is in my hair and his chest is pressed against mine and his lips are mere inches away. Trying to close the distance, I push up on my toes, but he brings his other hand to my throat and holds me in place.

"Have you been fucking yourself with a dildo named Thor?"

"Well," I gasp, neck straining as he tugs my head back. "Calling it 'Byrd' seemed a little on the nose."

My fingers burrow behind the strap across his chest, and the hitch of his breath is a memory carved of hopeless desire.

But this time, he doesn't turn away.

This time, he crashes his lips to mine and plunders my mouth with his ravenous tongue, and his familiar taste—cedar and caramel and Spirits under stars—trickles down my throat like ambrosia.

"You brought me my bag," I mumble when he lets me come up for air. My brain is apparently still back at the front door.

"You noticed that, huh?"

"It's kind of in the way."

Stepping back, he shrugs the strap over his head and lets the duffel fall to the floor, and I immediately launch myself back into his arms. He catches me with his hands under my ass and doesn't even flinch under my weight.

"I can't believe you're here." His stubble scrapes over my cheekbone as I pepper his neck with kisses and thread my hands into his glorious hair. "I really, really missed you."

He carries me to the back room without answering and tosses me onto the bed before reaching back to rip his shirt over his head.

Holy fucking Hercules. If he was ripped before, now he's fucking *intimidating*, all corded muscle and taut, tanned skin.

And splayed in vivid color over his heart...

Wings.

"You got a tattoo," I blurt. *My wings. And...a raven?* He grunts without taking his predatory gaze from me, toeing off his shoes as he unbuttons his jeans. *Okaaaay.* "Are you gonna say something or just keep looking at me like you're about to make me your snack?"

"Oh, I'm gonna say something. But first I want to see it."

My dick? I shove my thumbs in the waistband of my cutoff sweatpants and start to slide them down my hips.

"The dildo, Echo." His lips twitch, but his eyes are definitely glued to my half-exposed erection. "Show me this toy dick that's been taking what's mine."

"Oh." To be fair, all of my brain cells have taken up residence significantly south of the space they're supposed to inhabit.

It seems like a bad idea to turn my back on him right now, so I scramble up the bed on my ass and fumble under the pillow while he sheds his jeans and boxer briefs.

Keeping an eye on him was definitely the right call. Thor is a top-of-the-line sex toy, but it's nowhere near as impressive as the hulking Shiva looming over me.

The mattress dips as he throws a leg over my hips, caging me between his knees. When he holds out his hand, I hastily relinquish the dildo.

"The little dial is for levels of vibration, and the button—"

"Lube."

Oh my god.

Conveniently, the bottle is still within reach, tucked under a corner of my rumpled sheets, where I stashed it after my last session. I squirt some into my palm, and he watches with lethal fascination while I spread it over the silicone shaft. Low tremors course through my body, potent with lust and alarm, and my eyes dart between Thor, Byrd's face, and the larger-than-life erection jutting up between his thighs.

"What are you gonna do with it?" The words come out hoarse and breathy, and I thrill at the dangerous lilt that lifts the corner of his mouth.

"First, I'm gonna toy with you until your deviant mouth can't do anything but beg, and then I'm gonna use it on your ass." He hovers over me, bracing himself on one arm as he flicks the dial, and the vibrator hums to life. "And then I'm gonna fuck you again with the real thing. Maybe I'll make you take us both at once. How many times do you think I can make you come screaming before the neighbors complain?"

"*Oh.*" My hips cant of their own accord, my cock hungry for contact, but instead of crushing his body to mine the way I want him to, he leans in and drags Thor along my jaw. The hum sinks into my teeth, saliva floods my tongue, and I arch my head back into the pillow with a gasp.

"We're done with these games, Echo," he says, dragging the vibrating tip down my neck and placing his lips against my ear. "No more fucking teasing me with Josha or Thor or Gale fucking Shepard. You want me unleashed? You want me feral and possessive? *I'm right there.* Every fucking minute of every fucking day."

His teeth sink into the sensitive spot behind my ear as Thor brushes over my recently pierced and extremely sensitive nipple, and everything fucking short-circuits. An embarrassingly high-pitched whine escapes me, and my hands clutch at his biceps, carving half-moons into his impeccable skin. He rewards me with a far-too-brief but still highly effective grind of his cock against mine before sitting back on my thighs to consider his handiwork. "You don't need to push anymore, baby. I'm ready to *take.*"

"Can you start by taking off my shorts? Please?" I add hastily when his eyes flash.

"Not yet." He turns Thor over in his hands and thumbs the dial to the next setting. "Hands on the headboard." His grin is wicked. "Let go, and I'll stop."

"I love you like this," I confess. My heart is back in the 4-Runner, racing to the rhythm of memory. All these moments with him—each one a tipping point. *How much deeper can we dive before we come full circle and start to fly?*

"I know."

"To be clear, I love you spread out and whimpering for me, too."

Fuck me. I could drown in that smile.

"Next time."

And I'm ready to soar.

I thought Thor and I had a pretty good rapport, but under Byrd's merciless attention, I discover we've only been flirting at the edges of the possibilities. With devastating care, he rewrites the language of my body—delicate over my ribs, vicious along the V of my groin, fucking catastrophic on the sensitive hollow beneath the head of my cock.

My first orgasm paints my chest before he's even bothered to remove my shorts, and his eyes gleam with satisfaction as he studies my writhing, wretched remains.

"Look at you," he says. "Not so cocky now, I think."

"Don't say 'cock' unless you're planning to give me yours."

"That smart mouth." He smears his thumb over my lower lip, and I chase it with my tongue. "What should I do with it?"

"Anything you want."

How he could possibly look any more erotic, I can't fathom, but his lids go heavy as he toys with my mouth, and when he sucks his own lip between his teeth, I almost sob with jealousy.

"So hungry." He smirks, dripping with this new, alluring confidence. "Should I feed you my cock next?"

I can't speak around his fingers, so I nod eagerly, swirling my tongue in encouragement and fighting the urge to peel my fingers from the headboard and reach for his hips.

Hooking my lower teeth, he pries my jaw open and uses his other hand to smear his cock through the cum on my chest.

Holyfilthyfuckinghell.

"Suck me clean," he commands, bringing himself to my lips.

Yes. Sir.

The taste of him is rich with reunion, the clean musk of his skin mingling with the sweet salt of my cum. A satisfied hum ripples from my chest as he guides himself deeper, filling me at last.

"That's it, baby. Fuck, you look gorgeous with that smart mouth gagging on my cock." Lacing his fingers with mine, he anchors us both to the bed frame and starts to fuck with steady, plunging strokes. My insatiable cock fills again as I suck in air through my nose and flatten my tongue along the thick vein running up the underside of his shaft.

I want him frenzied, incautious, unfettered. I want my jaw to ache for days and my voice to burn tripping over the tracks of this claiming.

"You keep looking at me like that, and I'm gonna come," he warns, but he recognizes my unspoken urgency and lets himself go. "Gonna make you choke on it." His fingers tangle in my strands, and he yanks me up until the short hairs of his groin tickle my lips. My throat spasms and he groans, punching savagely deeper to bury himself with short, punishing thrusts.

The world swims to a haze of textures—pain biting at my scalp and jaw, the heady scents of sex and sweat, the swell of his velvet crown filling my ravaged throat—and then the hot slide of his cum floods the back of my tongue.

A string of praise and curses spills from his lips, and I am so gloriously *used,* it becomes worship.

He releases me with all the drugged reluctance of a junkie relinquishing their favorite fix and slumps back against the headboard. I turn my face into his hip as he brushes his thumb along the tear tracks leaking from the corner of my eye.

The move is so unspeakably tender after the spectacular ferocity of the throat-fucking I just received that I lift my head, searching his face for signs of remorse.

"No apologies." He smiles, reading my worry. He nods at the bed frame. "You can let go now."

Peeling my cramped fingers free, I give him a relieved grin. "Can I take my pants off, too?"

His eyes dance over the erection trapped behind my waistband, and his lips twitch.

"Go ahead."

"Thank god." I shimmy out of my shorts and climb up to straddle his waist. Cupping my face in his hands, he brings me in for the kind of kiss that curls my toes and has me moaning into his mouth—all slow, sultry exploration, like he's capturing the imprint of my soul with his thorough tongue.

"I missed this mouth," he murmurs when we finally come up for air.

"Even when it's being too smart for its own good?"

"Even then." He drops his head against the wall and trails his fingers down my neck. "Every shape and sound."

"Is this a dream?" I whisper.

"No, baby. I'm right here."

"Me too."

But it *feels* like a dream—too full of Byrd and wonder and bright with sticky sunlight to be real. And Byrd himself—all his cautious, careful edges, forever fragile beneath the burden of my need. Are they really now strong enough to bear my weight?

"Tell me about the tattoo," I say, tracing the raven's watercolor tail feathers. "Is this us?"

"The seraph and the bird," he confirms.

"Are we falling?" The forms are entwined, a carousel of limbs and claws and wings of muted black and brilliant blue.

"We're diving."

Diving is different from falling. *Diving is on purpose*.

I lean in to press a kiss to the raven's head upon his heart, then peek at him through my lashes. "Do you want to see mine?"

"Do I?" He rolls his eyes. "Audrey told me that was real."

Pausing in the act of twisting to show him my new, very sexy ink, I raise an eyebrow. "You saw Audrey?"

"She did mine."

He drove all the way to LA to have his body marked by the same woman who covered my scars and scribed my story across my skin. It's—staggering. And poignant. And it makes me instantly, irrationally, *incredibly* horny.

"I need you to fuck me now," I inform him. "You can check out my tattoo while you're riding my ass."

42

Echo

His pupils blow like an eclipse, black swallowing the summer gold, and he throws me back onto the bed between his thighs.

"I seem to remember promising Thor a turn first," he says in that growly voice that I fucking love. My hole clenches with giddy anticipation, and I hurry to retrieve the silent, discarded toy from the sheets. When I hold it out to him, however, he shakes his head.

"I want to watch you do it. Show me how you'd fuck yourself if I wasn't here."

"If you weren't here, I'd have gotten off an hour ago, had a smoke, and probably be napping," I tease, but I bring the dildo to my mouth. Working up a generous helping of saliva, I toss him a wink before letting it drip onto the smooth, flared head.

"There's my dirty boy." The rasp in his voice thrills up my spine, and I lean back on my elbow, drawing a knee to my chest.

I'll be your anything.

And I know how to put on a show.

"I like to start with the swivel. You haven't seen that feature yet." Pressing the button, I show him how the tip rotates. "It feels fucking amazing on my rim. I pretend it's your tongue—*ungh*—warming me up."

Said tongue flicks out to swipe at his bottom lip as his eyes track my movements.

How long will the voyeur win out before he breaks? He's already hard again, pumping himself almost lazily, but I can read the quivering tension in his thighs as he rests on his haunches like a stallion waiting for the spurs.

"When I'm ready, I switch to the vibrator. The lowest setting, to start, but it feels fucking insane when I press it inside. Just the first inch, but if I clench like this? It gets so intense I can feel it all the way to my balls."

Fuck. My voice is starting to shake, as if his avid gaze alone is heating the air in my lungs to leave me gasping. I'm not sure how much longer I can toy with him before I beg him to take over.

"Now I'm imagining your cock—how you work me open with those deliberate thrusts. And when I hit my prostate—*shit*—I amp up the dial and hold it there until I'm drenched with precum and my dick is begging me to jerk it off."

My whole arm is shaking with the strain of propping myself up, but I don't want to fall back and lose the intoxicating view of him. Easing back on my self-torment with a sigh, I wave the white flag.

"It's *begging* to be touched, Coen. *Please*. I don't want to come again without your hands on me."

I hold my breath as he holds my gaze, and then release it in a grateful gasp when he lunges forward, trapping my bent leg between our chests before drawing a fingertip lightly down my aching shaft.

"Like this?" His knee finds the hand between my thighs and urges me to spear myself deeper.

"More," I plead, as my head falls back and his body blazes above me.

"Like this?" His palm gathers precum and rolls over my throbbing head, callus on silk.

"More."

"How about this?" The hot length of his own erection scorches along mine, and he wraps us both in his fist.

"Fuck. Yes. Fuck. *Fuck...me.*"

My hand is still trapped between us, Thor shoved farther up my ass than I've ever dared alone. I can't move enough to change the setting, and each rock of his hips sends sensation crashing through me, reaching up and out through my flesh to collide with the euphoric glide of our cocks in his hand.

"I'm gonna come, *I'mgonnacomeI'm—*"

"Give it to me. I want it all."

And there's no part of me that can resist him. Everything explodes, pulsing, shattering, nails raking down his chest.

"There it is. Fucking gorgeous, baby."

"I..." My lashes flutter. "I can't—" My knuckles struggle against his knee. "Turn it off."

"I don't think so." Another slow grind and a sob escapes me, but my dick pulses out another jet of cum. "You keep *Thor* right where he is. I wanna feel that buzz on my cock when you strangle us both with your slutty little ass." His breath lays a line of fire across my cheek. "I'm gonna fucking *defile* you."

And...

I'm done.

Echo has officially been replaced by an incoherent puddle of lust.

With lidded eyes, I watch him coat his cock, and I shiver when he spreads more lube onto my already stuffed hole. One finger probes gently along the silicone shaft, burning past the first ring of muscle.

"Fuck," he hisses. "That's fucking tight."

"Mmm." I squirm, caught between discomfort and greed as he crooks the digit, seeking my prostate.

"You good?" And then he brushes over the spot, and I arch off the bed with a cry. "I'll take that as a yes."

"Definitely yes," I gasp.

The finger withdraws, and he lines himself up, holding me open with his other hand on my thigh. Sucking in a gulp of heated air, I brace for the invasion, my hand on the vibrator trembling with sympathetic expectation.

"Echo."

I lift my eyes to find him studying my face—not with the old haunted fear but with clear awareness. "Are you ready?"

No.

I've always been ready for you.

"Yes."

After a last, searching look, he nods, gripping my thigh and shifting his hips experimentally against the resistance of my body.

"C'mon," he encourages. "Let me in."

He's too much, too big. There's no way he's going to fit, and I shake my head against the tragedy of it. This is the Byrd of my wildest fantasies—sure and confident, generous and selfish, poised to take me exactly the way I want. *How is it fair for my body to betray me now?*

His fingers bite into my jaw, and my eyes fly open, prickling with tears.

"Baby." The faith in his gaze is luminous, spilling over into mine. "It'll fit. You can do this. You just gotta relax and let me in."

"Kiss me."

He does it wide open, letting me drown, and drinks my sigh as my body surrenders, *letting him in*.

"*Fuck*," we groan together, and his smile curves against my lips.

The burn is immense, straining at the edge of endurance, and for a moment, I just breathe his air, my fingers floating in his tangled hair. He holds himself still, waiting for me to adjust, weight balanced on his arm and his thumb rubbing slow circles on my inner thigh.

It happens all at once—a tide of heat that ripples through every grasping muscle to leave me languid and pliant. My fingers flex, brushing against his balls, and his whole body shudders, slipping a little further inside.

"Coen." I trail my other hand down his cheek and press my palm to the art over his heart. "Make me come screaming."

He still has to fight for every inch, but *holy shit,* what a glorious fucking battle. When his hips finally meet my ass, I flip Thor's dial to the next setting and watch him struggle not to fall apart.

"Holy fucking *hell*, Echo." His hips rock helplessly, and I'm beyond full, beyond stimulated, but he's *right there with me,* so I bring my free leg up to wrap around his waist.

"You should see what you look like right now," he continues, staring mesmerized at where we're joined. "Your ass is a fucking vision."

"Is that an invitation?" There's nowhere left to go, but I move anyway, tilting my pelvis to meet the next agonizing thrust. His laugh turns into a tortured groan.

"Fuck, baby. I wanna fuck you so hard right now, but this is..." He huffs out a harsh breath. "I'm gonna last about two seconds."

"I don't care. Take what you need."

His fingers spasm at my hip and thigh, and he draws back to drive into me hard, twice. Then he shakes his head and tears himself free, taking Thor with him. The dildo hits the floor and rolls under the bed, still humming softly, as Byrd flips me over and smashes my chest into the mattress.

Instead of pushing my legs apart, he shifts to straddle them, trapping me between his knees and laying a sharp smack across one ass cheek.

"*Shit*." I writhe into the sheets, but he holds me captive.

"Hot for teacher, huh?" His palm soothes over the sting, and his thumb traces the words etched between the dimples of my ass.

"Always," I pant, nothing but nerve endings and need.

This time, he's not slow or careful. He notches himself at my entrance, grips my shoulders, and hauls me back as he surges forward, impaling me on his cock.

With my legs pressed together like this, he's impossibly huge, irrevocably hard—bruising and brazen and staking his claim.

"Tell me you love me," he demands, drawing himself back to the tip.

"I love you," I husk, leaking all over the sheets.

"I love you too."

The rest is a blur of vibrant skin and blunt nails and his hot mouth sucking at my spine, my neck, my eager tongue. It's ecstasy so sharp, I forget to be broken or fixed or lonely or brave. I stop being *Echo* at all. I'm just *here*, being his.

Being me.

He takes me with all the fervent ardor of a man set free, and I come screaming until my voice is gone.

Sorry, neighbors.

43

Echo

"How come all you have in your fridge is Nutella and beer?"

"Those are Tilburg college staples."

Guys in their thirties are supposed to be tired after mind-blowing sex, right? But Byrd is walking around my apartment—his apartment?—in nothing but his faded jeans, grumbling about my lack of groceries. Not that I haven't missed his cooking, surviving mainly on takeout as I currently do. And I've seriously missed watching him cook for me, punctuating his efficient movements with stories about how he learned to make a certain dish or where he found the elusive ingredient starring in the evening's culinary adventure.

Tomorrow, we should definitely hit the Jumbo.

If he's still here.

Today...

"We can order a pizza."

He closes my pathetic fridge and comes to lean against the door to the living room.

"Pizza?"

"They have this thing where they deliver it right to your house."

"I'm vaguely aware of the concept." He's so infuriatingly *relaxed*.

"You want mushrooms?" I scan the floor for my forgotten phone, determined to match his casual tone. "They only have the regular kind. Not that gourmet shit you like."

"You look good."

So do you.

"Yeah?" There's my phone. *How'd it end up half under the couch*? "You could have seen me more than once in the last two months, you know." I wave my retrieved phone at him. "This does more than text." Okay, so maybe I'm not feeling exactly casual. But he shows up on my doorstep with no warning, completely rocks my world, and now he's just going to act like it's all normal?

"I was trying to give you space." He has the nerve to look mildly amused, dropping his arms from the doorframe to cross them over his chest.

"Yep. Good job." My sarcastic gesture takes in the—admittedly small—apartment. "Lots of space."

"Are you sorry I'm here?" His brow creases with confusion.

"Of course not."

"Then what—?"

"*Why* are you here, Coen?" The way his eyes glow when I use his real name resurrects all those damn butterflies. "You didn't come all the way here to find out about Thor. You were already on my fucking doorstep when I sent the stupid text."

"I was at the train station, actually. I don't have my EU SIM card yet, so I lost service when I left the Wi-Fi."

"Stop it. You know what I'm trying to say. What does this *mean*?" My hand flutters vaguely between us, woefully inadequate to harness the immensity of the question.

"It means I'm here." He takes a step toward me and frowns when I back away. "It means I'm staying."

"Until when?"

"Until forever."

Forever?

Don't fucking pass out, Echo.

"What about your job and the cabin and your life?"

"I quit my job and rented out the cabin."

"What? No. You're not supposed to do that shit anymore. You're not allowed to sacrifice things for the people you—" *Love*. The word sticks in my throat, bitter with the names of everyone who came before me. "—For me."

"Are you telling me to leave?"

Fucking hell. *Is he being deliberately obtuse?*

Whirling from his earnest confusion, I stalk back into the bedroom. If I'm doing this now, I need him to put on a fucking shirt. He follows me—because this is what he does now, apparently. Like all the pain he put me through since I left him in SF was pointless, and everything I did to him...*was exactly what he expected.*

"Are you mad at me?" he asks, startling when I throw one of my shirts at him. Not that it will fit his massive caveman chest. "I thought—"

"Shut up." I scrub my hands through my hair as he slowly tugs my shirt over his head and sits gingerly on the edge of the bed. "Okay, look. I know the last time we really talked, I gave you a lot of shit about not *knowing* me. I was fucking hurt that you hadn't told me about your past, and that you didn't trust me to know my own heart and what was best for it.

"But...I get it—even if I don't want to. Because I *told* you I was broken and then made my weaknesses your responsibility. And I didn't just dump all the work of fixing me onto you, I decided what that looked like and made up my own rules—the same way everyone else in your life always has."

No more greedy, childish Echo.

It's my turn to confess.

The worn carpet chafes my knees when I sink to the floor, and the late-afternoon sunlight is a brand across my bare shoulders and a halo in his hair.

"*I* was the selfish one, Coen. I constantly demanded things you weren't ready to give, without ever stopping to consider what it might cost you.

"So yeah, maybe you should have told me about Gabe before you said you loved me. But not trusting me to make decisions about our future? *Your* future? That was more than fucking fair. Please don't make any more choices you'll regret for me. I won't survive it. I'd rather live off a hundred video calls than think I was anything like...them."

"Are you done?"

"I—yes." And maybe I fucked it all up, but it feels weirdly liberating, coming clean. Letting myself fall without any expectation that he'll catch me, even though he's right here.

"Okay, good. Thank you for saying all of that, baby, but it's bullshit."

I start to shake my head, but he slides from the bed to straddle my lap and tilts my face to look at him, fingers laced behind my neck and thumbs pressed to my galloping pulse.

"Yes it is. I *should* have trusted everything about you, because even at your most vulnerable, you were a thousand times stronger than me. You didn't just see something you wanted and go after it fearlessly, you saw something in me that deserved you. You knew exactly what I needed but was too afraid to reach for, and you refused to accept my cowardice or my excuses. You gave yourself to me without restraint or compromise again and again, and all you ever asked in return was for me to be as brave as you.

"There's nothing selfish or petty or small about that. No one's ever been as generous with their heart or their body or their soul as you've been since the day I met you. I'll chase you to the ends of the earth if you'll let me, Jericho Wash, and the only thing I'll be leaving behind is my fear."

"Wow," I breathe. Or try to—there's no space left behind my ribs with my heart overflowing into all the cracked and empty spaces. "That was...really fucking romantic." My hands relinquish their death grip on his thighs to snake around his waist. "But maybe no one needs to do any more chasing. Maybe we just keep each other now, and that means I'll never let you make yourself small again, and you'll never let me fall. And where we go next, we choose together."

"I think that sounds like a perfect life."

There's no choice left but to kiss him then—not like the world is ending but like it's beginning.

Like we're breaking the surface, with nothing in front of us but sky.

44

Four Years Later

Coen

"Look at you, all grown up," Shilo exclaims, sweeping Echo into a fierce hug. "Thank you for coming."

"I saw you last summer, Shilo." He grins when she gives his ribs a poke.

"For about five minutes. You and Byrd holed up at the cabin the whole time you were visiting. Very antisocial of you."

"Blame it on Coen. He doesn't like to share."

I give him my own poke, and he dances away, eyes wide with feigned innocence.

"That was a busy year," I explain, very reasonably. "Echo started his minor studies, and I was on tour all spring."

"What he means is, we barely saw each other from January to June, so when we got here, we had a lot of catching up to do."

"Is that what the kids are calling it these days?" Wicked humor sparkles in her gray eyes. "I hope you wore this old man out."

"Please don't encourage him. I get enough of the old-man jokes at home."

But when he sidles back up to me and slips his arms around my waist, I can't help laying my hand on the back of his neck to steal a little of his warm exuberance. "And you better be careful," I warn him, pressing my thumb against his pulse. "Twenty-five is halfway to thirty. You'll be as old as me before you know it."

His scoff tickles my shoulder before he nips it.

"Worried I'll outgrow you?" he teases. "Now that I'm a college grad?"

"Speaking of college grads, I know it's not my place to be proud of you, Echo, but I hope you're proud of yourself for all you've accomplished," Shilo says, then gives my arm a fond squeeze. "And I know this one thinks the world begins and ends at your feet."

Because it does.

We're grinning at each other like lovestruck teenagers when Shilo shakes her head.

"Enough of that. Go say hi to Josha, Echo. Let the grown-ups catch up."

"You just said I was all grown up. Make up your damn minds." But with a roll of his eyes and a kiss on my cheek, he heads off toward his friend.

Shilo watches him go, her amused expression fading to wistful melancholy.

"Have you heard from Gem lately?" I ask, sympathy stealing into my voice. The new lines at the corners of her mouth suggest the answer, but I'd be a bastard of a friend if I didn't ask.

"Not since Hals had to bail him out of the Chico lockup back in February."

"Shit. Any idea where he is now?"

She shakes her head. "It was almost a relief when he first took off, you know. The year after he lost his place at ENC, he was a nightmare to be around. Drinking too much, snapping at everyone who offered anything resembling comfort or advice. I felt so helpless, seeing his pain and self-loathing and then being forced to watch it turn slowly into rage. Hals was lost in his own anger, and poor Milla didn't know what to think, so when he left, life got a little easier." She sighs. "But he's my first baby. It's unbearable some days, not knowing what he's doing or if he's okay."

"I can't even imagine. You know how sorry I am. We both are."

"I know."

We share a moment of useless silence.

"For what it's worth, I believe he'll come around eventually. He's always been a fighter. One day, he'll realize your love is stronger than his shame and be ready to accept help."

"I hope so." She leans her head briefly against my arm, then gives herself a shake. "Enough of my depressing shit. Are you ready for tonight?"

I glance at Echo, elbows resting on his knees and dark head bent to Josha's ginger one. Whatever he's saying coaxes a reluctant smile from the younger man's lips.

How much do I owe to a similar sight?

But there's no trace of flirtation now, and the only feeling stirring in my chest is pride.

"He's a good man, your Echo," Shilo observes, following my gaze. "And a lucky one."

"I'm the lucky one."

"You are *so* fucking gone," she laughs. "We need ice for the party. Go and get him out of here for a few while we finish setting up."

"How's Josha holding up?" I ask once Echo and I are out on the road.

"He's worried about Gem, of course, and hurt, but mostly he's pissed. Shilo and Hals—all of Big Top—they're his family, and he doesn't understand how Gem could just abandon them because he made one mistake. I don't think Josha's ever given up on anything in his life. So he can't relate."

There's a note of self-deprecation in his voice that has me glancing over to study his profile. "And you can?"

"I know what it feels like to be convinced something's been taken away from you, and you can't see your way through to getting it back." His eyes are on the manzanitas sweeping past outside the window, but his hand clenches reflexively in his lap, faded silver scars stretching beneath the ink. Taking his other hand, I squeeze all the comfort of my unflagging love into his strong fingers to banish his restless ghosts. A wry smile tugs at his lips as he squeezes back.

"I don't tell you enough how grateful I am that you never gave up on me. I wouldn't be here today if it wasn't for you," he says.

"You would have found your way eventually. All I did was give you a safe space to try."

"You reminded me that I had wings, and you made me love them again, even though they had scars. You showed me that they could still take me where I wanted to go. You made this"—he raises his wrist to flash his tattoo—"something strengthening instead of shameful. Something to overcome rather than hide behind." He turns toward me, pulling his leg up onto the seat so that his knee brushes my thigh, and fuck, I don't want to be driving right now. He should be wrapped in my arms for these confessions so I can spill my sorrow for his struggle and my gratitude for his strength into his sable hair.

"You loved every fractured piece of me. How could I do less?"

"Falling in love with you was never a choice," I assure him. "And your pieces always fit together flawlessly from where I was standing."

We've hit the stop sign at the end of Little Lake, thank god, so I tug him across the console to claim his mouth before his defenseless beauty makes me weep. He comes willingly, surrendering to the urgent sweep of my tongue, and his lips curve in a smile beneath mine.

"You were always right about me going to school," he says when I reluctantly release him to make the turn toward town, and his voice is lighter now, touched with the self-aware amusement of battles long won. "I wouldn't have been able to compete at Cirque du Dumain if I hadn't gone to Cici, and Terry Crane would never have hired me if I was only the tagalong boyfriend. Now we get to spend next year touring with the premier rope company in the country. Together, because of you."

I'm not about to argue, although I'm pretty sure Acrobatic Conundrum would have taken him in a heartbeat, with or without his NCC diploma.

"It goes both ways, baby," I say instead. "I wouldn't be touring at all if you hadn't pushed me out of my comfortable self-pity and given me something to go after."

"For our next gig, maybe we can come back and work for Big Top? I like the idea of doing a season here, where we started. I wanna develop some of the duo stuff we've been working on and create a new act. Something hot as fuck and hopelessly romantic that will make the audience fall in love and want to fuck us at the same time."

"You mean the duo stuff that always ends with us naked?"

"Whose fault is that, Mr. Baardwijk?"

To be fair, more often than not, I am the one who loses focus and drives our private training sessions into the bedroom—if we even make it that far. Partly because being restrained in a basing wrap with Echo's lithe body climbing all over me is more than a little distracting, but also because there's something intoxicating about the level of trust involved—that his faith in me extends to my grip on the rope when it's the only thing between him and another fall. Seeing him grow beyond his wild potential and mature into a dynamic, confident artist makes my heart pound and my dick hard. From his sassy, delicious mouth to his bright grace to his honest vulnerability, it's only grown harder to keep myself from claiming him at every opportunity.

And the smartest thing I ever did was stop resisting.

Echo

It takes us an extra half hour to make it back to Big Top with the bags of ice because Coen insists on a detour to the Navarro overlook, where he proceeds to wreck me in the backseat with one of his out-of-body blow jobs. Which means *of course* I have to return the favor.

By the time we get back, the Edison lights are glowing like mammoth mutant fireflies under the twilit trees, and laughter spills out of the open tent flaps. A wave of nostalgia hits me, and my fingers twine with Coen's in the gloaming.

"Good graduation gift?" he asks with a soft smile.

"The best. Is it weird that I lived here for less than four months, and it still feels more like home than the house I grew up in?"

"I think we rewrote the definition of 'home' when we found each other."

I guess we're both feeling a little sentimental tonight.

"Sap," I tease, even though I love this side of him. I love all of his sides—every layer peeled back as his guard came down over the last four years, revealing another piece to enchant and ensnare me.

Like his surprising competitive streak at PvP video games. Or how he loves to mother hen the shit out of me when I'm sick but turns into a miserable, cranky toddler if he gets so much as a cold.

And the way he still goes all growly and possessive every time we hit a club, only to become sheepishly attentive as he tends to my bruises in the inevitable aftermath.

Twining my arms around his neck, I part his lips with a warm swipe of my tongue and kiss him until Shilo comes to find us.

They've put together a private show to celebrate the end of my four years at Cici. It's small and intimate—just the family taking turns on stage while I sit on a bench piled with cushions, holding Coen's hand. Milla, seventeen and striking on the silks. Shilo and Cheyenne with an almost whimsical duo hoop routine. Hals and Josha making everyone gasp with a knife-throwing act that's only slightly less terrifying than it is impressive.

"Didn't want to join them this time?" I whisper to the man at my side.

"Just wait," he replies, and I'm still gaping at him when he disentangles himself from my arms and starts to unbutton his shirt.

"What are you doing?"

"Giving you your present."

The opening chords of Pink's "Glitter in the Air" fill the tent, and with a last wink, he vaults onto the stage, all feline prowess and masculine grace.

Fuck. Me.

It's the same routine from the first time I saw him, swimming to the surface of my screen in black and white. But this time...

Coen Baardwijk, shirtless on the rope in living color, dancing through the ether above a dark stage.

For me.

The final move is a slow wheeldown into a flared dismount that leaves him kneeling at the edge of the mat, eyes locked on mine. I'm standing rapt at the edge of the stage, hands poised for an ovation that never comes, because the music fades and he starts to talk.

"Baby, when you found me, I was lonely and lost. I'd let the people I thought I loved put me in a cage and convince me I deserved it. Then you crashed into my life and showed me love could give more than it takes—even when it's messy and complicated—and taught me to see myself through your eyes. You set me free while rebuilding yourself, and even in the midst of your own pain, you never tried to clip my wings. You're an absolute miracle, and I want nothing more than to spend the rest of my life learning to deserve you.

"Will you let me be your husband, Echo Wash, and fly off into the sunset with me?"

In the breathless silence of the dark tent, his words hit my chest like a fucking sunrise.

"Yes, Coen. Fuck, of course. Yes, please." I'm laughing as I leap onto the stage and launch myself into his arms. "Every word for yes."

Milla darts from the wings to place a small velvet box in his hand.

"I get a ring?"

"You get everything." He slides it onto my finger like a promise made real—I'm his, and he's mine, and I can shout it to the stars for the rest of my life.

The platinum band sparkles in the stage lights, inlaid with onyx and aquamarine. The colors of a young man fighting his way back from the brink of destruction. The colors of the tattoo over another man's heart.

Everything goes a little surreal after that—a whirlwind of congratulations and excited hugs, toasts and drunken speeches and questionable choices on the rigs. Basically all my favorite things about a Big Top party. My joy surrounds me, vibrant with friendship and family and *love*.

We're both cruising comfortably in that hazy place between a little drunk and not-quite-tired by the time Coen and I are finally alone.

"Why are you looking at me like that?" I ask, dropping my head back onto his shoulder.

"Like what?" He's leaning against the edge of the stage with my back pressed against his front, and I'm not sure who's holding who up at this point.

"Like you're expecting the other foot to drop, and you want to gobble me up before I disappear." I snap my teeth at him. "Afraid I'm gonna change my mind?"

"It's shoe. And you better not." He pinches my lower lip and gives it a tug. "I'm just waiting for that sassy mouth of yours to make some comment about my biological clock or second trophy wives."

"I would never spoil one of your perfect romantic gestures like that."

"You thought it was perfect, huh?" His eyes twinkle.

"Everything about you is perfect. Besides—" I tilt my chin to give him my best sassy grin. "I've always wanted to be a trophy wife."

If you enjoyed Echo and Byrd's story, please consider leaving a review. Reviews and recommendations are GOLD to an indie author like me.

Want more Broken Boys of Cirque?

Broken Boys of Cirque Book 1

Wristlocked: A Dark College Sports Romance
Available Now!

Broken Boys of Cirque Book 3

Josha and Gem's story coming in 2025!

Shoutout time!

Nothing about indie publishing happens in a vacuum. Even though it sometimes feels like we have to do it all, the bottom line is that none of these words would ever reach a single reader without the tireless support of a whole team of amazing people.

First shoutout goes to my alpha readers: Becky and Amy, whose unhinged comments give me a reason to get out of bed in the morning and keep putting words on page. Char, who gently reminded me that my boys can't solve ALL their problems with dirty sex—sometimes they need to actually talk to each other. And Jen, who helped me plan the most romantic circus proposal when all I wanted was to type "The End."

To my beta readers who stuck it out to end with Echo and Byrd and helped me battle the imposter syndrome that comes with the self-editing phase: Jenny, Danielle, and Elisa, you are gold. Please don't ever leave me.

To my hype team, Blythe's Baddies, who hold my hand through the twisty world of of social media marketing with unflagging humor, patience, and support. I'm sorry I'm so frequently clueless and occasionally forget what day of the week it is. I couldn't do this without you.

To my editor, Brooklyn, who puts up with my vocabulary and my obsession with italics, and who keeps me (mostly) following the rules while remaining one of my biggest cheerleaders.

To my family, who tolerate my smut obsession and keep asking questions and believing in me even when all I've managed so far is a very expensive hobby. I love you.

And to all the readers who took a chance on a baby author—Thank you from the bottom of my greedy, needy little heart. You make it all worth it.

xoxo, AK

Content Notes:

- Graphic sexual content (multiple scenes)

- Homophobic language (one scene, not by MCs)

- Injury/Hospitalization (brief)

- Divorce (not between MCs)

- Shitty sibling dynamics

- Light bondage

- Underage drinking (US)

- Smoking (tobacco)

- Anal sex

- Rimming

- Sex without a condom

- Cum play

- Explicit language

- Sex toys

- DAP (double anal penetration)

*Please DO NOT use the contents of this book as an instruction manual for exploring kinks of any kind.

About the Author

AK Blythe recently moved back to her small home town in Middle America after fifteen years in Northern California. She copes with the tragedy of leaving her real-life circus community behind by creating beautiful, broken, extremely horny circus characters to share with her readers. Her grown children are both horrified, but her three cats, two dogs, and her horse are very supportive.

You can find A.K. Blythe on these social platforms:

Website: akblytheauthor.com
Instagram → @ak.blythe_books
TikTok → @akblythewritesbooks
Facebook → @ A.K. Blythe
Goodreads → http://www.goodreads.com/akblytheauthor